Want You More

NICOLE HELM

ZEBRA BOOKS
KENSINGTON PUBLISHING CORP.
http://www.kensingtonbooks.com

ZEBRA BOOKS are published by

Kensington Publishing Corp.
119 West 40th Street
New York, NY 10018

All Kensington titles, imprints, and distributed lines are available at special quantity discounts for bulk purchases for sales promotion, premiums, fund-raising, educational, or institutional use.

Special book excerpts or customized printings can also be created to fit specific needs. For details, write or phone the office of the Kensington Sales Manager: Attn.: Sales Department. Kensington Publishing Corp., 119 West 40th Street, New York, NY 10018. Phone: 1-800-221-2647.

Zebra and the Z logo Reg. U.S. Pat. & TM Off.

First Printing: December 2017
ISBN-13: 978-1-4201-4280-8
ISBN-10: 1-4201-4280-1

eISBN-13: 978-1-4201-4281-5
eISBN-10: 1-4201-4281-X

10 9 8 7 6 5 4 3 2 1

Printed in the United States of America

Books by Nicole Helm

Mile High Romances

Need You Now

Mess With Me

Want You More

Gallagher & Ivy Romances

So Wrong It Must Be Right

So Bad It Must Be Good

*To all the trails I've hiked
that led me to my happily ever after
with my very own hero*

ACKNOWLEDGMENTS

Every book I write gets done because of a group of amazing women who help me every step of the way: Maisey and Megan, my cheerleaders as I write; my hard-working agent, Helen Breitwieser; and my supportive editor, Wendy McCurdy. They all make writing a joy and I couldn't do it without them.

Chapter One

Tori Appleby had fallen in love with Gracely, Colorado, almost the moment her Jeep had driven over the boundary. It was gorgeous, for starters. Settled into a valley where mountains brackcted either side, craggy, snow-peaked sentries that seemed to look out over the tiny Colorado town.

She'd felt . . . protected. Which was overly fanciful and unlike her, but she'd liked it just the same. She'd lived in a lot of beautiful places, and they all held different pieces of her heart. From a never-ending wheat field in Kansas, to the poshest resort in Vail or Telluride, she'd always found ways to appreciate the land around her.

When you were alone, it was all you had.

But Gracely was special. Back in college, when the Evans brothers and Sam Goodall had been her best friends, when they'd planned a future business endeavor together, Brandon and Will had spoken of Gracely like it was the center of the universe. They'd given it a reverence Tori hadn't believed, even back then when she'd been a little softer, a little more naïve.

But they were right. Some seven years later, separated from the little family she'd built after leaving her own, she'd come to Gracely and found it *could* be the center of the world.

If only that center didn't include Will Evans, the biggest mistake of her entire life. Which was saying a *lot*.

Today, Tori had parked at the east end of town, taking a meandering walk around Gracely in an effort to find a place to live so she could get out of Sam's hair. More because Sam's hermit cabin in the woods didn't offer the amenities she would have preferred. Like a microwave.

Parking on the east end meant quite a walk to the one and only apartment complex, but she needed that kind of movement, that expending of energy. Because she'd decided to stay, which meant somehow, some way she had to forget about everything with Will and a past she'd let dictate her life for far too long.

Sarge obediently trotted at her side as she walked at a brisk pace, her German shepherd keeping up with her easily despite his age. Her pet the one constant of the past decade.

Before she reached the apartment complex that had been her destination, Tori got distracted by a row of shoved-together houses, many with FOR SALE or FOR RENT signs.

The morning Brandon had gotten back from his honeymoon, he'd handed her a check and called it a signing bonus for agreeing to work at Mile High Adventures. She knew it was bullshit and charity, but she hadn't had a choice.

She needed a place to live that wasn't Sam's, and she needed to feed herself and her dog. It required money, and she was about out. Two months of unemployment had completely depleted her savings, meager as it had been since she'd been focused on sending money home to her parents before Toby had ruined her.

Still, no matter how damn weird it was to be here, with Brandon and Sam offering her a job with Mile High Adventures no questions asked, and Will acting like he wished she'd never been born, she'd come to a realization in the past few weeks of haunting Gracely.

She belonged here. Gracely was perfect. Mile High was exactly what she'd dreamed it could be when she'd been in college with the boys.

She stood at the corner of two streets, one that would lead to the apartment complexes once she walked past the row of houses.

The first house was a cute little green structure. It was one of the few houses without a sign in the yard. It struck Tori as sad that so many people were giving up on this pretty little mountain town. Clearly, this was something of a mass exodus with so many signs.

Of course, if there were this many houses for sale or lease maybe a house was financially feasible? She'd never had a house before, and she wasn't sure she wanted to buy one right this very second, but it would be nice to have somewhere kind of isolated and her own instead of another bland apartment where she had to listen to people stomp around all day or complain about her having a dog.

She walked down the street. The house next to the green one on the corner was a pretty buttery yellow. Normally, Tori would've had no interest in it. Girly, sunshiny colorful stuff just wasn't in her wheelhouse. But something about this house had her stopping and staring.

Maybe sunny cheerfulness was out of character, but what if it was exactly the kind of thing she needed? Even though joining Mile High had been the plan all those years ago, returning to that plan didn't mean this wasn't a fresh start. Far away from Toby and his lies and his reputation-ruining scandal.

She could start over in Gracely. Yes, it would mean dealing with some of her past, a past she really had begun to think would never have to be dealt with, but the minute she'd been fired and turned down for every ski instructing job in the area, she'd known that she had to come here. Facing the past was pretty much the only road to take.

As a teenager, she'd run away from one family. It had been necessary as her brother's violence had started to center on her, and so she'd always known she couldn't go back. She tried to pay off her parents' debts, but that was all it was ever going to be.

But she'd created a family with Brandon, Will, and Sam all those years ago, and this was a family rift she could fix. She could deal with it now that time had matured her and completely eradicated her problematic feelings for Will. *Completely.*

"Hello!"

Tori turned toward the cheery feminine voice that rang out. A young blond woman was coming out of the green house next door.

"Hi," Tori offered carefully, wondering if the woman thought she was a burglar or something. "I was looking at the 'for lease' sign there in the yard." She pointed at it.

"It's a great house. At least I think it is. Ours is great and we've been here quite a few months now, and the people who were living there were like this cute little couple who took such good care of everything."

"Oh, well, thanks," Tori returned as the woman approached. "I . . . guess I'll check it out."

The woman stuck her hand out between them. "I'm Cora."

There was something a little familiar about the woman, but Tori couldn't place it. She took the woman's outstretched hand and shook it. "Hi, I'm Tori."

Cora cocked her head. "Oh. Tori. I know you!"

"You do?"

"You were at the wedding. My sister is Lilly. You know, she married Brandon and you were there. An old friend of the Mile High boys, right?"

Tori tried to smile, though she was uncomfortable with the connection. She'd only met Lilly briefly, and she'd seemed nice enough, the perfect woman to stand up to Brandon's bulldozer tendencies, but leasing a house was supposed to give her a break from all those old connections.

"Anyway, this is a great house and I'm a great neighbor. You can even ask Lilly." The woman's wide smile faded a little. "Well, don't ask her too many questions. Lilly has very high standards."

Tori usually found overexuberance obnoxious, but something about the honesty in Cora's retraction was endearing.

A boy, probably not quite a teenager, flew out of the house Cora had come out of. Tori remembered him from the wedding. A blur of edgy energy combined with a kind of surly exterior that reminded Tori a lot of herself when she was a kid.

"Mom! Where's my Xbox controller?"

Cora rolled her eyes, looking far too young to have a son that old. "Duty calls," she said brightly. "But if you do end up leasing it, stop by and let me know. It's hard to find friends around my age here." She started walking back toward her house. "And now that Lilly's married to Brandon, it's just me and Micah."

Tori had never been very good at making female friendships. She tended to be too abrasive and suspicious of women who knew how to dress or fix their hair. Growing up with brothers and a poverty-stricken mother on a farm and then in a trailer park, she'd never quite acquired the art of femininity. But something about Cora and her cheerful prettiness wasn't off-putting at all.

"Yeah, I'll look into it. It was nice to meet you."

Cora waved and disappeared inside with her son. Tori took a step back to examine the house. She pulled her phone out of her pocket and typed the address into her notes.

It would be nice to have friends. It would be nice to have a connection and a house and all the good things a new start could be made out of.

For nearly the first time since she'd stepped foot into Gracely knowing a showdown with Will was imminent, she smiled without an ounce of sarcastic gleam behind it.

Will Evans knew that getting drunk didn't solve problems, but it certainly diffused the messy tangle of emotions currently existing in his chest.

Tori was here to stay. To *stay*.

Will squinted out into the thick pine forest that lined the back of Mile High Adventures. The dusky green, murky and thick, reflected his mood.

He'd much rather be in his own cabin, but hell if he could swallow Brandon and Lilly's lovefest. He was happy for them. More power to them. In his current mood, he'd rather gouge his eyeballs out than have to witness them.

Damn, but he had to get himself together. He had convinced *everyone* he was a good-time guy, and he'd barely been cognizant of doing it. Until the past few weeks, when everything seemed to be unraveling, including his usual façade.

He'd been an ass. To just about everyone. His brother, his new sister-in-law, his best friend, his half sister. Hell, he'd been a prick to Skeet, Mile High's grizzled, old secretary.

Will was in bad shape, and he didn't know how to fix it.

The door to the porch opened, and Will didn't have to guess it was his brother. Brandon was too quick to speak for it to be anyone else.

"I won't let you turn into an alcoholic, if that's your plan."

Will took a deep breath. He didn't *want* to be an asshole

to Brandon. Or anyone. "Don't you have a pregnant wife to flutter around?" Oops.

"I do, and I'd much prefer to be doing just that, but everyone is worried about you."

It was new. People being worried about him. It was uncomfortable, all in all. He much preferred everyone thinking he was fine. He *liked* people coming to him for a laugh or a joke or a fun night on the town.

"And you drew the short stick, eh? Pull up a chair. I'll drink to your—"

"Will."

Will stopped, if only because he hadn't heard that kind of grave note to his brother's voice since Brandon had delivered the news Dad had died.

"I need you," Brandon said simply. Baldly. In a way that had Will squirming in his seat. "I need you healthy and whole. A lot of changes are happening, and Gracely is still dying, and we are, in fact, its only hope that I can see. Mile High needs *all* of you."

"I'll be fine."

"Will you be? Because you seem to be hitting the bottom of those bottles a little too much for anyone's comfort lately."

"You want me to stop drinking? Fine, I will." He held out the bottle, and when Brandon took it, Will did his best to shrug. Yeah, he'd been drinking too much lately, though he was an adult and that was *his* choice to make, but if Brandon wanted to play moral police, Will would let him. No skin off his nose.

"I know you don't want to talk about it, but if this is all about Tori, you need to tell me."

All of Will's attempts to be unaffected fluttered away like ash in the wind. That's what he felt like, actually. His marriage was over. His brother was happily married and procreating. Mile High was doing well, and maybe that hadn't trickled down to Gracely yet, but it would.

And Tori was back.

"Don't worry about me. Don't worry about . . . her."

"You're not hearing me. If it's about her, you need to tell me."

"Why?" Will demanded, all that edginess leaking into his tone no matter how much he tried to bury it.

"Because I will tell her to leave."

Will whipped his gaze to his twin brother. "You outvoted me," he said, pushing down the clawing temper trying to free itself. Brandon and Sam had decided they wanted Tori back and Will had been *outvoted*.

"I will change my vote if it brings my brother back."

Will swallowed. Hell, wasn't that tempting? Say the word and she'd be gone. He could go back to pretending that night seven years ago had never happened. That *Tori* had never happened.

But somehow it wasn't a relief, in the least. It settled all wrong in his gut. "You don't want to do that," he managed to say, though it sounded far more strangled than he wanted it to.

"I don't, no. But I can get her a job somewhere else. I can give her money to leave. If you simply cannot coexist with her, then I will fix it."

"You can't fix everything, Brandon."

"Yeah, so I'm learning." Brandon let out a long-suffering sigh, and Will had to admit for a newlywed the guy looked *tired*. And not for the right reasons. "But I do have some control over this."

Will looked back out at the quickly darkening mountain forest in front of him. "You outvoted me," he repeated, because, well, because it had hurt. Even if that hurt was his own damn fault for not explaining things to Sam and Brandon.

But who would want to relive ancient history? He certainly didn't.

"I thought whatever happened between you two . . . Look, I thought if you got over your initial reluctance you'd be fine, but she starts tomorrow. She's been around for a few weeks, and you are decidedly not fine. I would love to include Tori in Mile High, but you rank, brother. So, if you need her gone, I'll do the dirty work."

Because Brandon never hesitated to stand up and do the work. Will might not always agree with what the work should be, but he'd always, *always* admired his brother for a whole myriad of things. That being one of them. Not that he'd ever told Brandon.

It would be wrong to take him up on this. Not because he thought Tori belonged here. By his way of thinking, she'd made it very clear she didn't. That she'd desert all of them if things didn't go her way.

Something tightened in his gut. A familiar old something he'd spent a lot of years ignoring. Refusing to identify.

"Lilly's having twins."

That jerked Will out of any past feelings. "Twins."

Brandon raked his fingers through his hair. "Yes, twins. She had some bleeding, so we went in and . . . Anyway, found two in there. Then they started going on about all the risks and terrible things that could happen and I . . . I can't control any of that. Even if I could wrap her up in Bubble Wrap and tie her to a bed, she wouldn't let me. So, I . . . I need you one hundred percent, because God knows I'm not going to be for the next six plus months."

Will's chest tightened, at a million things. Concern for his brother, for his sister-in-law, for his future nieces or nephews. An odd, blanketing grief that he'd never had a chance to have that kind of worry, because Courtney had ended their chance before . . .

"I need to know you're present. I need to know you won't

snipe at Sam and Hayley. That you won't dump on Tori. That—"

"I'll handle it."

"I need—"

Will stood, forcing every last swirling emotion inside of him down and away. He clapped Brandon on the shoulders and gave him a little shake. "I've got it. You can trust me. I've been off a little, I get it, but consider it fixed. I've got your back."

Brandon let out a sigh of relief, and Will realized Brandon wasn't just *exhausted*, he was sick with worry.

"Mom had us just fine. Lilly's made of sterner stuff. She'll be a freaking Wonder Woman."

"Do you not recall Mom's dramatic renderings of you being in the NICU for months?"

Will managed a smile, a real one, for the first time in weeks, he thought. "And look at me now."

Brandon was quiet for a while, too long, studying Will with that all-too-assessing hazel gaze.

"And Tori?"

Will tried not to tense, but he probably failed. "I was caught off guard, and I'll admit I've been wallowing in it. But . . . I can put all that in the past." For Brandon, he'd do anything.

"You sure?"

"Positive. Go home to Lilly. Do whatever you need to do. You can count on me. You can trust me with Mile High."

Brandon let out another sigh, something shuddering that had his shoulders slumping. Will wasn't sure he remembered ever seeing his brother quite like this. There'd been a grimness to him when he'd figured out Dad had been cutting corners at Evans Mining Company, an exhausted certainty when Dad had died and Brandon had had to clean that all up.

Brandon had been shoulders-back determination since he'd gotten it in his head that Mile High Adventures could save Gracely from its near ghost town status. He'd been humorously felled by Lilly Preston earlier this spring.

But Will had never seen him *wilt* under all the pressure.

This was why you didn't go falling in love and shit. All it did was make your life harder, scarier, and far more full of hurts.

"Thanks," Brandon said, giving him a little back thump, which was about as close to a hug as they ever got.

Will watched Brandon go, back to the family he was building. Will stood on the porch of Mile High Adventures, which was *his* future. He'd do whatever it took to make sure it kept succeeding.

Even if that meant forgetting everything that had ever happened with Tori Appleby. One way or another.

Chapter Two

Renting the house had been easy enough. The leasers had been happy to offer the place to someone who might be interested in buying sometime in the future. Tori was glad to have a place to call home. A place to really start building her new life.

Again.

Luckily, the house was moderately furnished, which meant that aside from some kitchen appliances, she was good to go even with her meager belongings.

Last night she'd settled in and Cora had brought over a bottle of wine and some brownies. Tori had been surprised to find herself enjoying the woman's company before Cora had had to go home and check on her son.

Today though, Tori was starting her first official day at Mile High Adventures. She'd have to get to know the area better before she led any excursions, but it would only take a few weeks to get that training down. She already knew all the ins and outs of climbing and camping and kayaking.

Of course, instead of sleeping in to be bright eyed and ready to go, she was up at the crack of dawn. She hadn't slept well at all because she'd been plagued by the knowledge that things with Will had been antagonistic at best and she had to . . .

Well, they had to stop sniping at each other or glaring at each other or, worst of all, pretending the other was evil incarnate. They had to face the problem between them. Figure out how they were going to move past it.

She was here for the long haul. She wasn't backing out of this because Will was uncomfortable. Especially if Sam and Brandon were both happy to have her.

She'd ferreted out from Hayley and Cora the fact that Lilly and Brandon were currently living in the cabin that had once been shared by Will and Brandon, and that most nights that meant Will slept at the Mile High offices in the bed Tori had seen the day she'd asked Brandon if he wanted her at his wedding.

So, even though it was the last thing she *wanted* to do, Tori was going to head to Mile High headquarters far earlier than her shift required and confront Will about how they were going to work together.

It scared the hell out of her.

Over seven years of separation had obviously changed them both, and it wasn't like she was going to have a conversation with him and they could magically go back to being best friends. It wasn't like he was going to flash a smile and she would grow back all those old romantic feelings she'd had for him. They were dead and gone.

So fear and anxiety and nervousness were stupid. But no matter how often she repeated that thought to herself as she drove to Mile High, the nerves jumped in her stomach until she felt downright sick.

She shook her head as she drove. She'd let emotion and fear drive her to this place, and that was the woman she didn't want to be anymore. The one who led with emotion, and always, *always* suffered the consequences.

She would approach Will, and they would have to discuss finding some way to exist around each other. Reasonable. Calm.

She parked her car in the parking lot and took a deep breath, trying to calm and center herself. This was fine. More than fine. She was being a responsible and mature adult, and if Will couldn't be the same, that wasn't her fault.

But her steps up to the beautiful cabin that acted as headquarters were decidedly slow. She was very nearly dawdling.

The cabin was beautiful—picture perfect both in its exterior and how it was set into the mountains. The gray snowcapped slate framed the dark woods of the cabin and was the perfect neutral to make the green roof and trim of the cabin pop.

She could stand here forever and look at this beautiful sight and be perfectly happy.

Coward.

No, she wasn't going to be that. She forced herself up the porch and ignored the shaking in her arm as she lifted her hand to knock on the door.

She could do this. She could handle this. Will was going to understand.

Wasn't that what you thought seven years ago?

She steeled herself against that stab of pain, pushed it away. This was something else entirely.

She knocked and she waited. She knocked again, and she waited again. The longer she waited, the more irritation started mingling with nerves and fear and pain.

He couldn't know that it was her. There weren't any windows or peepholes that would reveal her, that she could see. It was a little early, so maybe he was still asleep. Even though Will had always been an early riser. But things changed. People changed. *She* had changed.

She lifted her hand again, this time to *really* pound on the door, but it swung open and because she was shocked by the sudden movement, she couldn't quite stop the forward motion of her arm. Her fist landed right in the center of Will's chest.

His very, very bare chest. Hot. Hard. Shirtless chest.

For a second they both stared at her hand lodged against his skin. Just . . . *sitting* there. Her fist to his bare, *muscled* chest. She could feel the crisp hair beneath the edge of her palm, and the warm heat of Will Evans's sleep-rumpled body against her own skin.

It was like a weird dream from all those years ago, except it wasn't then and it wasn't a dream. She was real-life touching Will's naked chest. *Naked chest.*

It was only once her gaze rose to his that she finally got her brain to engage enough to pull her hand away. She cradled it with her other hand, trying to work her way through the unsteady, edgy way her body responded.

"What the hell are you doing?" he asked, his voice all sleep gravelly.

It wasn't fair that heat pooled in her belly, a sharp, erotic pang. But more than that, an undeniable tug of loss that echoed across the years. The way her heart used to skitter when he'd smile at her, or she'd dream that just once when he bent to whisper some stupid joke in her ear, his lips would linger somewhere, anywhere.

She swallowed at the overwhelming *swamp* of memories and current physical responses.

"I came to talk to you." She was very impressed with herself. Her voice sounded almost normal. Maybe a little hushed, but not like *you are too hot to breathe* panting.

Sure, it had been seven years since she'd had to pretend like Will didn't affect her, but she'd spent the six years prior to that perfecting her *I do not find you attractive, Will Evans* demeanor.

He took a deep breath, all the tension in him loosening before he smiled. Actually smiled. "Make yourself at home. Be right back. I'm going to put a shirt on."

She could only blink at him as he walked away. After a week of nasty comments and nastier looks, Will . . . smiled at her. She didn't know what to make of that.

Gingerly Tori walked into the beautiful main room of Mile High Adventures headquarters. It was everything they had discussed in college. They'd wanted the headquarters to look like a cabin, like a *home*. So that the people who understood the beauty of the mountains and what it could offer would come here and it would feel like that mountain getaway. It would be perfect and cozy, and customers would want to come back to find that feeling over and over again.

Apparently, the boys had used her idea of putting prints on the walls of quotes about the mountains. It nearly brought tears to her eyes, this dream come to life. It ached that she hadn't been here to choose the sayings or to have a choice in the rugs or the couches. It hurt in a way it hadn't up until this very moment, that she hadn't built this with them as she was supposed to have done.

"Is it what you pictured?"

She had to compose herself. She had to find a way to not cry in front of him. She couldn't allow him to see how hurt she was. Tori'd had to be strong her whole life, and this was no different.

"You guys did everything we talked about. It's very impressive." She didn't turn to face him. She couldn't quite yet. The tears in her eyes would be too visible.

She'd promised herself a long time ago she'd shed no more tears in front of Will Evans, and it was a promise she intended to keep.

* * *

There was an ache in Will's chest that was so much worse than the anger he'd been using to hide it for the first few weeks of Tori's arrival.

He had to figure out some new way to deal. Something aside from anger, and definitely something aside from this hurt. Memories that felt like they cracked open his chest were the kind of wallowing bullshit he couldn't allow. Not when Brandon was counting on him.

"Well, we've put a lot of work into it," he said, affecting his breeziest tone. "Brandon won't be in today, but Sam and Hayley should be here later. Skeet usually gets in around eight. Lilly put some paperwork together for you to fill out to make the employment official. Insurance liability and that sort of thing. Knowing Lilly, she probably has a whole schedule for you too."

Tori finally turned to face him, her pale eyebrows drawn together, confusion darkening her blue-green eyes. They'd always reminded him of the ocean, and it was so damn *weird* to be pushed back into that old reminder, these old feelings.

What did he do with a woman who'd been his best friend, then disappeared without a good-bye? All because he couldn't give her what she wanted.

"Okay," she said after a few seconds of silence. "I can handle a little paperwork, I suppose."

He offered a bland smile. "I know you know how to do all the excursions, but we need to make sure you know the area well enough before you can lead one. Once you've got the area down, you'll get scheduled. Between you, me, Sam, and Hayley we should be covered even with Brandon in and out."

Her drawn-together eyebrows didn't smooth out, the

skeptical expression on her pixie face didn't change. He'd always admired Tori's composure. She'd never had to effect a sunny disposition, she'd just been a brick wall of whatever the hell she'd wanted to be. She'd been a tiny blond force of nature and nothing, *nothing* about that seemed to have changed.

Damn her.

So he kept yammering on about procedure, anything to ignore the fact they were suddenly being civil to one another. "I bet she's even put together a few maps for you to help familiarize yourself. Stay put. I'll go grab everything."

She didn't say a thing, but he didn't exactly give her time to. With as much nonchalance as he could muster, he walked back to Lilly's office and found the little folder with Tori's name on it.

For a second, he could only look at her name. Tori Appleby. Something like a ghost that had haunted him for years. After having been one of the steadiest influences in his life for his early twenties.

He still couldn't get over what she'd done to him. To them. Or what he'd done in return.

He couldn't think about that. All of it had to be in the past. Brandon was counting on him, and he'd done a lot of stupid things in his life, but he would not let his brother down.

He got the folder and walked back out to where Tori was still looking at everything in the office with too bright eyes. Regret so clear in their blue-green depths, awe in the slight curve to her wide mouth. Things he'd felt himself while building this place.

That she hadn't been there, when she should have been.

"Here we go," he offered, irritated when his voice came out a little rusty. "As I predicted, Lilly has everything you could possibly need in here. Including maps."

Tori took a deep breath, and he could feel her gaze on him though he didn't lift his eyes to meet it.

"So, you're really just going to act like the past few weeks didn't happen?"

He stilled, though he'd give himself some credit for not freezing completely. He gathered all his acting skills and put them to use. Because anything he felt had to be put on the shelf right now. That was where he preferred deep, complicated feelings anyway.

"I'll admit your reappearance took me a little off guard." Understatement of the year. "A lot of things have been going on around here. Brandon got married. Sam is dating my half sister I only just found out about. It's been a strange summer. Things are settling down though, so . . ." So what? He didn't have a clue.

"What about me?"

He looked at her then, but realized it was a mistake. Such a mistake, because she looked like she looked in his memories. Exactly the same. Not a fraction of her looked any different. She was still a tiny thing, all muscle and mouth, that thick blond braid ever present down her back. Eyes like the ocean, deep and unfathomable and full of secrets he never wanted to know.

Exactly the same, as though seven years of separation made no difference, and that same confusion and anger and fucking *fear* she'd incited the last time he'd seen her back then still swirled in his gut.

But he was older. Wiser. He knew how to lock that shit away these days. "You're here. You were always supposed to be here."

"So, we're going to pretend like it didn't happen?"

"I think that's the best course of action. Don't you?"

Not an ounce of the confusion etched into her face changed. "Actually, that's why I'm here so early. I thought we

should . . . well, clear the air before we had to work together."
But she still stared at him as though he were some mythical
creature whose existence she didn't understand.

He looked away, made a grand gesture with his hand still
holding the folder. "Consider the air cleared."

He could tell she wanted to push further. If he had to
guess, she wanted to push into what had happened between
them all those years ago. He didn't have the wherewithal for
that. Not today. Hopefully not ever.

"Well, I'll get you a pen and you can fill out the paperwork." He thrust the folder toward her, not wanting to be
any closer to her than he had to be. Not out of childishness
or pettiness, but out of survival. Staying as far out of her
orbit as he could would be damn survival.

She took the outstretched folder, and gave a little nod.
"Sure."

"Where's Sarge?" he asked, because apparently his brain
hadn't received the *stay out of her orbit* message.

She blinked for a second, as though the question took her
off guard. Though it shouldn't have. She knew he'd cared
about Sarge as much as she had.

"I'm leasing a house with a yard and a fence. I didn't
think you'd want him running around the office." She
paused and he caught a glimpse of her mouth curving, but
he immediately looked away, because that old familiar gut
pang was not welcome here.

"Scratch that," she said, a note of humor in her voice. "I
didn't think Brandon would want him running around the
office."

Will almost, *almost* smiled at that, but it hurt too. This
whole thing would, but maybe . . . maybe with enough time,
it would stop. Instead of being this big, open wound, maybe
it could heal?

God, he had to hope so.

"Bring him to work with you. We'll figure something out. Gracely gets a lot of out-of-the-blue afternoon thunderstorms. You won't want to leave him outside."

"All right. I'll bring him tomorrow then."

"Great."

"Great," she repeated.

Silence descended over the room, and with it that nostalgic ache for a friendship she'd ruined and abandoned. But that was seven years in the past. The *past*. He couldn't let it live in him like this.

"I'll get you that pen," he muttered. He walked over to Skeet's desk.

He thought he heard her mumble something that sounded suspiciously like "This is going to suck."

Then again, he might just be projecting.

Chapter Three

It was the weirdest thing in the world to be living a dream Tori thought she'd abandoned. For seven years, she'd grieved over losing this. The chance to build an outdoor adventure company with her surrogate family.

Some days, she blamed herself for that loss. Some days she blamed Will. And some days, she realized that was just how life *went*. Never quite what it should be or what you could expect.

And this, right here, was always the problem with hiking. Too much time to think. When she'd been a ski instructor in the winter and a climbing instructor in the summer, her mind was constantly busy. Or her mouth was.

Hiking with Sam was allowing her brain to coil itself around in all those old ways she'd thought she'd grown out of.

Apparently, she'd just outrun them for a while.

"Solace Falls is the easiest hike we've got," Sam said as they hiked. "It's hard to get lost on. I figure you'll want something more challenging than leading this, but it gives you a good view of what you'll be working with. Which is a good place to start."

Sam started to climb the outcrop, so she followed. Even

if being back with the guys was a million shades of weird, it was nice to see Sam like this. Something close to content, which even before his family tragedy had been something he'd struggled to find.

But after his sister's death, Sam had changed. Tori had been around when Will and Brandon had gotten through to him to get out of Boulder and try to find some peace. But she hadn't been around to see if he'd ever found it.

Based on what she'd witnessed from spending some time in his hermit cabin in the woods, he had. Or at least was in the process of finding it.

Isn't he lucky?

They reached the top of the rocks and at the end of the path there was an open space of overlook. She stepped toward it with Sam, taking a deep breath of pine-scented air.

She smiled as Gracely came into view, stretched out before them in the green valley between towering mountains.

It was a truly beautiful spot for a truly beautiful town and state. Even with all her complex feelings for the people involved, it was good to be here. Pretty much every time she looked around, she was reminded of that. How lucky she was. That even after what had happened, the way she'd left, she had friends who would welcome her back into the fold. It was a blessing, and she had to stop taking it for granted just because Will was being all . . . normal.

He was on board with pretending nothing was wrong between them. So things were great. Everything was fine and great and *back to normal*.

She wondered if she'd ever believe it.

"Well, I guess they didn't exaggerate, did they?" Tori said, gesturing out toward the beauty before them.

"No. Gracely is everything they said it would be."

A rugged beauty. The perfect landscape to build not just a company, but a *life*. That had been the dream.

She wished she could be happier to get back to it, but

under the excitement, and the hopefulness, there was this constant ache. She'd wanted more.

"So, where's your girl?" Tori asked with absolutely no finesse. But she had to get out of her head and picking at Sam would do that.

Sam slid her a look. "If you're referring to Hayley, she had her own excursion to lead today."

"Well, for what it's worth, I like her. I think I like Lilly, too, but she honestly scares me a little bit."

Sam laughed, smiling easily in a way that surprised her. Even knowing he'd changed, it was odd to see Sam so demonstrative. "I believe that's the normal response to Lilly. Which makes her just about perfect for Brandon."

"Yeah, I can see that."

Silence surrounded them, though she could hear birds trill and the occasional animal moving around in the rocks or brush.

There was an elephant in the room, or the wide-open sky above them as the case may have been, but Tori didn't know how to approach it without making it look like she still had feelings for Will. She didn't know how to ask any questions about what had happened with him without making it seem like . . .

Wasn't that her problem? Always a little too worried about someone seeing her weaknesses. Maybe Toby had been right, and if she'd just opened up to him . . .

She rejected that thought immediately, hating herself for even having it. Toby had been an expert manipulator, convincing her he was harmless and sweet. Proving he was anything but.

She'd realized in the aftermath of all *that*, that Brandon, Will, and Sam had been something true and real—truer and more real than any other relationships she'd had. She'd stayed away out of fear—fear that Will would have twisted the story to make her the villain, to make everyone hate her.

But for all his faults and flaws, she should have known that wasn't Will's way. Clearly Brandon and Sam were a little in the dark about everything that had gone down. Maybe he'd saved that for stories to his wife? But where was the woman?

It wasn't that Tori was interested in the state of Will's relationship. It was just that it was weird. She'd heard nothing spoken of Courtney. Will seemed to be staying at Mile High by himself. Of course, models traveled a lot, so maybe they were just apart until she got back from some jet-setting trip. Maybe she'd return in a cloud of fancy underwear and giant boobs and . . .

Tori couldn't do this again. She could not get all wrapped up in what Will was doing or not doing, or *who*.

She just needed to find out what was going on so she could move forward with all the facts. If Sam wanted to give her a hard time for that, so be it. She was stronger than withering at a few well-placed jabs.

"Get over yourself, Appleby," she muttered under her breath.

"What was that?"

She looked at Sam, whose gaze was on the world beyond the overlook, a soft smile on his face. So weird to see any softness in this man.

But life had gone on, and people had changed, and it was time to dive into that. Headfirst. No matter what.

"So what's the deal with Will?"

"The deal?" Sam repeated, his expression far too satisfied for Tori's taste.

But she forged ahead. "Yes, the deal. Where's his wife?"

Any enjoyment Sam had been getting out of the conversation faded, melted right off his face. "He still hasn't told you," he said quietly. Seriously.

"Told me what?"

Sam ran a hand over his beard, scraping his palm up and

down across his jaw. "I don't know that it's my place to say anything."

"Look. I'm not . . ." Tori kicked at a few loose pebbles. "I was asking because she's not around. Quite frankly, we never exactly got along, so if I'm going to have to deal with her, I'd like to know when and where so I can protect my eyes from the avalanche of breasts."

Sam's mouth curved briefly, but it quickly went back to the grave expression that was some mix of a million things that had probably happened while she was gone in her own little world trying to escape the Will Evans curse.

"They got divorced."

"Divorced," Tori repeated lamely.

"Yeah. Couple months ago it was final. Not sure exactly when they decided, but it's final now. She was never around much, but she really won't be around now."

Tori didn't know what to do with that information. Will was divorced. Which did not matter in the least little bit. His relationship status was as moot as hers was. She'd walked down that road once, and she wasn't about to do it herself a second time.

"Don't go telling him I told you that. He doesn't need any I-told-you-sos."

"I wouldn't tell him I told him so." Even though she had, though not about marriage, just about Courtney in general. "I'm not the same girl I was."

"Good, because it's been a rough few months, and he doesn't need anyone busting his chops."

"Maybe he shouldn't have married a lingerie model," Tori muttered. Because, hell, maybe she wasn't the same girl, but getting rejected had been pretty shitty, so being rejected in favor of *Courtney* had added insult to injury.

"Would you have preferred he married you?" Sam asked pointedly.

"Don't start with that nonsense," she returned, her whole chest seizing up, hurting. Would it always hurt?

"I don't think it's nonsense."

"You're quite the Miss Sassy Pants who butts his nose into other people's business these days," she returned, because she couldn't linger here in all this old hurt.

"Well, shit. Lilly must be getting to me. I'll knock it off," he returned, good-natured and casual, but the way he studied her was anything but.

And if she was on this fact-finding mission, asking about Will's past, she might as well figure out some things about her own. "What exactly did Will tell you about back then?"

"Will told me nothing," Sam replied, his voice far too gentle for Tori's liking. "He mentioned you had some feelings for him, and it didn't work out. That's all I know. I don't know that I even want to know the whole story, but as long as there is this whole story none of us know, shit's going to be weird, Tori. It just is."

"We'll get used to it," she returned, because she had to believe they would, or this wouldn't be the new start she needed it to be. "Will and I talked this morning, and we're putting everything behind us. It's like a fresh start." She was glad she sounded a lot more chipper and certain than she felt. Because she felt none of those things. She felt a kind of dread, and confusion, and slight irritation that Will could flip a switch and be back to the carefree man she'd once known.

Worse, that that reaction pulled at her heartstrings more than it should. Her poor little rich boy and his legion of issues.

"Well, I'm glad. Because I'm happy you're here. We're all happy you're here."

Tori wanted to believe it, but of course it wasn't true. Will was not glad she was here. But he was willing to put up with it, so she had to deal with the emotional upheaval of putting up with it too.

Lilly Preston-Evans sat on her bed slowly going insane. She had no doubt she was also driving her new husband insane, but it was either that or worry herself into tears and she flat-out refused to do that.

When Brandon appeared with another glass of water, she nearly screamed. He kept foisting them on her like it would magically keep the babies healthy and growing inside of her.

Babies.

But instead of insisting she drink the water under his watchful eye, or piling another blanket around her, Brandon smiled. "I brought you some visitors."

"Ooh!" Lilly straightened in the bed, smoothing her hands over her hair. "It better be someone from Mile High with work for me to do."

"Never say I don't understand you, wife. Sam and Hayley came by to give you a full report."

Lilly clapped her hands together, she couldn't help it. Finally, *finally* something to think about that wasn't the past few days. Nothing had been scarier than finding blood and rushing to the doctor.

Or finding out she was carrying twins. That multiples tended to complicate pregnancies, and she would need to be on bed rest until the bleeding stopped.

She was too damn scared to ignore the doctor's orders, but Brandon kept hiding her computer, and she had nothing to take her mind off the worry, the fear, the prospect of *two* babies coming out of her.

Sam and Hayley entered her bedroom and she grinned broadly at them. She couldn't remember ever being so happy to see random people in her bedroom in her life.

"I want a progress report." She ignored her husband's disapproving look and fixed Sam and Hayley with a look that she hoped would trump Brandon's.

"Hello to you, too, Lilly," Sam returned dryly.

She waved a hand at him, completely undeterred. "Oh, don't act like you want chitchat. Out with it."

"Things are going great," Hayley offered. "Plenty of excursions."

"I, uh, took a meeting with Corbin," Sam added, rocking back on his heels.

"*You* did?" Lilly demanded, shocked that Sam would take any meeting, let alone such an important one. Forming a partnership with Corbin to get Mile High's customers staying in Corbin's lodge had been a special feat for Lilly when she'd started with Mile High as public relations manager. Introverted, grumpy Sam taking on any responsibility in that vein was . . . well, a shock.

"Between Will's history with him, and Brandon being busy, and Hayley so new, I seemed like the only choice. Much to my dismay."

"And?" Lilly prompted, her mind whirring over what she would have wanted to say to Corbin if she'd been able to take the meeting. She tried not to worry over Sam handling . . . well, any of it.

"We agreed on some terms for winter specials. I e-mailed all the information to you before we came over."

"I think I married the wrong man," Lilly said fervently.

"He only did all that stuff because I told him to," Brandon returned.

She smiled over at him. "Okay, maybe I married the right one, then." She didn't know why, but knowing what was happening at Mile High sent relief coursing through her. She managed to relax a little bit, which hadn't been happening at all.

She needed more. "How's the Will and Tori thing going?"

Sam and Hayley exchanged a glance that did not bode well for the answer.

"It's actually really, really weird," Hayley said.

"Weird not World War Three?" Brandon asked.

"No," Hayley said carefully. "Considering how antagonistic they were toward each other before, this week has been . . . I mean, I know I don't know them like you guys do, but it's . . . They're very civil."

"Tori told me they agreed to put the past behind them. But . . ." Sam trailed off and shook his head.

"You can really tell that something happened," Hayley continued. "No matter what they say to each other, or how polite they are. It's obvious something bad went down between them. There's so much tension brewing it's downright uncomfortable to be around."

A problem to fix. One she couldn't control, but could at least focus on without crying. "Well, then, we need to do something about it."

"Lil, you can't sweep in and fix everything. Isn't that what you're always telling me?"

Lilly waved Brandon's question away. "This is different. The way Will and Tori are with each other affects our business. We have to pay attention to it. We have to act on it."

"You're reaching."

She was. Totally. She couldn't bring herself to care, so she focused on Sam and Hayley instead of her disapproving husband. "We need to find a way where they'll have to spend a lot of time together."

Sam burst out laughing and only stopped once he met her gaze. "You're not serious."

"Of course I am. We can come up with some kind of excursion where they'd have to go camping together, and work together. It could help them work out their issues."

"I repeat, you're not serious," Sam said.

"Well, what's so wrong with my idea?"

"Aside from the fact that they are two grown adults who can deal with their own shit without our interference?"

"Yes, aside from that. They need a catalyst. Hayley, what do you think?"

Hayley stood next to Sam wide-eyed. She'd only joined Mile High this summer, only met Brandon and Will, her half brothers, this summer as well.

But Hayley was a sweetheart. She had a softness to her that Mile High desperately needed. A vulnerability that was somehow steeled with a strength Lilly admired. It couldn't be all bearded testosterone all the time.

"I . . . I don't know anything that happened with them. I don't know their history. Don't ask me."

"No one knows what happened, do they?"

Brandon sighed. "No, not exactly. But clearly they had a gigantic argument that ended a friendship."

"See?" But Lilly noticed that Sam was expressly looking anywhere but her. "Sam?" she said in a warning tone. The little bastard *knew* something he'd been keeping from them.

"I don't really know what happened," Sam said carefully.

"But you know something," Lilly pressed.

"You do?" Brandon and Hayley asked in unison.

Sam scowled. "All I know is that Tori told Will she had feelings for him, so to speak. Which happened about the time he disappeared and came back married to Courtney. So, shutting them together probably isn't the best route to take here."

"Well, I don't know," Hayley said hesitantly. "Sometimes you have to face things to get over them. Maybe sticking them together is exactly what they need."

"Thank you, Hayley. Now, it's two against two. Which one of you is going to cave and agree with the women?" Lilly asked sweetly.

When Brandon and Sam both looked at her with steely gazes, she rolled her eyes.

"An excursion where they work together just gives them the opportunity to talk. They don't actually have to do it. If they come back still tense and uncomfortable, then that's all there is to it."

"And if they come back and nothing has changed, you will let this and them be?" Brandon asked.

"Of course not."

Sam and Hayley laughed until Brandon glared at them.

"Well, you two are no help, why don't you get out of here," he growled at them.

"He thinks he's going to change my mind in private. Isn't that cute?"

"I have no delusions of changing your mind, sweetheart," Brandon muttered. "But I think you've had enough excitement for one day."

"Fine," Lilly said with a dramatic sigh. "But I'll be in touch," she said, pointing at Sam.

Sam and Hayley exited the room, and Brandon took a seat next to Lilly on the bed. Her wheels were already spinning because she really thought her idea was brilliant. What would be better for two people who thought they could ignore everything than having to face whatever they were ignoring?

"You know that Will and Tori's issues are none of our business and claiming they have to do with Mile High business is a little bit insane."

Lilly let out a sigh. He was right, kind of. But . . . "I have to concentrate on something or I'll drive myself crazy trying to figure out how we're going to take care of two babies." Or, so much worse, the alternative. No babies at all.

Tears pricked her eyes and she ruthlessly blinked them away. Will and Tori were a much, *much* better focus.

Brandon's hand rested over her hand, which she hadn't realized she'd placed over her belly.

"I don't know if pushing Will and Tori together is a great idea. You should have seen the fireworks those two sparked off when they were the best of friends."

"Then maybe that's the answer."

"What?"

"Fireworks. Explode. Burn out."

"We're in the mountains, Lil. I think you're supposed to heed Smokey the Bear's warnings about starting fires."

"Shows what you know. What Will and Tori need is a controlled burn, and we're just the people to facilitate it for them."

Of that Lilly was sure.

Chapter Four

Will had spent a lot of years being easily distracted by whatever the next fun thing might be. He'd honed that part of himself. Spontaneity and fun. A disorganized kind of chaos that would lead him from one thing to the next without a whole lot of time to plan or obsess over the details.

But, as it was so often in his life, Mile High was the exception. It was easy to be as detail-oriented and conscientious about things as Brandon always was—as long as Will cared, especially when survival depended on it. For so long Will had assumed he was something short of worthless in that department, but Mile High had opened his eyes.

He just needed to be in a place that suited him. In a field that interested him on a variety of levels. Mile High and the building of it had become linked with his soul.

He paused in his current prep for a weekend backpacking trip that was going to act as some kind of employee bonding experience for their clients. Souls and whatnot was not something he wanted to think too deeply about.

He really hoped the clients knew as much about backpacking as Hayley had assured him they did. There was nothing worse than customers who overplayed their strengths and underplayed their weaknesses.

When Will's phone rang, he didn't even glance at the caller ID before answering it.

"Hey, Will, it's Hayley."

Will noted Hayley sounded strange. "Hey. What's up?"

"Um, well, the hikers wanted to get a bit of an early start, so you're going to meet them . . ."

He lost his concentration on Hayley's words in his ear when Tori walked in, cell phone cradled to her ear, bright pink backpack—if he wasn't mistaken the same one he'd given her for her birthday as a joke ten years ago.

Tori hated pink, and she probably hated him, but she was here and she was wearing that backpack.

Their eyes met across the meeting area of Mile High headquarters, and if she was paying attention to her conversation, she was doing a much better job than him.

But he was friendly, easygoing Will, no matter that the mere sight of her made his ribs feel like they'd tied together and squeezed everything inside of him.

That feeling would go away. He'd always, *always* been something close to sure about that. But seven years had passed and here he still was.

"Will?"

He blinked, realizing he'd zoned out on his conversation with Hayley. "Yeah, meet them there."

"And the other part?"

He flicked a glance at Tori again, despite every voice in his head telling him to stop. Her expression was grim, she'd shifted so she now held her phone to her ear with her hand, her knuckles white from the pressure.

"Will!"

"Yeah?"

"Are you okay?" Hayley asked, concern lacing the already weird tone to her voice.

"I'm fine. Just distracted trying to get ready. What's the other part again?"

"Sam can't make it. We're going to send Tori instead."

His brain came into sharp focus then. Tori and her backpack. Tension-filled phone calls. The weirdness in Hayley's voice.

A setup. So clear and damn interfering he almost laughed. What had he expected, really? For everyone to let it go? For everyone to pretend? That was his expertise. The rest of them were pokers and prodders and obnoxious as hell.

"She needs the experience, and—"

"And please spare me the lies. You aren't any good at it." Though he was irritated, his voice didn't come out as sharp as it could have. He couldn't muster anger, not when he was the idiot who hadn't seen this coming.

Hayley didn't say anything, though the call didn't end so she was still on the line. Something shifted inside of him, mostly against his will, but Hayley was his sister, half or not; kept a secret for most of their lives or not, she was his little sister.

He felt protective of her, some weird biological thing, and it had been a long time since he'd felt the need to protect someone, the desire to. He was the youngest—even as a twin. He'd always been the one at the bottom of the totem pole, so to speak. Having something of a purpose was . . . Well, he'd always liked that. It was why he threw himself so wholeheartedly into Mile High. Purpose.

"Tori and I will meet the clients at Healing Point, and if you set it up with that much symbolism, you and Brandon and Lilly need to work on your subtlety."

She let out a little huff of breath. "Will."

This time when he looked at Tori, she didn't have the phone to her ear, and she looked . . . wary. Pissed. And, worst of all, uncertain.

Because it mirrored all his feelings and then some, he smiled at her, but in that Tori way, it felt as though she saw right through it to everything he was trying to hide underneath.

In his twenties, he'd been fascinated by that. Until she'd wanted more. How was it fair to want more than that? She could already see through him. What more was there?

"Anything else pertinent I need to know?" he asked Hayley with as much nonchalance as he could manage. He could do a backpacking trip with Tori. Even with that damn pink backpack and all the memories and old weirdness, because it was just that.

Old. Gone. A lifetime ago that no longer existed. Like his childhood, like his marriage, things that didn't exist anymore, so they couldn't possibly matter.

"No. The rest of the information is the same. Just . . ."

He waited, but Hayley wasn't finishing her sentence. Which meant it was something he didn't want to hear.

"Have a good time, I guess," she finished, quite lamely.

"Of course." He hit End on his phone and focused all his energy on sending a bland smile Tori's way. "I guess it's the two of us."

"And this doesn't reek like hideous setup to you?"

"Of course it does. Why do you think I'm agreeing to it with a smile on my face?"

Her lips twitched a little, the first hint of any amusement she'd had toward him. It shouldn't unlock something inside of him. It shouldn't affect him at all.

So he wouldn't let it.

"Let them think forcing us to work together will create . . . Hell, I don't know. We've been civil to each other for days now."

She studied him in that oh-so-careful way of hers. Somehow different from Lilly's concern or Hayley's curiosity. A world in itself, that blue-green look filled with a history he didn't know how to erase.

"Civil isn't always comfortable, Will," she said, and her

voice was calm and quiet, and it was nothing like before. Because Tori had been loud and brash and had barreled through any conversation.

He didn't recognize this careful stranger, even when he did.

"Where's Sarge?" he asked, because the dog always seemed safer. A buffer. Happier memories. A better past.

"My neighbor's looking after him overnight. I wanted to read up on the dog rules in the National Forest before I brought him along for an overnight trip, and this was a little last minute."

"Leashed on common areas and campgrounds, fine in the backwoods."

She gave a little nod. "I'll know that for next time. But I imagine clients should have to sign off on agreeing to backpack and camp with a dog."

"I'm sure Brandon can draw up something for future trips."

This was all civil. Easy back and forth. He didn't understand why everyone felt the need to maneuver them into working together.

"It's this, right here," she said, not looking him in the eye.

"What?"

She shook her head. "The long pauses. The awkward silences. Oh, we can pretend the past didn't happen, Will, but it's in every quiet moment."

"Then let's eradicate the quiet moments, shall we?" he offered with a grin he didn't feel, hefting his backpack onto his shoulders. "I hope you're prepared for one chatty hike."

Will lived up to his word. They hiked. For *hours* and he talked basically nonstop the whole damn time. Tori had lost count of how many times she'd seriously considered kicking him in the ass.

The only thing keeping her from doing it was the fact it

was something she might have done *then,* and she was
trying to avoid that line back into the friendship they'd had.

Civil might not be comfortable, but it had a lot fewer
land mines than friendship.

There'd been a sparkle of it. The old him. The old them.
When he'd asked why she thought he was agreeing to the
setup, because Will could be counted on to never quite react
the way you thought he would.

One night in particular.

She wished she had brought Sarge, rules and clients be
damned, if only so it would give her heart somewhere soft
to land when her brain and memories were trying to be a
dick.

"The backpacking camp area is up here." Will pointed, a
frown crossing his face. "We should hear someone by now.
If they left when Hayley said they did . . ." He trailed off and
increased the pace of their hiking.

Tori followed, more than ready for company that
wasn't Will Evans. It was easier to ignore all the silences,
all the ways they stared at each other—lost in thought and
memories—when other people were around. She knew
they noticed, but still. She could focus on them instead
of him.

Him who hiked up mountains with ease, whose voice
was the same rough timbre of her memories. Oh, she'd
gotten over all those old feelings, but it didn't mean the
ghosts of them didn't still haunt her.

He'd been a first, so many different firsts, friendship and
love and utter heartbreak in a way she hadn't even felt with
her family when she'd left them, so maybe he'd always
haunt her.

Gee, isn't that a cheery thought.

Tori followed Will into a little clearing where the camp-
site should be, if the map was right.

"Where are they?" Will wondered, pulling his walkie off

his pack, but before he called back to Mile High, he scowled deeper and strode over to a tree at the edge of the clearing.

Tori hadn't noticed it before, but now she realized there was a bright pink piece of paper nailed to said tree.

"What the hell?" Will muttered, stepping toward it, before letting out a curse.

Tori moved closer and squinted at the piece of paper to read it herself. All it said was *sorry*, but she supposed that's all it needed to say.

"There are no clients," she said tonelessly. Just her and Will—not just having to work together, but there was no way to get back to their vehicle by nightfall. They had to camp.

Together.

Just the two of them.

It was her turn to curse.

"Lilly's always a bit sneakier than I think she'll be," Will muttered, tearing the piece of paper from its nail and crumpling it in one hand.

"You think it was Lilly?" Not that it mattered. Someone from Mile High had plotted to get her and Will alone together for *some* reason. Did it really matter who?

"It was all of them, but it started with her. You'll find, soon enough, when it comes to Mile High, everything starts with her."

"Not Brandon?"

Will shrugged out of his pack and placed it on the ground. He rubbed a palm over his beard as if he was trying to plan how to get out of this, but Tori knew. They were stuck.

"Brandon's part of it, but Lilly . . . She came along and I barely remember what it was like before. She swept in and changed everything, Brandon included. They fight. They disagree constantly. And yet, when it comes to Mile High, it's like that all twines together and becomes some idea, some plan, some *scheme*." He gestured disgustedly with the crumpled piece of paper in his fist. "And everyone's on board. Everyone's falling in line to do the bidding of the Brandon-Lilly Express, and you know what the worst part is?"

She shook her head, a little too interested in the fact a woman could sweep in and change anything about the Evans brothers. What would that look like? What would it take?

"They're always fucking right."

Tori didn't particularly care for the implication in this case. Mostly because she didn't know what any of the people at Mile High were trying to prove.

"I wouldn't even be surprised if we head back down tomorrow the best of friends," Will muttered disgustedly as he rifled around in his pack.

"I would be," Tori returned. What could be said that would erase all that had kept her away for so long? She had a hard time believing years could eradicate it. She had no trust a day could.

"We should set up camp before it gets dark," he said.

"Joy."

"Just be glad they didn't somehow confiscate one of our tents so we had to share one," Will returned, unclipping his tent from the outside of his backpack.

Tori shuddered. Yes, she would be very grateful for that. Sharing a tent would be pure and utter torture. Really, he had a good point on all of this. It could be so, *so* much worse.

She shrugged out of her pack and worked on getting out everything she would need to set up her backpacking tent.

Will did the same and they did it in silence. Oddly enough, it wasn't that uncomfortable, tense silence she'd hoped to get used to. This was an almost companionable one. Working side by side had always been easy, but it was a surprise it still could be.

"I'm sorry. I don't get what they're trying to accomplish. You know them better. What could possibly come from this that would benefit them? What's their endgame here?"

Will sat back on his haunches and looked out over the forest around them. The air was heavy with pine and sun and it'd be very nearly relaxing if she didn't have a million things going on in her head.

"I really don't know," he finally said. "Unless it's just . . ."

He trailed off. Completely. Then started busying himself with setting up his tent. Oh, he was not getting off that easily.

"Just what?" she demanded.

He glanced at her sideways. Assessing. Wondering. Finally he shrugged, as if it didn't matter at all. It didn't, so she couldn't figure out why his nonchalance made her bristle.

"Maybe they think we should rehash all that old shit."

Tori had a lot of snide comments for that, but she couldn't quite make any of them come out of her mouth. Her throat had tightened and something far too close to panic fluttered and jittered in her chest.

She thought she'd accepted rehashing the past was a possibility. In all the weeks leading up to coming to Gracely, to facing Will, she thought she'd accepted that at some point they might have to discuss that horrible night.

She had moved on. She'd lived a whole life without Will and those feelings. She didn't feel the same way anymore, and she wasn't the same person anymore. It shouldn't matter.

It shouldn't, but it did. Not because she felt the same way, but because if they rehashed she would feel that old pain. No matter that she was over it. The memory of it would hurt, and having the memory of it hurt with him witnessing it was too much to bear. It had always been too much to bear.

"There isn't much point in that, is there?" She was beyond gratified when her voice came out strong and clear.

"No. Can't change the past, right?"

"Right."

They both returned their focus to setting up their tents, and Tori could only hope that was that.

Chapter Five

Will had never much cared for the softer sides of adventure stuff. Those activities that might be hard on the body, but gave the mind too much time to think. Hiking. Camping.

He preferred throwing himself into a raging river in a kayak or raft, or flinging himself up the side of a mountain. Things that required agility, strength, skill, and focus.

But putting up a tent only took so long, and he was currently debating the need for a fire. They didn't need one at all, even with night falling and the temperatures cooling off. An MRE to eat, a sleeping bag to keep warm, they were set.

All that was left to do was wait. For night to fully fall. For it to be late enough to sleep. For it to get light enough to go back to Mile High in the morning.

Waiting had never been his strong suit.

The problem was he had a little niggle of unease that Lilly and crew had set this up. She hadn't been wrong about almost anything since she'd shown up in Gracely, but surely she'd have to be wrong at some point. Why not about this?

"H-holy shit."

He glanced at Tori, who'd stumbled backward from her tent, eyes wide, hand over her heart.

"Wha—" But he saw it then, or more heard it, then

turned to it. Ambling out of the tree line around the clearing was a bear.

. A big fucking bear.

He'd seen a lot of bears over the years, but never this close, and never this big. Christ. The large creature stood at the edge of the clearing, its nose in the air clearly sniffing.

"Do you h-have bear spray?" she asked, her voice quiet and a little shaky but not panicked. "Mine's in the tent."

"Yeah, just need a few steps." He took a deep breath, trying to calm his over-beating heart. "Why don't you come closer?"

He didn't take his eyes off the bear to see if Tori would listen. Instead he edged toward his pack, which was only a few inches away. As much as the advice to make lots of noise usually worked in getting a bear to go away, the bear was so calm Will was loath to startle it with yelling.

Tori moved next to him and for the first time since he'd noticed the animal, he flicked a glance away and toward Tori. She stared at the bear, but her jaw was set. Whatever fear might have lurked she had locked down.

"Stand behind me."

She snorted, and the bear tilted its head toward them.

"I'm going to start making noise, and if I have to spray it, you don't want to be downwind. So just stand behind me like a good girl." Which he said to get a rise out of her, yes, at the least sensible moment.

"Say 'good girl' again and I'll feed you to that bear myself," she muttered, but she took a step behind him.

The bear ambled along the edge of the trees, mostly sniffing at shrubs, but occasionally looking their way.

"Shoo, now," Will said in a calm voice, trying to sound forceful but not startling.

"Oh my God, you did not just tell a bear to *shoo*."

"What would *you* suggest? Be my guest." He made a

gesture toward the bear, who seemed utterly unaffected by both his *shoo* and their arguing.

"Hey, bear! Get out of here!"

"Hey, bear," Will muttered. "You think it responds to 'hey, bear' more than 'shoo'?"

"I think it doesn't matter what we say, it matters that he goes the hell away," Tori huffed. "Thus far, neither of us have figured out the right words."

The bear munched on some bush, continuing to pay them no mind. Will didn't want to go up and spray the thing when it wasn't being antagonistic, but he also didn't want to stand here all night with Tori all too close.

Somehow her proximity seemed way more dangerous than the bear, though all in all, both were minding their own business—lurking about the edges of his clearing and or life like a potential threat—whether to life and limb or emotional and mental well-being.

He gripped the bear spray in his hand. He couldn't get rid of Tori, but he could get rid of the bear. It was something, anyway.

He stomped his feet, and yelled "Hey!" a few times. Tori followed suit, adding clapping to the mix. The bear looked at them, damn near quizzically, and then took a step forward.

Without even discussing it, he and Tori both stopped making noise. Will held his breath, and he had a feeling she was doing the same. Especially as the bear took another step their way.

Will fumbled a little but got the bear spray cap and safety off, but before he could even worry about how to spray the bear, it stopped, sniffed the air again, turned around, and lumbered back into the trees.

Will let out the breath he'd been holding. Coming into contact with predators wasn't exactly uncommon, but it wasn't common, either. Especially that close up.

He turned to Tori and she had her hand covering her face, and she was shaking.

"Hey, you okay?" he asked, wrapping his hand around her arm before he thought better of it.

It was only as he tried to draw her closer to offer a little comfort that he realized she was laughing. *Laughing*.

"I just kept thinking . . ." She laughed again, trying to take a gulp of air. "If that bear ate us, boy, wouldn't everyone back at Mile High be sorry they'd set us up."

It shouldn't be funny, but his own laugh bubbled up and out. Maybe a little adrenaline-induced, but a loud, long laugh nonetheless. "I would have haunted their asses."

She laughed even harder, and he couldn't help but laugh too. Getting killed by a bear would have been quite the story-worthy end.

It took him a few minutes to realize Tori had stopped laughing, that she'd sobered, and mostly that his hand was still wrapped around her arm.

She held it tense now, frowning at his fingers, and for some reason he couldn't get his brain to turn on and release her.

Because the day had been hot, they were both wearing T-shirts, so his hand gripped her bare forearm. Tori had always exuded a gritty kind of toughness, but her skin was soft, tanned, a little mole right where his thumb imprinted into her skin.

He heard her inhale sharply and it was a reminder he hadn't done that in too long, so he gulped air he belatedly realized he needed.

It broke whatever spell had settled over them and she jerked her arm from his grasp. She took a step backward, not meeting his gaze as she wrapped her arms around her midsection.

Nothing was funny anymore. It was heavy and weighted, that ugly thing that existed between them because of one stupid night a million years ago when she'd told him she was in love with him.

Love. She'd used that word like it wasn't a weapon or a threat. Like it was something soft and easy, but he'd known better.

Love hurt. Love broke things and people. Love was *hard*, and he wasn't any damn good at hard.

Tori was trying to breathe through her body's torturous response to Will's hand being on her arm. Her *arm*. Why should her heart beat against her chest like it was trying to escape? Why should her breathing be uneven, her legs shaky?

It was a touch, a simple one, and it meant nothing.

Except Will always meant something even when she desperately wanted him not to. Because it was as much the look as the touch that shoved her back seven years to her heart breaking all over again.

"We should build a fire. Maybe that'll keep the bear away overnight," he offered into the all-too-heavy silence.

"Yeah," she managed to mutter, though she still felt thoroughly shaken. If only it was because of the bear and not because of a little arm touch. "I'll find some firewood."

"Get your spray."

She bristled at the command, more because she was irritated with herself for being such an idiot to have her head full of Will when she should have her head full of not getting attacked by a bear.

They worked in utter silence doing everything needed to collect supplies and then build a fire. The sun was slowly setting, but it'd be a while before it got full dark, and then what? Every creak and crack of the forest would convince her the bear was back, and how was she going to sleep through that?

And then, worse, so much worse, would be the places her mind would wander in her non-sleeping state. Mainly Will's tent. Will.

Will, Will, Will, damn it, how was it so easy for her life to revolve back to this point? Where Will Evans was the center of the universe she revolved around.

She cursed as she missed the piece of wood she'd been cutting down into kindling and scraped her finger with the blade.

She sucked her finger into her mouth, and realized disgustedly she was lucky she hadn't cut her whole damn finger to the bone. As it was, she'd at least need a bandage to stop the bleeding to protect the cut from the work she was doing.

"You need a bandage," Will said, so matter-of-factly she wanted to argue with him out of spite. Who was he to decide that? Maybe she could do just *fine* without a bandage.

But she wasn't going to repeat the mistakes of twenty-five-year-old Tori. New life. New person. She needed to accept there was a time and a place to be contrary, and alone in the woods with a bloody finger and a bear ambling about probably wasn't it.

Will had pulled a first aid kit out of his pack and grabbed some disinfectant and a Band-Aid. He paused for a second, standing in front of her, and in that pause she felt something jittery and light.

Anticipation.

She was like an addict. Only her drug was too-handsome men who would never, ever give her what she needed.

After that all-too-potent moment of hesitation, Will took her hand and sprayed the disinfectant. Out of sheer force of will she didn't flinch or hiss though it burned like a bitch.

He held her hand in his, competently wrapping the Band-Aid around the cut. It was far too much like the arm-touching thing before. All that awareness coursed through her, as potent and dangerous as it had been when she'd been young and stupid. Just like then, she was *certain* he felt it too—the way the air warmed and something sparkled to life between them.

But she'd been wrong then and she was wrong now, and that meant something had to change. It meant she had to be stronger than she'd been back then.

"Maybe they were right." Avoiding wasn't working. Pretending wasn't doing jack shit, so maybe she needed to do the thing she'd never done before. Maybe instead of pretending or running, she needed to face the thing she least wanted to.

Will's hazel eyes met hers, wary and confused. "Who was right about what?"

"We need to hash it out. All of it."

He dropped her hand, his eyebrows drawing together, his eyes searching her face as though he were waiting for the punch line.

"Maybe it'd be good." Could it be any worse than this? Maybe if they talked that night through, bit by excruciating bit, she could dull that shiver of want when he was too close.

"I don't think so," he said softly, but she knew that tone. Will was only soft when he was sure, when there was no changing his mind. But she would try to, God she had to try.

"It isn't working. Whatever this is doesn't work for me. We need to try something else, and you said yourself Lilly is always right. Maybe this was her plan all along, because everyone can see it, Will. They can see this doesn't work."

The idea of talking about it made her shaky, but she was sure now—especially in his reluctance. This was the thing they needed to do. Maybe they'd both moved on, but they hadn't healed. She was tired of this feeling like a picked scab. She needed it to be an old scar that couldn't crack and bleed.

There was no change in Will's expression. He stood there stiff and blank and when he met her pleading gaze, all she saw was emptiness.

When he spoke, his voice was flat. Final. "It's working for me."

Then, much too much like that night on their favorite Boulder overlook, Will turned his back on her and walked away.

This time though she wasn't left with a broken heart. There were no tears in her eyes, no pain in her chest.

No, this time, all she was was angry.

Chapter Six

Will woke the next morning gritty-eyed and pissed off and dreading leaving the safety and solitude of his tent.

He would fully admit to anyone who would accuse him of it that he was a coward. He'd never had to be brave, and he'd never had to fight. That was Brandon's expertise, and Will had never learned it.

Ever since his mother had blamed *him* for telling her about his father's affair, and the possible child he'd created with someone else, Will had learned that being brave and doing the hard thing only got you a cart full of shit.

So it didn't bother him he had spent the night hiding from an angry woman in his tent. It was a better alternative to the shit.

He'd heard her stomp around outside for a while after he'd zipped up his tent. He'd listened carefully, not willing to fall asleep until he'd heard the zip of her own. Once she'd paced off her anger or whatever and gotten into her own tent, he'd gotten snatches of sleep, always straining to listen for any possible bear sounds.

Every time he'd woken up, listening too hard to the sound of a Colorado wilderness night, the same thought had run through his head.

Christ, why would she want to dredge all those old memories up? So they could be more uncomfortable around each other? So he could be reminded of all the ways her confession all those years ago had betrayed his trust? So he could be reminded of all the ways his terrible response had been a betrayal of hers? Why would either of them want to relive one of the most terrible days of his life?

Right up there with Mom's anger at *him* and threatening to cut him off, and when Courtney had flippantly announced she'd had an abortion.

Odd, he could rationalize those both away. Mom had needed a target for her hurt to land, or maybe she'd come to love her reputation more than her children. Whatever it was she'd needed him to be the scapegoat. Shitty? Sure, but there was some reason, some need behind it.

With Courtney, well, it wasn't like they'd had a typical marriage. They'd always had fun together, and they'd never communicated. They'd never talked about what they wanted, and he'd been more than happy to stay in Colorado with Bran while Courtney spent most of her time traveling for her modeling career. Sure, it had hurt that he'd lost the chance at his child without even a say in it, but he couldn't blame her for looking out for herself without consulting him. That had always been who they were.

Both incidents had cut him open, bled him dry, but he'd found a resigned kind of understanding.

He'd never in a million years understood why Tori would admit she loved him that night, when he wasn't worth the trouble, and she was worth infinitely more.

Now she wanted to rehash it? Hell no.

He climbed out of his sleeping bag, trying to ignore the itchy feeling building in his gut. He wouldn't name it and it would go away.

The morning was cool and in any other situation that might have been something like calming and relaxing. He loved a cool mountain morning and the quiet promise of a new day. He liked the hope of dawn and dew. It restored him most days, but today he felt none of that hope for renewal or the excitement at facing the day. All he felt was dread.

He grabbed a sweatshirt out of his pack and pulled it on. He shoved his feet into his boots and then, with a deep breath to steady himself and remind himself she couldn't make him relive one of the most painful nights of his life, he stepped out into the cool mountain morning.

Tori was already standing outside her tent, her gaze on the eastern sky that was growing pink behind the trees. She had been stretching her hands above her head, leaning back and then spreading her arms out wide, but she stilled as he stepped out.

It only lasted for a second or so, and then she went back to stretching, her eyes never darting toward him.

He should look away, be the coward he always was, but the way she moved was still as mesmerizing as he'd tried to pretend it wasn't all those years they'd been friends.

She wasn't blatantly gorgeous like most of the women he'd dated or, in Courtney's case, married. He'd always gone after women who had the kind of bodies that matched their big personalities, but Tori's gigantic personality had been trapped in this tiny body. Short, compact, everything about her reminding him of a scrappy little fighter. The gleam in her blue-green eyes, the way she went after what she wanted—stubborn and dogged. She walked through the world as if it was a constant fight, and she was always ready for it. Always determined to win.

She was a force, and something about that made her too pointy chin, and too big eyes, and too sharp face gorgeous. She was tiny, but everything about her was strong and even at his weakest, he recognized that strength and envied it.

He'd always wanted it in ways he'd never been able to make sense of. So he'd befriended it, even though she'd always intimidated him. He'd circled around it, like the earth to the sun, he'd orbited around Tori helplessly attracted and desperately afraid of getting too close in case he'd burn up.

He'd always known she'd burn him up.

A pertinent reminder that he couldn't look at her like this, think of her like this. He'd survived their friendship because he'd done an excellent job of pretending none of those feelings or fears existed inside of him. Pretending had been the Will Evans way of surviving the world since he'd been a teenager.

Today though, in the pearly light of dawn, and the emotional upheaval of the past who-knew-how-many days, he felt that old want shudder through him. Some weak part of him could imagine his hands on the smooth lines of her body. Something in his mind dared wonder what she might taste like, and as it always did, those thoughts made him hate himself.

Because if there was anything he knew without a shadow of a doubt, it was that Tori Appleby—in her infinite strength that hid some infinite vulnerability she'd never be willing to show—was not for him. He wasn't strong enough or brave enough or *good* enough to be the man who touched her.

It was a shame for Tori that she had shitty taste in men.

"Good morning," Tori offered cheerfully.

He knew not to trust that cheerfulness because Tori was never cheerful except when she was about to kill you.

"Morning."

"Sleep well?" she continued in that syrupy sweet voice.

"Like the dead," he replied, because he felt like the dead. Gritty-eyed and numb and as though nothing but blackness lay before him.

"Isn't that nice? Wish I could say the same. I was too busy thinking about all the hours I put into planning how I was going to tell you I loved—"

"You can't make me do this," he growled. She couldn't force him to relive it. She couldn't.

She smiled at him, sharp and dangerous, that smile he'd always admired because it had never been aimed at him. Now it was on him, and he knew a weapon when he saw one.

"Can't I?"

A sense of foreboding stole through him because last night he'd been certain that all it would take was a few well-placed words and to walk away, and she wouldn't push this. Who would want to push this?

But he should've known better because Tori was the woman who'd set this horrible thing between them in motion in the first place, and she was not a woman who let things go. Who sulked away, who played the coward.

Which was why, he realized with a clarity he didn't want, he'd been so mad when he'd come back to Boulder after he'd married Courtney and she'd been gone. It was why he'd been so livid that she'd reappeared seven years later as if nothing had happened.

Because it wasn't Tori to be a coward, to run away. It wasn't Tori to give up the fight.

Now she wanted to rewrite the ending? Come back into his life? Face all those old things he'd cut out of himself?

The itch in his gut got stronger, more of a searing, boiling thing. But if he didn't name it, everything would be fine.

For Brandon, and for Lilly, and for Mile High, Gracely, and the Evans name, he could not give in to this ugly thing inside of him.

Which meant he had to fight, for once in his life, he had to fight.

There was something passing over Will's face Tori didn't recognize. It reminded her a little bit of when she'd first seen him at Mile High on the day of Brandon's wedding.

He'd been so . . . angry, and while she'd imagined their reuniting in a lot of different ways, blind fury on his part had never been one of them.

Everything about his expression was hard, and it made him look older somehow. Older and dangerous, and though Will had always been a danger to her heart, he'd never appeared *dangerous*.

Unease shivered down her spine, and that was certainly new and different. She'd been so certain she had everything right, and that she was going to win this fight.

For the first time possibly ever, she wasn't so sure she would. Not against this man she didn't recognize.

But he didn't say anything, and eventually he stopped staring at her like he thought he could dismantle her piece by piece. She was a little shaky at that because her saving grace had always been that he didn't think he could win against her. If he ever thought he had power over her control, she'd be toast. Because it was true. He absolutely had all those things—power and control. It would only take a few little words for him to dismantle her completely. He'd just never known it.

Ignoring the way her stomach curdled and her chest got too tight, she forced her body to relax. "I've always wondered what it was," she said conversationally, "because even if you didn't have feelings for me back when we were friends, why did you have to—"

"Yeah, we were friends. That was it," he interrupted gruffly, a steely, furious note to his voice she thought maybe he was trying to hide. "Should I remind you that you ran away a lot faster than I did?"

It was the flat-out lie that unwound some of her control. "Bullshit. You disappeared. I stayed in Boulder. I . . ."

He stepped toward her and even though she wanted to be strong and formidable, her words trailed off. Because he looked dangerous and intimidating, and he'd never been those things. Even that night when he'd flat-out told her that there would never be anything between them, he hadn't been aggressive.

"What is it you're trying to accomplish?" he asked, his voice threaded with that same deadly calm it'd had when he'd told her love was never going to be a thing they experienced together.

That question made her hesitate. The answer gave away too much. How would she survive being here, having come here basically homeless and penniless and on her knees, if he knew so many of those old hurts still thrived inside of her? Like he was some sort of disease, one that lived in her blood no matter how many years and treatments she'd employed to get rid of it. A cancer that was never truly eradicated.

"I want to erase it," she said, more than ashamed when her voice wasn't the sturdy, determined thing she wanted it to be.

"I guess that's the difference between you and me, Tori. I erased it a long damn time ago."

It hurt. She knew he wanted it to hurt. He was good at that, finding the thing to push the dagger deeper.

But beyond her hurt, beyond her anger, she saw something else. Older and wiser and used to the hurt, she couldn't help but wonder if Will was hurting her on *purpose*. Not because he was mean-spirited or awful, but because when you hurt someone else it sometimes felt like you were protecting yourself.

Because why would he have been angry when she first arrived if he'd erased it so effectively?

It was a lie, and that stirred her anger all over again. Will had always been adept at pretending, but he'd never lied to her face.

"You've already erased it and me," she said, pretending to ruminate over his words. Putting a few new ones in his mouth because it would piss him off. "And yet here I am. Here *we* are. But I'm not going anywhere this time, and I don't think you are either."

"No, I'm not."

"Then I guess we'll just see how erased it is for you." Because she wouldn't let him have his lie. She'd poke at him until he broke, and then maybe she'd finally have the truth, and some closure. A foundation to build her new life on.

Because damn right she wasn't going anywhere, and neither was he.

Chapter Seven

Will stared blearily at the computer screen. Brandon said he'd make it in this afternoon, and Will wanted to double-check and make sure he'd done everything right in Brandon's absence. He wanted to be certain, absolutely certain, he hadn't fucked things up.

It was a nagging worry, and he wished he could blame that on why he hadn't slept for two nights, but even in his best denial shape he couldn't make himself believe it.

No sleeping was all Tori. The subtle threat she'd left him with the other day, and the gnawing worry she had something up her sleeve.

But he hadn't seen much of her that day, and she'd spent the day after on an excursion kayaking with Sam. Yesterday she'd taken the day off due to a few deliveries at her new house.

In that break from having Tori in his space, he'd dreamed of that night every time he'd fallen asleep. It never quite went the same as the reality had, but in every version of the dream she was wearing that flowery sundress she'd been wearing, and her thick blond hair had been down at her shoulders, and she'd said those damaging words.

I love you.

Will scrubbed his hands across his face. This was his penance for lying, he supposed. He'd told her he'd erased it, so now he was going to relive it till he went insane. Seemed apt, all in all.

A mug of steaming hot coffee appeared at his elbow and Will glanced up to find Skeet hovering over him. The gnarled old man acted as Mile High's secretary, refused to use computers, grunted more than he spoke actual words, and never, ever made drink deliveries—except to Lilly. Skeet did have a soft spot for Lilly.

Will must have been in worse shape than he'd thought to have earned Skeet's rare caregiving tendencies.

"Thanks," he offered wearily.

Skeet shrugged looking around the office, his bleary blue eyes taking in the rumpled twin bed shoved in the corner.

"You been looking for another place?" Skeet asked in his age-graveled voice.

"No," Will returned, keeping his attention on the computer screen.

"Has it occurred to you it might be a good idea?"

"Nope."

"You can't spend the rest of your life living out of the office, boy."

Will grunted. Instead of arguing further, Skeet thankfully disappeared. Living in the office was fine for now. Surely with twins on the way, Lilly and Brandon would want a bigger house. What was the point in finding a place if he was only going to be moving back into the cabin eventually?

The cabin Brandon had designed, and had built, and you had no say in?

He pushed the thought away because he hadn't wanted

a say. He didn't care where he lived. He could live any damn where.

Skeet reappeared, holding a jar in front of him, and Will groaned.

"You can't be serious," Will said, eyeing the jar and Skeet's beady-eyed glare.

Skeet held the big plastic jar Lilly had made months ago when she'd been irritated with their preference to grunt rather than actually answer a question. Whenever one of them grunted at her, she made them put a dollar in it.

"Promised Lilly," Skeet said easily. "Now pay up."

Will muttered curses under his breath as he grabbed his wallet from the corner of the desk. He pulled out a one and shoved it into the jar. He opened his mouth to say something obnoxious, but a bark stopped him.

Sarge bounded into the office and skidded to a stop, tongue lolling to one side.

"There's a boy," Skeet said, not needing to lean down to pet the dog's head. Sarge sat dutifully as Skeet scratched behind his ears.

"Sarge!" Tori called from what Will assumed was the main area up front.

"Like her," Skeet said in his usual gruff way, before giving the dog one last pat and disappearing.

Sarge stayed where he was, panting seemingly happily up at Will. It twisted in his heart that the damn dog might *recognize* him.

"Come here, boy," Will said softly, patting his knees. With a little yip, Sarge jumped up and put his paws on Will's knees, just like he used to. Will rubbed his hands over Sarge's head and down his neck.

Sarge offered a rough, sloppy lick in return.

"Well, that's about as much action as I've gotten for . . ." He trailed off because he heard Tori's heavy footsteps in the doorway. For a little thing she sure could make a lot of noise.

He glanced up at her meeting her gaze. He was immediately wary because she had that warrior stance about her. She was here to do battle. It wasn't a shock. God, he was just tired. He didn't want to fight today. He just wanted . . .

What the hell do *you want?*

Whatever the answer was, today wasn't the day to figure it out.

"Isn't it funny how he hasn't seen you for seven years, but knows exactly who you are?" she asked, crossing her arms over her chest.

It reminded him too much of Brandon's wedding day, when seeing her had been like a sledgehammer to the chest, and she'd had the nerve to look pissed off and ready for a fight while he was still reeling from the blow.

"Yeah. Funny," he intoned, because until he had a better option the whole pretending-like-he-didn't-give-a-shit routine he usually used was going to have to work. "You're taking the Solace Falls hike today, right? With Hayley?"

"Actually, Hayley has family in town unexpectedly, I guess. So I was thinking I could take the hike by myself. It's the easy one. Shouldn't be too much of a problem."

Will frowned at that. It was an easy hike, and he wasn't worried about her hiking it in the least. But *leading* people in a hike was a whole other thing, and it was the point of their business. They hadn't let Hayley take a hike of her own until Sam had observed her through one.

"Of course, you're welcome to come with." She smiled and it was not a nice smile. No, this was the smile of a woman who was going to twist the knife as deep as she possibly could.

He couldn't even blame her. No matter how angry and frustrated he got with her—being here, pushing at him—

eventually he'd cool off and remember she had nowhere else to go. She was fighting because she didn't have a choice.

It was the fundamental difference between them—that she'd always had to, and he never had.

He patted Sarge's head, finding some comfort in that. Going with her was what Brandon would do. So it's what he would do no matter how much he didn't want to.

"All right. I'll go with you. You'll lead it, and I'll just be there to observe. If everything goes well, then you'll be cleared to at least lead that excursion on your own from here on out."

"Fantastic. You know, I was just thinking about that hike we took in Estes Park that one summer. You remember that?"

He wasn't quite sure what her endgame was now. If she had brought up that fateful night, he would have known exactly what she was trying to do. What the hell was she after, bringing up old *good* memories? From before everything got broken and splintered apart.

"Estes Park. Yeah, when we saw the moose?" he asked warily.

"Exactly." She smiled brightly. "You told me about your father and why Brandon had to rush back to Gracely."

Will stilled, keeping his expression neutral, his eyes glued to the dog. He still didn't know where she was going, but he realized she was definitely going somewhere.

"I felt so sorry for you. To find out that your father was doing terrible things and to have to deal with it. Of course, you weren't the one who had to deal with it, were you?"

"You have a point to all this?" he ground out.

She shrugged, easy as you please. "Just trying to figure out a puzzle, if you will. When I try to put all those pieces together, they don't make any sense."

"Pieces of what?"

"You."

A simple word, amazing it could land like a punch. Or

maybe a stab. He didn't want her figuring him out, and he had a bad feeling she was one of the few people who could.

"What's the whole story on Hayley? I haven't quite figured out how that works."

Gently he nudged Sarge off his legs and stood. Because he could take a lot of bullshit poking at *him*, but he wouldn't let her bring Hayley into it.

"I'd watch where you step," he said with as much menace as he could muster, meeting her sharp gaze for the first time.

She widened her eyes, all fake innocence. "What do you mean?"

"Come at me all you want. You start messing with the people I love, I'll poke right back."

Her eyebrows drew together and she cocked her head, studying him in a way he didn't even begin to understand.

"Don't you get it? That's exactly what I want you to do."

"I remember that day in Estes as well as you do. You told me something about your family that you weren't particularly fond of talking about."

Her expression didn't change, but he could tell simply by the way she held her body a little differently that he'd hit his mark.

"Something about your brother? And why you had to run away from home."

"You'll notice there's a little bit of a difference there." She paused. "My brother threatened me. You just didn't help your brother clean up a mess."

"Oh, honey, if you want to make this a contest about who is best than you should know you've already won. Congratulations. I know what I am. You pointing it out to me doesn't hurt."

This time her eyebrows drew together with something other than confusion, fake or otherwise. It was a softness he didn't want to recognize but did. Tori had always felt sorry for him. Even when he hadn't wanted her to. But he remembered all too clearly a time when she'd been a soft place to go when he was feeling particularly self-pitying.

She'd never made him feel like crap for it. Which he'd never understood. She was such a hard, uncompromising person, but she'd been understanding with him. When Brandon hadn't. When Sam hadn't. When his family hadn't. Tori had always given him the benefit of the doubt.

He'd forgotten that about her. It hurt to remember it.

But the softness disappeared almost as quickly as it had appeared. Her gaze sharpened and everything about her hardened against him. "I felt sorry for you then," she said as if reading his thoughts. "Now? You are too old to still believe this self-defeating shit. You get to choose. The life you want. The life you lead. Acting like it's different is pathetic." With that, she turned on a heel and walked away.

He tried to breathe through this new anger she pulled out of him. He didn't know how to reset or pretend it away. He didn't know how to smile through it. He'd been through a million hurtful and terrible things, and he'd always known how to do that, without poking back, without giving away how it cut him.

But he didn't know how to do it with Tori, and he wasn't sure how much longer he could keep his reactions on a leash.

Poke, anger, and retreat. That was Tori's current strategy. She knew it would work. If it didn't kill her first.

It was awful to poke and feel that pain and be surprised at the ways he could hurt her right back. It sucked to run away when she knew that what they really needed was to face this thing.

But she had to maneuver him there. So no matter how it sucked, she had to keep at it. No matter how much she wanted to scream in frustration, she had to tamp down her temper and keep at it. Like a general leading her troops.

She watched Will engage with the group of men and women who would be taking the Solace Falls hike today. It was quite the conglomeration of people. Two older married couples who were taking their first summer of retirement very seriously and touring all of Colorado. Three younger women who laughed too hard at Will's paltry jokes. Two bearded guys Tori was pretty sure were high.

All in all, she supposed this was Mile High normal. Her life was going to be Mile High normal so she needed to pay attention to how Will dealt with things, no matter how irritated she was when he flashed a smile at the far-too-young women giggling at him.

In fairness, Will smiled at the young women, but he treated them no differently than the potheads or the retirees. He was cheerful and jovial with everyone. It was such an act that her head hurt. Because she could read the tension waving off him and no one else could.

Why did she have to be on any sort of frequency where she understood Will?

He had the clients sign the various paperwork required for going on a short hike like this. She paid attention to that, too. No matter how jumbled and unfocused she was, this was her future.

Tori sighed and tried to blow out all the emotional shit inside of her. She took the lead on the hike as Will stayed at the rear. She could hear him tell charming stories about wildlife and hiking to the giggling women who swarmed around him while she answered questions from one of the older couples about the weather and appropriate footwear.

Even with the women expertly flirting with Will, and the stoners clumsily attempting to flirt with her, the hike was oddly nice. It was comforting to do something she was good at and *knew* she was good at, with someone she knew and worked well with.

It was disconcerting to realize she and Will still made a good team, even more disconcerting to feel the bone-deep rightness of this whole thing. Being here. Leading hikes. She was *made* for this. Deep in her soul she knew that in a way she knew nothing else.

Tori Appleby was made for mountains and working outside and . . .

She glanced back at Will smiling that empty smile at some woman leaning against him as though she needed help up the rocks to get to the final summit.

For so very long she thought she'd been made for Will Evans, and vice versa, and it would kill her to allow herself to believe such fictions again. But she could imagine it, working together, a deep, soulful camaraderie, for all the years that stretched out before her. It would be *so* easy to fall back into all those old thoughts and feelings and wishes.

Lucky for her, she'd never taken the easy path, and she didn't plan to start now.

Chapter Eight

Will had just about enough of Giggly McSorority Sister. Maybe on another day his ego would have been assuaged by a woman in her early twenties falling all over him, but under Tori's all too watchful eye he just felt *old*.

He'd been married. He'd been divorced. He'd had a town love him then hate him, watched his family's reputation and business and shaky foundation crumble before him. He'd built a business with his brother in the aftermath. He'd lived lifetimes, and this woman had lifetimes ahead of her instead of behind her.

Plus, no matter how perky her breasts she kept rubbing against him were, the fake clumsiness she was employing had about tripped him up twice, and he wasn't really keen on the idea of falling down a mountain for a pair of tits.

Why on earth that thought process led him to glance up toward Tori and *her* tits was utterly beyond him. He knew better. But she was on top of the outcropping of rock they had to climb to get to the top of the falls making sure the older couples had made it up, and, judging from the look on her face, saying something snarky to pothead number one.

A tiny warrior queen, with the strength to fell a hundred men ten times over. She smiled down at the older woman and offered her a hand, everything about her in control and at ease.

What would it be like to have her real smile aimed at him again? Probably fatal. No matter how much life he'd lived in her absence, he was the same feckless fuck.

Something uncomfortable shifted in his chest, and if he thought too much about it, it might feel like denial. He might recall Tori saying he was too old to still think he was worthless. If he focused on that he might have to accept he had changed. He'd stepped up a few times and—

The little "whoops" and subsequent giggle were the only warning he had before a body all but crashed into his.

Since he was on an uneven portion of trail, he lost his footing. He scrambled for balance, reaching out to grab on to anything steady, but it was too late. He stumbled backward, unable to use his arms to break his fall. There were about three moments of impact. Shoulder, hip, and then his head.

He saw a flash of light, but then he was rolling a bit, and he at least had enough brainpower to use his legs and arms to stop his momentum. He stopped on a rocky, uneven patch of land a little ways off the path, and he rolled to his back, breathing hard and trying to move past the shock enough to figure out if he was seriously hurt.

He heard some shouting and screeching, but he was a little too concerned with his own well-being to worry about anyone else. Everything pulsed with pain and he gritted his teeth against it as he closed his eyes to shut out the bright, blinding sun above him.

When he forced himself to open his eyes and think about getting up, he didn't see the sun, but the ocean.

"Will."

He blinked, realizing it wasn't the ocean but Tori's eyes, wasn't a breeze on his cheek but the ends of Tori's braid. She was kneeling next to him, her head directly above his.

"I think I'm okay," he managed. He was a little out of sorts, but maybe it was the shock or maybe it was her.

He needed to get up.

"Stay still," Tori ordered, her hand firm on his shoulder. "Let's make sure you *are* okay, not just think you are. Now where does it—"

"Oh my God, I'm so sorry. I didn't mean to. It was just . . ." He couldn't see the girl because Tori's head was still over his, but the cause of his fall was all but blubbering apologies between little sobs and hiccups.

"I suggest you get her away from me," Will muttered between clenched teeth, because he was a little too tempted to yell at her for her idiocy and he didn't want to yell at a client no matter how much she deserved it.

Tori murmured a few things and people shuffled about. He didn't pay attention to what was being said or who was where, he brought his hand up to the spot on his head that burned. His fingers came away bloody.

"Well, shit." He tried to sit up again but Tori's hand firmly pressed his shoulder into the rocky ground.

"I don't think you should move."

"There's a rock in my ass. I have to move."

He didn't try to stand quite yet, he just scooted off the sharp rock that was digging into his butt.

Tori's hand was still on his shoulder, strong and sturdy, like a beacon to center on while he got his wits about him.

Except getting his wits about him just meant he realized how much his shoulder and hip hurt.

"What hurts? Can you move everything?"

Will did a mental tally of his body, moving his fingers and arms and legs and toes, making sure everything worked the way it was supposed to. Things were sore and achy, but nothing felt broken or sprained. The only thing he was a little concerned about was the blood dripping from his head.

"Ash, give me your squeezy water bottle," Tori ordered to someone in the group before her face was all up in his face again. She studied him intently. "Do you have a concussion?"

"No," he muttered, irritation moving through him along with the pain.

"Follow my finger."

He glared at her, not paying any attention to her damn finger. "No."

"Don't be a dickbag. Follow my finger." She moved her finger from left to right in front of his eyes and he sighed and did what she asked. What was the point in fighting her? She would just poke at him until she won.

"Now this might sting or feel a little jolting, but try to sit still," she said in an even, no-nonsense tone, as if he were anyone else. A stranger. A client. Why that pissed him off in this moment was anyone's guess.

"That doesn't sound ominous at all. Why don't you—" He yelped as she sprayed some water onto his head. Ice cold water at that.

Then she started running her fingers through his hair and over his scalp and that was somehow worse than the cold and the sting. She was close and he could smell something that must have been soap or shampoo because Tori didn't wear perfume, and as she maneuvered around him looking at different areas of his head, her body brushed against his.

It shouldn't matter, but it did, and she came to a stop kind of in front of him, peering at the top of his head, her chest basically shoved into his face. A cruel cosmic joke when she had on a stretchy exercise pullover that left little to the imagination.

His imagination did not need any help in that department. "Could you maybe not do that?"

"I have to make sure you don't need to be rushed to the hospital for stitches or something," she returned.

"I don't mean not look at my injury, I mean not shove your . . ." He cleared his throat. His mind stumbled through all of the words for breasts, but none of them seemed appropriate in this situation so he just sort of vaguely gestured. "You know, in my face."

She blinked down at him and then scrambled off to the side. If his head wasn't throbbing, he might've laughed at how quickly she scurried away. Like a scared animal. An oddly cheering thought.

"It looks like just a scrape," she muttered. "I can't find any sort of gash or cut, but it's hard to tell with all your hair."

"I think I'm fine."

He let out a little yelp as she poured more water over his head. When he glared at her, she smirked.

"Just making sure you're all cleaned up."

"Let me up. I'm tired of people staring at me."

She didn't move out of his way, still holding the water bottle perilously close to his head. "You took quite a tumble."

"Wasn't my fault," he returned, scooting a little to get some room to stand up where she wasn't hovering over him.

"Oh, I know."

Will glared up at her. "She fell on me."

"Literally. Figuratively." Tori cocked her head. "Are you sure you weren't just distracted and lost your footing?"

He scowled. "I'm sure."

Tori shook her head and got to her feet. She held out her hand to him. "Come on. Let's get you up."

"I don't need your help to get up."

"Take my hand, you dipshit."

Grumbling and irritated and aching, Will curled his hand around hers and got to his feet. He didn't feel dizzy or light-headed, although it took a few seconds to feel sturdy.

Tori's hand slipped out of his, and it sent a little pang through him. It was nice to do something with her without that roiling old shit in his gut, but that was never going to be anything more than short-lived, was it? The shitty past existed. End of story.

He rolled his shoulders and twisted his torso back and forth. "I think I'm more bruised than broken."

"I guess that hard head came in handy for something."

"Ha. Ha." He looked grimly up the hill. Everyone was lined up on the trail looking on, and even though it wasn't his fault, taking the spill had been damn embarrassing.

"Let's head back to Mile—"

"No," Will said, taking a hesitant step and gratified to find his legs seemed fine. "We're taking the clients up to the overlook. That's what they paid for."

Tori pursed her lips together and studied him. It almost looked like concern lurking in her blue-green ocean eyes, but he was probably imagining things. She probably got quite a kick out of seeing him take a header down a mountain.

"I think we should get you back and make sure that you're okay," Tori said carefully.

"I've taken a few falls in my day. I'm okay. Trust me. It'll hurt like a bitch for a few days, but nothing's broken or sprained and you said yourself you couldn't find a cut that'd need stitches. No point in going back and lying around. Eventually the body heals."

She cocked her head and looked at him strangely, but he was too tired and irritated to read the look.

"You can stay down here while I lead them up—"

"Like hell I'll stay down here like some kind of pansy ass."

She rolled her eyes and shook her head and then started tramping back up to the trail. He followed her, trying not to wince at every step. His legs were fine, but his hip ached.

But he knew from experience it would be better to move around now, no matter how painfully, rather than lie still and let everything get stiff.

Tori was instructing everyone on trail safety and making sure to have clear footing before taking the next step. The girl who caused him to fall started rushing over the minute he stepped on the trail, but a sharp look from Tori stopped her in her tracks.

Thank God, because he didn't feel like being generous right now. No matter how apologetic the woman looked, he wasn't certain he could smile and say it was no big deal.

One of the retired women handed him a little bottle of ibuprofen. "Would you like a few of these?" she asked kindly without sounding patronizing.

He managed to smile at her. "God bless you." She smiled in return and let Will shake out a few pills before he handed the bottle back to her.

He tossed the pills back, grateful Tori was paying enough attention to hand him a bottle of water. Since she'd been leading the group, she'd been the one to shoulder the pack. He was probably lucky he hadn't been wearing it or he could have taken an even nastier stumble.

"Why don't you take the lead this time and I'll take the rear," Tori suggested as he handed the water bottle back to her.

He opened his mouth to argue with her, but she touched his arm.

Gently.

"Take the lead," she insisted, a little too gravely. "I get that you're a big strong man and just fine, but take the lead. Please."

It was hard to believe the concern he thought he saw in her eyes was a product of his own imagination now. Because why would she care if he took the lead if she wasn't at least a little worried about him?

If she was even a little worried about him, she didn't hate him quite as much as she pretended to. Which was certainly something to consider.

Thankfully, the remainder of the hike was uneventful. The sorority girls who'd caused Will's fall kept their distance and were much subdued. The older couples praised them both for the beautiful views and the wonderful experience, even despite the fall. The stoners asked her to party with them later, and Tori politely declined.

After the clients dispersed, she and Will walked into the office. Tori snuck a glance at Will as he eased himself into a big chair in the main office.

Skeet was sitting behind his desk and frowning at Will, so Tori turned to him. "Do you have ice packs around here?" She angled her chin toward Will. "Took a bit of a fall."

Skeet nodded and disappeared back into the kitchenette area while Tori continued to study Will. He looked a little gray, but she supposed if anything was seriously wrong he wouldn't have gotten this far.

Still, there was this uncomfortable rock in her gut. Something like worry. She hated that her heart could be so silly as to be concerned over Will's welfare when he was clearly fine, but when had she ever had control over her heart?

"I still think you should see a doctor just to make sure," she offered into the quiet of the room.

"Your concern is touching."

It didn't sound as sarcastic as she might've wanted it to sound. The last thing she wanted to do was touch Will. In any shape or form. Touching would be bad.

Skeet appeared from the kitchen with an ice pack. He handed it to Will wordlessly.

"He needs two more," Tori said. "He hit his head, his hip, and his shoulder."

Skeet gave Tori a little nod before disappearing, hopefully to find more ice packs.

Will looked over at her from beneath his lashes. She always thought it unfair that a guy had long dark eyelashes like that, when her pale ones were basically invisible unless she put mascara on, which always seemed like a waste of time.

"You were paying awfully close attention to my fall," he said, something odd in his tone.

Like he could see through her a lot more than she wanted him to. So she shrugged as nonchalantly as she could manage. "I was the leader of the hike. I was supposed to be paying attention." Maybe, *maybe*, she'd been paying a little too much attention to the woman flirting with Will so she had witnessed every landing point on his fall.

But that was neither here nor there.

"It wasn't your job to be paying attention to *me*." He winced as he put the ice pack on his head, which caused her to bite back her snotty retort.

She might be angry with him and irritated by him for a

million different reasons, but that didn't mean she liked seeing him physically hurt. The jerk.

Will let out a tired sigh and Tori felt like she should say something, but she didn't know what. Watching him fall hadn't exactly been fun for her. If she was being completely honest with herself and no one else, her heart had jumped to her throat when he'd toppled backward.

Skeet returned with the ice packs. Instead of handing the ice packs off to Will, Skeet crossed to her and held them out.

She stared at his outstretched hands somewhat horrified. "What do you want me to do with them?"

"Boy's only got two hands, and I have to answer the phone." With that, Skeet shoved them at her and walked over to his desk. To a phone that was most certainly *not* ringing. She glared at Skeet, then looked back at Will, who was smirking at her.

"Afraid to touch me, sweetheart?" he drawled.

She rolled her eyes so hard it nearly hurt. "The last woman who touched you knocked you down a mountain. You might want to be careful about engaging in females touching you."

He gave a little laugh, which was a surprise because she didn't think he was feeling too jovial about the whole ordeal.

"She said it was a dare."

"To knock you down the mountain?" Tori returned, taking a hesitant step toward him, his large body sprawled in that chair, his eyes drooping half closed, looking tired and soft. Everything in her softened at that, no matter how she tried to harden it.

"A dare to flirt with me. I told her she was very bad at it."

Tori's mouth twitched. "Did you really tell her that?"

"No. I told her next time she wanted to flirt with a guy to try not knocking him off a mountain."

"You know, it was only a few feet down a mountain. You're being very overdramatic about it."

His eyes met hers, and where she'd thought he'd looked tired and soft not more than a minute or so ago, the look was sharp. Assessing.

She feared it saw way too much. Feeling unaccountably nervous and weird, she stepped toward him again. It didn't make any sense to be nervous when not that long ago she'd been shoving her fingers through his hair searching his scalp for a cut.

But there'd been a weird feeling then too, it was just that shock and fear had hidden it. She didn't have those things anymore to hide behind. She just had . . .

"Here," she said, clearing her throat when her voice came out scratchy. "Put that one on your hip. I'll hold this one on your shoulder."

His eyes had never left hers and her nerves intensified. She didn't even know why or what this was. It was just . . . silence. Or something.

After a few humming moments of she didn't know what, he took the outstretched ice pack and shifted in the chair to slide it against his hip.

Trying to stand as far away as possible and still be able to reach his shoulder, she plopped the other ice pack on his shoulder.

His hand closed over hers on top of the ice pack, and she sucked in a loud breath against her will.

Tonight, when she was lying in her bed berating herself for this moment, she would have a good reason for why she felt all shivery and affected. She'd find the best excuse for why she couldn't breathe properly, or why her heart beat too hard, but for right now she couldn't come up with excuses or reasons because his warm, calloused hand was on top of hers. She felt that warmth more than she felt the cold of the ice pack.

He curled his fingers around her hand and she all but squeaked, but he just shifted her hand and the ice pack to the side of his shoulder rather than the top.

"There," he said, his voice too low and husky. "And since the chair is keeping the ice pack on my hip, I can probably hold this one myself."

"Right." So she should probably tug her hand away. Or something. "I can hold it if you need me to. I mean, if your other arm's sore." Was that *her* voice coming out sounding so breathless and far too close to the giggling women on the trail?

There was a beat of silence, heavy and meaningful, but she tried to ignore the meaningful part of it. The way he studied her. All the jittering feelings inside of her. If she ignored them . . .

But wasn't that the problem? Ignoring didn't work. She needed to find a way to face it. To acknowledge it and eradicate it. A surgeon couldn't cut out a tumor if he didn't know what and where the tumor was. He had to identify it first, map it out, have a plan and know what the hell he was dealing with.

She opened her mouth to say something—God knew what—something inevitably stupid, but the front door opened and in came laughter and other people.

Hayley, Sam, and someone Tori didn't know filed into the room. Tori jerked away from Will, which was stupid because of course everyone noticed. If she'd just stood there like a normal person, no one would have questioned it.

Luckily, Hayley was immediately distracted, Tori assumed by the ice packs on Will's head.

"Oh no, what happened?"

Hayley rushed over to inspect Will, but Sam stood where he was, impenetrable blue gaze still on Tori.

"He fell," Tori said lamely, trying to break Sam's all-too-assessing gaze and failing.

"Did he have help?" Sam asked, quirking a brow at Tori.

"Just a dope of a hiker knocking me down by accident," Will offered. "But I'm fine."

Tori wished she was.

Chapter Nine

Will was irritated by Hayley's appearance for a lot of reasons. First and foremost because he'd been certain Tori had been about to say something. Maybe even something conciliatory. But it was nothing more than wishful thinking to imagine they could be friends again.

"Are you sure you're okay?"

Will forced himself to smile at Hayley, forced himself to be gratified by her concern. This half sister he barely knew.

"I'll live. Though I'll be a grumpy son of a bitch for a few days."

She patted his good shoulder sympathetically. "I think you deserve it."

Will glanced over at Sam and then realized there was someone he didn't know in the room.

"Will," Hayley said, walking over to the tall, dark-skinned man. "This is my stepbrother. James, this is Will and Tori. I'm showing James around and then we're going to go to dinner. I was hoping you guys could join us, but if you're hurt . . ."

Will was about to agree. Too hurt to go out to her awkward dinner, but James stepped toward Tori with a wide smile and offered a hand.

When Tori smiled back, shaking the man's hand, Will clenched his teeth, glancing at Hayley. She was grinning over at Tori and her stepbrother, self-satisfied, as if . . .

Oh, hell no.

He shoved to his feet, ice packs be damned. "Dinner sounds great."

Hayley blinked at him. "But if you're sore and grumpy, you should probably stay home and relax."

And let Hayley try to set up some guy Will knew jack shit about with one of his best friends? No way in hell. Maybe he and Tori had . . . issues, but that didn't mean he was going to let Hayley indiscriminately throw guys at Tori. It was a well-documented fact Tori had shit taste in men.

He being a prime example.

James lived hours away, and as far as Will knew had a somewhat tenuous relationship with Hayley. That was not enough to give a guy the green light to be thrown at your friend.

Besides, Hayley didn't even know Tori. She had no idea the kind of guy she would need. Tori had just gotten to town and . . .

"You okay, buddy?" Sam asked, an all-too-knowing look in his eye.

Will realized he was walking a very fine and weird line here. Something between friendly concern, which was all this was, and Sam reading far too much into it, or Hayley getting bent out of shape that he thought she was wrong about clearly trying to shove her stepbrother at Tori.

But that was fine. He could handle all this.

"I feel great. I could use a really good dinner fixed by someone else." He grinned broadly, which only served to earn him odd looks from everyone.

"O-okay. I asked Brandon and Lilly, but Lilly's checkup is tomorrow and she wanted to make sure she'd stayed off her feet all day. Um . . ." Hayley looked sort of helplessly at Sam, and whatever passed between them, Will couldn't read.

He was a little too busy trying to read the looks James sent Tori's way.

"We can't get everybody in either of your Jeeps, so why don't you and Tori meet us at Steak House in Benson. Say, around six?"

Will looked at Tori, who was clearly trying to find an excuse not to go. But if he was going, she was damn well going. Which he knew didn't make any sense, but maybe he did have a concussion. Either way, they were both going to dinner, and he was going to make sure Hayley didn't try shoving her brother in Tori's direction.

Because somehow that made sense.

"Sounds great," Will said, smiling, though he realized a little belatedly it must not have appeared like a smile since Sam and Hayley were looking at him very confused.

"Ookay, um, well, I'm going to show James around. We'll see you guys at dinner." Hayley smiled, though her eyebrows drew together as she gave Will a once-over. "And if you're not feeling up to it, I won't be upset if you cancel."

"I'll be there," Will replied resolutely. He gave the trio a little wave as they filed out the back, making sure to stand without a grimace until they were completely gone and on the back porch.

He collapsed back into the chair with a groan.

"What the hell are you doing?" Tori demanded, coming to stand in front of him, hands on her hips, irritation in the line dug across her forehead.

"Planning to have dinner with one of my best friends, my half sister, and her stepbrother, plus you. That's something like the new American normal, I think."

"You're hurt, and what's more, why are you dragging me into it?"

"You seemed rather dragged of your own accord."

"What?"

"All that *smiling* at Hayley's stepbrother."

She scoffed. "Your brain's jumbled."

"I saw the look on Hayley's face. She's trying to set you up."

Tori huffed out a breath. "That's ridic—" Her features softened as she seemed to mull it over, and then her mouth curved. "You really think so?"

"Yes," he ground out through clenched teeth. "So I'm saving you."

"Saving me? From the hot guy Hayley's trying to set me up with? At a dinner you all but forced my hand into going to?"

It was a wonder his teeth didn't break due to the pressure they were under from the way his jaw clenched. He took a deep breath in through his nose, then forced himself to unclench, to relax.

Tori crossed her arms over her chest and glared at him. "I can, have, and *will* handle anyone trying to set me up with anyone, as I'm in charge of my own life and who I spend time with."

"Because you have such great taste in guys."

She stilled, and he realized far too late he'd gone about this all wrong. Tori would only take this as a challenge, not what it was—which was friendly concern. So to speak.

"I'll pick you up at five-thirty," he said with the best smile he could muster. His mustering skills were sorely lacking.

"Oh, I'll be ready at five-thirty, Will." She stormed out,

grumbling something that sounded a hell of a lot like "but I don't think you'll be."

Whatever *that* meant.

Tori knew it was mean, but after everything that had happened today, she felt mean. He'd gotten her all soft then . . .

She didn't know what that little display with Hayley was, but she knew she did not like it. Had she interfered with women drooling all over him on the trail? No, she hadn't.

How dare he say she had bad taste in men, no matter how true it was. Him at the top of the list.

Which even in her irritated state she couldn't let go. Toby had been worse, far worse. Will had been . . . oblivious and ignorant, and it had made him more callous than he would have been otherwise. Toby had been a total dickweasel in just about every aspect.

She blew out an angry breath, but if she breathed too much she'd lose the anger, and she'd have to deal with all the vulnerability swimming underneath it.

Will's fall. Will's touch. Will's too weird certainty that Hayley was trying to set Tori up with James.

Who was nice-looking, but that was the extent of what Tori knew about the guy.

She looked at herself in the mirror and cringed at what she saw. Because she looked nice, and she rarely looked nice. She looked like she had that night, and for a brief, crazed moment she'd wished she hadn't burned that dress.

She would have worn it. Like an amulet of power or something.

As it was, she had her hair down, which she never did because it was so thick and unruly and took forever to dry. She'd chosen a floral sundress Toby had bought for her, which she should've burned too. Maybe she still would, but for tonight it would suit her purposes.

If she didn't break Will open, he was going to worm his way back into her heart, and she couldn't let that happen. So she had to bring out the big guns. She had to force as many reminders of that night down his throat until . . .

She sank onto her bed feeling unaccountably lost. What was the point? Ignoring it didn't fix it or make it any less painful. Why did she think making him talk about it would? She should change, braid her hair, and then go out to dinner with her *friends*.

And learn more about James and open herself up to the possibility of a future where the past didn't matter.

Except Will was future and past and she didn't know what else to do but barrel on with her plan. Crack him open. Right down the center.

Which would crack her open in return, but hell, hadn't everything she'd built come on the heels of the worst things in her life? She'd met the Mile High boys only a year after she'd finally left home, and they'd given her so much. She'd learned how to be alone in the years after her breakup—so to speak—with Will, and she was here rebuilding that old plan in the wake of everything Toby had done to her.

So.

A knock sounded at the door and Tori took a deep breath.

She couldn't let herself be swayed by softness. Softness had gotten her clobbered time and time again. To save her life, to build a life, she'd had to be hard and unrelenting time and time again. When she lost sight of that and let emotion or softness rule, she always ended up bloody and bruised—either literally or figuratively.

She pushed off the bed and walked to the front door. She opened it effecting the most casual demeanor she could. She refused to soften when she saw Will's complexion still seemed a little off. Instead, she focused on the little thrill of success when Will's eyes sharpened and his jaw clenched together.

Dressing like this had hit the mark.

"We're not going to the fucking Ritz," he grumbled.

She cocked her head, something like an avalanche of hair falling over her shoulder at the move. God, she hated leaving it down. "Oh, aren't we?" she asked sweetly.

His eyes narrowed and there was something lurking in their depths, but she didn't want to think too hard about it.

"Remind you of anything?" she asked, doing a little twirl.

She thought she saw a flash of hurt cross his features, but that couldn't be. Why would it hurt him to remember the night when he'd so coolly dismissed her as if her being in love with him was some hideous affront?

He turned his back to her.

"You know, I always wondered," she said conversationally, closing the door behind her and locking it. "I realize you were taken off guard that night, but I never understood why you had to be so mean about it." She stepped into stride next to him down the uneven walkway to the sidewalk and where Will was parked on the street.

"I'm not doing this," he said, his voice low and threatening. "Your hair down and wearing a dress with shit on your face isn't going to make me do it."

"But I think Benson is something like a thirty-minute drive, so we have a whole car ride together to talk." She sauntered toward the Jeep, heart beating a little too fast, something like panic clawing at her chest.

Will walked stiffly to the driver's side. She gave him a quick once-over. He'd cleaned up since the hike, and now he was wearing nice jeans and a button-down shirt.

She focused on getting in the Jeep instead of doing what

she really wanted to do, which was ask him how he felt. But how he was doing after the fall was not the point of tonight. Whether his hip, head, or shoulder ached, it didn't matter. Not to her. She was here to get under his skin. Because he thought he was *saving* her from a very nice thing Hayley was maybe trying to do.

Will climbed into the driver's seat, his large, broad body taking up far too much room. He shoved the key into the ignition and turned it, his jaw clenched tight. He jerked the wheel to get the Jeep on the road, but he winced with it.

It took everything in Tori not to wince with him. Took every ounce of self-preservation she had not to offer to drive.

"So you don't have an answer then?" she poked instead.

He gave the most imperceptible shake of his head. "Nope. Sure don't."

"Do you want to hear my theory? Because, you know, I've had a lot of years to make up theories." She smiled sweetly, but Will didn't even bother to look over. His eyes were glued to the road, his hands tight on the wheel.

"The thing is, I assumed that you knew. I didn't think I was capable of being subtle about it. I know I wasn't some sorority girl flirting expertly, but we did spend a lot of time together. I thought for sure you saw through me."

Still nothing. Her stomach was starting to turn in nauseous circles, but she had to do this. To save herself. To build her life.

"I mean, I get it, Courtney's boobs were probably pretty distracting, and what guy wouldn't want to run off with a lingerie model?"

"Don't talk about her."

She blinked in surprise. It wasn't like Will to so obviously give away his weakness.

"Oh, I didn't consider the possibility that *she* might have left *you*."

The Jeep jerked to a stop with a screech. Will swore, his good arm moving up to grab his shoulder. Tori was too shocked by the hard slap of the seat belt against her chest to think.

She rubbed a hand over her chest and glared at him, but her glare died because he was looking at her with such sparkling fury and menace she actually shrunk back.

"Don't bring up my marriage. Ever. Do you understand me?"

Normally she'd argue out of principle, but there was something so wrong about the way he said that, as though there was a deep, awful hurt wrapped up in his marriage. She never thought she'd say the words to him, but in the face of his pure display of emotion, they just slipped out.

"I'm sorry," she whispered.

"Are you?"

She swallowed and looked down at her lap. "Look, I think we should talk about what happened between us, and I'm not going to stop poking about that, but I don't want to make you—"

He hit the accelerator again and was driving out of Gracely and toward Benson. The sun was setting in the mountains and the golden ball of light was so bright she had to close her eyes against it. A tear almost escaped, but she muscled it back just in time.

"I'm sorry if I hit a nerve," she managed.

"This is one giant fucking nerve, Tori."

"The Courtney thing . . . I'll leave it alone, but the rest has to do with *me*. I was there and my life changed irrevocably because of things that happened that night."

"I didn't do shit to you that you didn't start. I never wanted your confession. I never wanted your emotions."

"You made that crystal clear."

"Damn right I did," he said in something so close to a yell it was disorienting. Even that night Will hadn't *yelled*. "I was . . ." Whatever he'd been going to say he bit off. Violently.

"You were what?"

He shook his head, his eyes squinting against the bright sun setting. "I never asked for it. Any of it."

Though he was emphatic and angry and a million emotional things, she knew that's not what he'd been about to say. She was a little too shaky in her heart and scared and hurt to push it right now, but she'd come back to it.

She'd have to.

Chapter Ten

Will couldn't remember the last time he'd felt so much like punching someone in the face. Oh, there were a lot of times he'd threaten bodily harm against Brandon or Sam. Hell, he and Sam had almost come to blows a few times over Hayley last month. But it wasn't like this.

This boiling emotional thing. Wrapped up in Courtney memories and Tori and talking about a past he wanted to erase. She wouldn't let him. How dare she not let him. He just wanted peace. Why wouldn't anyone give him any damn peace?

James was telling a story about some guy he'd arrested. Tori was leaning on her elbow, listening to his every possible inflection as though rapt. Hayley was clearly enjoying the hell out of herself. Watching her stepbrother interact with her friends. Even Sam seemed at ease.

When had Will become the surly, awkward one?

When the steaks arrived, he decided he was just hungry. He would eat and then he would turn on the old Will Evans charm. Because he was fucking charming, damn it. People liked spending time with him, and he liked spending time with people, and . . .

He attacked his steak and did everything in his power not to look at Tori.

Not the way her golden hair glinted in the lights of the restaurant. Not the way she smiled at James and the little dimple on her right cheek appeared, which only happened on her soft smiles. Those he never saw anymore. All these details he'd forgotten he knew. All these pieces of her that he missed and wanted.

Because that's what her little car conversation did. It reminded him of all the ways he'd wanted to give her exactly what she'd wanted from him. He'd wanted to be the kind of man who could give her the love she deserved, but he'd known that was never, ever going to be him.

Why couldn't she just accept that? Why'd she have to keep pushing? Bringing Courtney and all those complicated emotions up.

He felt like he was being ripped in half, and it was so damn painful he barely noticed the throbbing in his shoulder or his head. All he knew was his chest felt like an anvil was pressing against it. Like a bear was clawing out his heart. It didn't matter that he was being all kinds of over-dramatic because that was how he felt.

And all Tori could dare to do was smile at this yapping stranger like he had any right to deserve her smiles. No one did.

"You might want to consider getting your shit together," Sam mumbled to him under his breath.

"What do you mean?" Will returned, equally quiet, their little conversation going unnoticed by the women who were just *so* enthralled with James the fucking cop and his grand tales of heroism and bullshit.

"It's not escaping anyone's notice that you're pissed off."

"Well, you can blame Tori for that because I was fine until she started poking at me on the way over." Which was true. It *was*.

Despite keeping their voices low, they were starting to attract glances from Hayley and Tori, and occasionally even James.

"Get it together. Now." It was the fact Sam of all people was the one lecturing him about his behavior that managed to knock some sense into place. Sam had been something of a hermit for years and was just now slowly emerging from that hard shell he'd built around himself. If Will's behavior was setting off Sam's discomfort, Will absolutely had to get ahold of himself.

"I haven't spent too much time in Aurora, but it's a nice town, yeah? Pretty out there close to Denver." See? He could be engaging and shit.

James shrugged. "It's really got nothing on Gracely. I gave Hayley a hard time about moving here, but I haven't been able to stop thinking about it since my last trip up."

Conversation continued with everyone talking about Gracely and its many charms. Will managed to calm himself down enough to be civil if not charming. Though it got harder and harder the more James smiled at Tori and asked questions about her time as a ski instructor or her hobbies or whatever.

It irritated him even more that Hayley kept smiling every time he did, as though she'd won some matchmaking lottery by pushing James and Tori into sitting next to each other.

Even as they all so cheerfully walked out of the restaurant, Tori and James lingering together a few steps behind, Will fought to smother the ticking time bomb inside of him.

Will glanced back as James pulled a card out of his wallet and said something close to Tori's ear.

It shouldn't matter. It didn't matter.

"We should probably head back, yeah?" Will said too loudly, using every last ounce of control to keep himself from grabbing her arm and jerking her away from James's proffered card.

He knew he was being an ass. It didn't stop him in the least.

Tori frowned at him, but there was also a little flash of worry. He liked that too, too much. That she might care enough to be worried.

She stepped toward him, of course not before she took the card from James. She offered the man a smile and then a different smile to Sam and Hayley. Which was important to note, for some reason.

"Thanks, guys. This was fun. I'm glad you invited me."

"Thanks for coming, and hopefully we can do it again soon with Brandon and Lilly too." Hayley leaned in and said something to Tori that Will didn't catch. Tori gave a little nod though, and Will could only assume it was about James.

Good-byes were murmured, and James, Hayley, and Sam went in the direction of Sam's Jeep, while Will and Tori started off in the opposite direction toward his. After a few seconds of walking, Tori touched him on the elbow gently.

"You want me to drive?"

He glared at her, irritated by any gentle from her right now. "No, I don't want you to drive."

"No need to be a growly ass. You're acting so weird, and Hayley thought it might have something to do with your head bothering you. If it is, I can drive."

"My head is fine."

"Okay. Great." He could hear the eye roll in her voice more than he could see it on her face.

They climbed into the Jeep and Will thought he did an admirable job of not bringing James up. They didn't talk at all as he maneuvered the Jeep through the mountains and toward Gracely. Which was how he liked it. She wasn't poking at him about things that had happened a million years ago, and he didn't have to feel jumbled because . . .

He pulled up to the curb in front of the house she was

renting. It was a sunshiny little house situated next to where Lilly's sister lived. The cheerful exterior wasn't exactly what he associated with Tori and yet it somehow worked. Because Gracely always seemed to work when it shouldn't.

He glanced at Tori, then forced himself to look at the windshield. He wasn't going there. Or anywhere. He was dropping her off and going back to Mile High and . . .

"Dating Hayley's stepbrother isn't the brightest idea."

He'd known it was a stupid thing to say before it tumbled out of his mouth, and yet he hadn't been able to stop it.

She glared at him, her mouth open as if she was going to yell at him, but in the end she didn't. She snapped her mouth shut and threw the door open, shoving herself out of the Jeep.

He should leave it at that. He knew he should leave it at that.

He got out of the car and followed her across her yard.

"Go home, Will," she said, her voice low and dangerous, her golden hair flowing behind her as she strode with certain, hard steps toward her front door. "I don't feel like fighting with you."

"Then don't fight with me," he returned, following her, trying to figure out why. It was like his body had taken over and he didn't know what the hell he was doing.

She whirled on him, so he came to a stop. Her blue-green eyes flashed in the moonlight, reminding him of a mermaid. Or something.

"You're making this impossible," she said, flinging her arms toward him. "Telling me what to do. Giving some opinion on who I can date and who's a good idea and what taste I have in men. We're not friends anymore, Will. Maybe we could be, but not like this."

Which hit, sharper than a punch, something more like a stab. He wanted her in his life, but she made it so damn hard. They'd been friends, but *she'd* disappeared. *She'd* been the one to change things on him.

How dare she say they couldn't be friends like this? "Like what?" he demanded, taking a threatening step toward her, but she just lifted her chin. "Like you always poking at me? Like you bringing up my marriage and flirting with my half sister's stepbrother all night?"

She stared at him openmouthed as if he was the crazy one. But he wasn't crazy. She had a problem with him giving some opinions on her life? Well, he had a hell of a problem with her wanting to drag the past into everything.

"You are so un-fucking-believable. Even more so than usual, which was already pretty unbelievable."

"You started it."

"Oh, how mature."

"That's me."

It was her turn to take a threatening step toward him and she poked him right in the chest. "I didn't say anything on the way back. I kept my mouth shut the whole way. I stopped talking about the past. You know why? Because tonight was nice. I sat there and thought about my future. I still think we should rehash that night if only because it would get out this simmering resentment, but tonight was *nice*. I sat there and I thought . . . maybe this can be my life. Living in Gracely. Maybe I could date a cute cop. Maybe for the first time my future is as open as I want it to be, and the only thing standing in my way is you and your shitty attitude."

"Did it ever occur to you that I'm in the same exact place? I have nothing but the future ahead of me. I am single, and Mile High is thriving, and then *you* show up with your crap poking at old wounds."

"Ignoring it isn't healing them! Why can't you see that?"

"Because I know what rehashing it will do. I know what explaining it all will accomplish, and I don't want it."

"What? My God, what do you think it will do?"

It would bring up truths he never wanted her to know. It would speak to all the weaknesses he was ashamed to have. If they went through that night, it was nothing but . . . waste. His cowardice was nothing but a waste.

He had to get out of here. He didn't know what he thought he was trying to do, and he had to get out of here. So he turned to head for his Jeep before he said another thing he'd live to grieve and regret.

"That's it. Walk away. Ignore it all and walk away. Good old Will Evans."

Something snapped, sharp and painful, and if he wasn't so angry maybe he could have repaired it. But he was done. He was out of patience and denial and all the other things he used to wrap up and hide away those feelings inside of him.

He whirled on her, and he didn't care that she stumbled back as he advanced. Good. She should be afraid. She *should* run away. She needed to be just as damn afraid of this thing boiling inside of him as he was.

"What are you doing?" she demanded in a screech when he grabbed her, curling his fingers around her soft, strong upper arms.

Because, damn it, it was all there. Just like it had always been. The unrelenting desire to have his hands on her. The hellish idea that he would never be complete until he tasted her.

So that's just what he fucking did.

He crushed his mouth to hers, holding her tight against him. Pouring his rage and his confusion and all those other things she brought out in him into the kiss. Into her mouth. Into her blood. He wanted her to feel it, drown in it. He wanted her to hate it as much as he did.

It was wrong. Everything about it was wrong, and yet it

was the rightest he'd ever felt. Ever. Tori wrapped up in his arms, Tori's mouth under his.

This. This was what he'd always been so afraid of. He'd been right to be because it was burning him alive. The fact she hadn't fought him off, that she was kissing him back, that she was small and pliant in his arms.

Shaking and vulnerable under all that determined strength.

A thing he could break.

He released her as a wave of self-disgust washed through him. In a situation that had already been fucked to hell, he'd just screwed it up even more.

Tori was frozen. She ordered her body to move, but it wouldn't. She'd spent years dreaming of Will touching her like that. Intimately. Desperately. She'd imagined him kissing her in a million different ways, and then she'd spent the past seven years dreaming of quite the opposite.

She was shaken and unsteady and so many confusing things. Her lips burned. Her body hummed. A pathetic unfurling need had centered itself deep in her belly. She hated herself a little, but when she looked at him, she hated him more.

It wasn't the realization she'd kissed him back—that he had that kind of power over her. It wasn't the realization this was the worst possible thing he or she could have done. It was the look on his face that made her hate him. Something unreadable mingled with horror.

As though kissing her was the worst possible thing he could have ever done.

She curled her shaking fingers into fists and then she pounded them to his chest and pushed him as hard as she could.

He stumbled back and she was glad of it. She wanted

him to stumble and fall, so she stepped forward to push him again.

"Tori?"

Tori froze at the questioning female voice. She glanced to the side where Cora stood on her porch, bathed in the dim yellow light hanging above the door.

Tori had the horrible realization they must've made enough noise to attract some attention.

"Is everything okay? Do I need to call the police?" Cora called.

Will cleared his throat. "We were just talking."

"My question wasn't for you, Will," Cora retorted, a surprising acidity in her tone.

Tori wished she could muster the strength to find that funny or even sweet, but all she felt was defeated and awful and too close to tears to do this any longer.

"You don't need to call anyone," she said carefully, making sure every word sounded strong and sure—the opposite of how she felt inside.

She couldn't let Will read her weakness. He didn't deserve her weakness.

"Are you sure because—"

"I'm leaving," Will interrupted.

Will looked at her then, even as he took a step backward toward his car.

She lifted her chin, determined to be the defiant fighter she'd always been. He couldn't turn her into that girl on the mountain seven years ago. No one could. "Don't you ever touch me like that again," she said quietly enough Cora wouldn't hear, but solid and sturdy and certain.

No nod. No response. He just turned and walked to his Jeep.

She knew she was shaking, but she had to find a way to get a hold on it. Be strong and unaffected so she could assure Cora that whatever she thought she'd seen had been nothing to report to Lilly or anyone else. Nothing more than . . .

Who the fuck knew. Will had kissed her. Like a possessed . . . It wouldn't do her any good to find a comparison. No good at all.

"Come on over, sweetheart," Cora said, a surprisingly soft note of order to her voice. Like a mother, Tori supposed.

Tori wanted to beg Cora off, but the woman's concern was a little too much. Wouldn't it be nice to have someone on her side for once? Cora had talked to Will like he was a criminal.

Tori wouldn't get that at Mile High. She wouldn't get it anywhere else, so she trudged over to Cora's doorstep.

"Did he hurt you?" Cora asked, searching Tori's face.

God, yes, but Tori realized immediately that's not what Cora meant. Had it looked that bad from an outside observer? "No, not like that."

"Are you sure? You can tell me. I know what it's like . . ." Cora trailed off and bit her lip before taking Tori's hand. "Come inside. We need wine."

Tori let herself be led. She didn't have the brainpower to do anything but. Will's kiss—*kiss*—lingered, like she was an animal caught in an oil spill and her entire body was covered with the remnants of it.

Sparking anger, impotent want, a confusion she didn't know how to sort through. What had that been? Punishment? Proof of something? She didn't get it. He hadn't kissed her like his life depended on it when she'd admitted she'd loved him years ago, but *now* when they did nothing but fight and snipe.

Cora deposited her on a comfortable couch the color of the sky at dawn. "White or red? I have both."

"I don't think . . ."

"I spent half the night arguing with my eleven-year-old about social media. Indulge me and be my drinking buddy."

"White." It'd be easier to go along with it. She didn't have the energy to fight anymore. She didn't have energy—period—fighting with Will took enough energy and then . . .

Cora handed her a wineglass filled almost to the brim with wine. She plopped onto the couch next to Tori and took a deep, long sip.

"Micah's dad used to hit us," she said, as though that was the kind of sentence you could just . . . say. To a superficial friend at best.

Tori opened her mouth, but what did you say to that? When you were already scrambled.

"I say that because . . . Well, I just wanted to put it out there. I know Will, but I also know how easy it is for a guy to hide . . . Well . . ."

"He didn't hurt me like that. He wouldn't." Tori almost hated having to defend him when she was so angry, so hurt. But he wouldn't. Not Will.

"Okay. Well, then tell me what the bastard did."

"I . . . Your sister is married to his twin brother and you . . ."

Cora shrugged easily, taking another sip of wine. "I love Brandon. I like Will. But I kind of happen to think men are turds. Brandon is an exception. I hope to God Micah will be, but mostly . . . turd."

Tori laughed, somehow. But laughing also weirdly made her feel like crying. "We just have this history."

Cora's blue eyes were sympathetic and when had Tori ever had that? She loved the Mile High boys, they'd been her best friends and champions in the whole of her life. But they weren't sympathetic. They certainly weren't going to let her bitch about men without trying to defend their irritating species.

"I used to be in love with him. A million years ago."

"And the turd wasn't in love back?"

"No."

"But if it was a million years ago, why all the drama?"

Tori shook her head, settling deeper into the couch, taking a thoughtful sip of wine. "I don't really know. I guess the way we left things. I said I loved him. He accused me of ruining everything. He disappeared, came back married to a lingerie model, so then I disappeared."

"And now you're back."

"And now I'm back and it's all still there. I thought I'd moved on . . . No, I had moved on. I did." She blew out a breath, downing some more of the wine. That's what she'd missed at dinner tonight. Alcohol. "He kissed me."

"Out there?" Cora squeaked.

"We were fighting, but we're always fighting. But . . . I don't know. He grabbed me and kissed me. Like . . ." Like he'd wanted to for years upon years and what did she *do* with that?

"Like what?" Cora asked a little breathlessly. "Indulge me, please, as I have not even been on a date for *months*."

"It wasn't a nice kiss."

"But it was hot, yeah?"

"Oh, yeah." Tori finished off the wine and Cora took the glass from her, popping up and back to the kitchen.

"You need more."

"There's not enough in the universe."

"True enough, but I'll fix you up for tonight." And fix her up she did, with another glass of wine filled to the brim.

Tori took the proffered glass, drinking deeply. Oh, she'd wake up with a shitty hangover and nothing solved, but in the moment what else was there to do? Go home and cry alone?

"So what are you going to do?" Cora asked gently, taking a seat on the couch again.

The tears were back, and with an entire glass of wine downed, she didn't have it in her to fight them anymore. "I don't know," she said, followed by an embarrassing sob, but Cora just pulled her into a hug and let her cry.

Chapter Eleven

Lilly toggled between reading a book on her phone and watching the tedious reality show blaring on the TV. She'd tried knitting earlier and had thrown the knitting needles across the room in a fit of frustration.

She was pretty sure Brandon had thrown them away.

Tomorrow was her doctor's appointment, and if she thought bed rest was bad, waiting to hear if you could get off it was torture.

The front door slammed open and in stormed Will. *Uh-oh.*

He blinked at her on the couch as though he'd forgotten she'd moved in and that he didn't share the cabin with Brandon alone any longer.

"Um, hi," she offered, smiling at him. Oh, he looked stormy. She'd hoped her little plan with Hayley would've sorted things out for him, but he didn't look very sorted.

"Hey. How're you feeling?" he asked, his voice scraped raw.

Lilly got the feeling he was asking out of courtesy rather than true interest. At least in the moment.

"Better. How was dinner?"

His eyes narrowed. "How did you know about that?"

"Hayley invited me." Among other things, but Will was

looking a little wild, a little . . . Well, maybe her plan had worked.

"Hey, Will. What are you doing here?" Brandon asked, entering the room with yet another glass of water.

God, she needed to be off bed rest. She forced her brightest smile at her husband as he set it down next to her, and didn't fool him at all.

"Still live here, don't I?"

"Well, sure, but you haven't been around much."

Will shrugged, looking around. "Just needed to . . ." He glanced from Lilly to Brandon, some complex series of emotions crossing his face.

She couldn't read them exactly, but wasn't it interesting to see an emotion besides cheerful blankness or honest cheerfulness? Will was usually one or the other, occasionally temper, but never . . . this.

Interesting. Yes, maybe her plan *had* worked.

"Sit down. Tell us about dinner." Lilly smiled invitingly. "Tell me about Hayley's brother."

"He's . . ." Will jammed his hands into his pockets. "Nice, or whatever."

"Oh good. I bet it'd be nice for Hayley to feel like her stepbrother and her half brothers would get along."

Will hunched a little. "Yeah, sure."

"What'd Tori think of him?"

Will glanced at her sharply and she knew she'd overplayed her hand a bit, but what did it matter now? Dinner was over and clearly he was worked up about something.

"What do you care what Tori thought of him?"

Lilly shrugged, gesturing with her phone, ignoring Brandon's disapproving frown, because of course the obnoxious man she loved could see right through her. "Just curious."

"It was you, wasn't it? All along. You convinced Hayley to do it."

"Do what?" Lilly returned as innocently as she could manage.

"You told her to set Tori up with James. What the hell were you thinking?"

Interesting that he'd be so angry about it. Interesting indeed. "I wasn't trying to set Tori up with James."

"My ass. When will you stop playing puppet master? I don't—"

"I said I wasn't trying to set Tori up with James, and I meant it. I was trying to prove to you that you might have some unresolved romantic feelings for Tori, and what better way to realize that then having to face the prospect of her with someone else?"

Will stood unnaturally still after that, and the entire room was silent except the blare of the TV. Lilly's self-satisfied smirk slowly died as she realized . . .

"You didn't," Will said, his voice low and unmeasurably hurt.

Lilly's heart sunk. "I . . . I thought it would do some good. I . . ."

She looked helplessly at Brandon, but he had his eyes closed as he rubbed his fingers over his forehead.

When she looked back at Will, he stood there like some angry, vicious god of war, storms in his eyes and violence in the way he held himself.

"Stop fucking with my life," he said, his voice vibrating with rage, but underneath it hurt and something else. Something almost like fear.

She opened her mouth to apologize. She even moved to get up, but Will was out the door, the sound of it slamming behind him reverberating through the cabin even above the din of the TV.

"I went too far, didn't I?" She wished she could blame hormones for the emotions swamping her, but it was guilt and shame, plain and simple.

"I wish you would have told me first," Brandon said on a sigh. "Everything with Will and Tori is complicated."

"I only wanted to help," Lilly replied weakly. "I thought if he . . ."

"Aw, Lil," Brandon said, moving to sit next to her. He took her hand in his and squeezed, a little bit of comfort in the mix of all her guilt. "You're going to have to accept what I had to accept a long time ago. No one can help Will until he's willing to help himself."

Tori was not looking forward to this, but she also wasn't going to be intimidated by it. So Will had kissed her, and so she had to work with him today. Such was life.

A big old ball of fucked-up fuck.

She was used to dealing with the fallout from that. For as long as she could remember, she knew how to deal with awful curveballs. All in all, a kiss from the guy who'd rejected her love confession seven years ago was probably the least screwy her life had been. Certainly less scary than her mentally ill brother being convinced she needed to be killed, and, as she still had a job and home, a hell of a lot less problematic than the fallout with Toby.

This was a downright family-friendly sitcom right here.

Grim and determined to view it that way no matter what, Tori marched up the stairs, Sarge at her feet, and walked into the Mile High office, shoulders back, ready to brawl.

She stopped short at the sight that greeted her when she stepped inside. Instead of Skeet at his desk and the living room empty, there appeared to be a little powwow going on in the main room.

"Oh. Um. Hi," she managed when they all turned to look at her.

Lilly was seated in a chair, Brandon standing behind her, Sam, Hayley, and Skeet assembled on the couch opposite.

"I . . . didn't mean to interrupt."

"No interruption," Lilly returned, waving her in. "We're having a little impromptu staff meeting, but we were waiting for everyone else to really get started."

Tori didn't miss the look that passed between Lilly and Brandon. Something laced with worry. Tori couldn't imagine Will telling anyone about last night, but . . .

Well, everyone was certainly acting strange. Still, this was her job and all that crap she'd convinced herself of outside, so she moved over to an empty chair and took a seat. Sarge happily curled up next to the window where the sunlight beamed onto the hardwood floor.

"Brandon was telling me you'd set a climbing record," Lilly offered. Everything about the woman was polished and smooth, and Tori didn't quite know how to relax around her.

"Um. Yeah. Where I worked last I did rock climbing instruction in the summer and ski instruction in the winter, though the climbing was more what I was interested in."

"Good," Brandon said. "We've been working on putting together a slightly more organized schedule to get you comfortable in all excursions, but I think the rock climbing is where you'd best fit. Hayley will keep doing our shorter hikes. Sam's been doing a little bit of everything, so we're trying to spread things out a bit more. Let Sam focus on the backpacking trips, taking Hayley or you with him when we've got women nervous about backpacking with a man. We'll hand rock climbing over to you, focus Will on kayaking, and I'll fill in where necessary. Lilly came up with a chart."

"Of course she did," Sam muttered, and Tori felt a little pang that there was a note of affection in it.

Silly to be jealous other women had joined their group, helped the boys out, become their friends and wives and girlfriends in the various cases. Silly to feel a bitter regret over what she'd walked away from.

Hadn't last night proven she'd needed to walk away?

I think last night proved that you're both screwy.

"What's all this?"

Tori jerked a little at the unexpectedness of Will's sleep-roughened voice. She hadn't heard him come in, and when she involuntarily looked over at him he was standing in the hall to the offices looking disheveled.

Wearing the same thing he'd been wearing last night.

This was . . . She didn't know what this was, that was the problem. Firstly, she'd never had to deal with the aftermath of an *actual* Will Evans kiss—a few imagined ones—but not the reality. Secondly, she'd never shared a bottle of wine with a female friend and spent half the night tipsily cursing men. She was in over her head and confused, and usually she stayed firmly in anger or determination. She didn't wallow. She didn't waffle.

But the cherry on top of all this weirdness and confusion was Will himself. She'd never seen him so bedraggled. Even back in the day when he'd get falling-down drunk at a party, he'd look all put together and charming. Things rolled off him—emotions and bad hair days.

He looked like none of these things right now.

"Oh, you're back," he muttered in Lilly's direction. "Got the clear?"

"Yes, doctor gave me the go-ahead to return to work, and as long as no other problems occur, I can do just about anything. So we're having a staff meeting."

"Of course we are," he grumbled, glancing around the room.

His eyes went nowhere near Tori herself, and instead of taking the chair that would have put him next to her, he went and leaned on the arm of the couch—as far away from her as he could get.

Then the damn dog she'd sacrificed for again and again went over to Will and curled up at his feet. The absolute traitor.

"With the summer rush kind of petering out, but the fall rush getting ready to start, Brandon and I thought it'd be a good time to kind of . . . refocus," Lilly was saying. "We've added two new wonderful employees." Lilly smiled broadly at Hayley, then Tori. "But we've been sort of shoehorning in willy-nilly."

"Lilly and I worked on a schedule, but this is a democracy and we want to make sure everyone's on board before we enact it into law, so to speak."

Democracy maybe, but Lilly and Brandon stood and sat before them like some royal couple handing out a decree, but the thing was . . . how could you argue with sense? Or the two of them, looking so gorgeous together, Brandon so clearly devoted to her, both of them so clearly devoted to Mile High.

An uncomfortable longing wound its way through Tori's chest. Before she even realized she was doing it, she glanced across the room to Will.

She nearly jolted at the fact he was staring at her, hazel eyes steady on hers, eyebrows drawn together as though he was trying to figure out some puzzle. Trying to figure out *her*.

She looked away, something warm and tingling creeping up into her face. Oh. God, she was *blushing*. She never blushed. What the hell was wrong with her?

But the heat and the certainty she was indeed turning bright red against her will only intensified when Lilly's gaze landed on her and lingered. Studying. Then flicking over to Will.

"I think it makes sense," Sam offered, if not reading the tension winding around the room, having impeccable accidental timing. "To focus each of us on one thing. As long as we're all capable of stepping into someone else's place should the need arise."

"Agreed," Lilly said with a nod. "Tori will need a few more training excursions, and we've got those scheduled on here as well."

And, Tori noted, none of them had Will as her partner. Sam and Brandon only. After everyone plotting to get them to camp together, Tori didn't quite understand what this all was.

Unfortunately though, she couldn't take it at face value and ignore all the volumes it spoke to. She couldn't ignore that it pissed her right off. Clearly, if they'd changed their tune so completely, Will had *told* them to keep him off any excursions with her.

Oh, the bastard. *He* thought he got to decide when he'd have to deal with her after that kiss? Fat chance.

Brandon and Lilly kept talking, trading off, giving explanations and reasons for different things. Sam and Lilly discussed someone named Corbin, Skeet offered a few random comments about people who'd called to set up excursions, and Hayley discussed something about . . . something.

It was hard for Tori to pay attention. Had Will *told* Lilly and Brandon about the kiss and that's why they'd agreed to back off the whole throw-them-together thing? He'd probably even put the blame on her, even though he had been the one to instigate it. The one to end it.

You weren't exactly fighting him off.

She shoved that unwelcome thought away. She'd been surprised. He'd been the one to grab her. She ignored the little shiver of memory that worked through her, because she was mad. Angry.

He was going around telling people things he had no business telling them.

Lilly and Brandon must have ended the impromptu

meeting, because people started to scatter. Skeet to his desk, Brandon and Lilly down the hall, Hayley to the little kitchenette, and Sam outside.

Tori tried to focus on the schedule written on a white-board that now sat on the mantel. She didn't have anything for an hour, and then she was going on a rock climbing excursion with Brandon.

That's where her head needed to be.

"Seems a little odd we're not scheduled together at all," she said instead. Because how could she focus on rock climbing when Will was *clearly* spreading rumors.

"Does it?" Will replied, pushing off the couch and step-ping toward the whiteboard. His face was blank, and every time he glanced her way, everything about him was unread-able. His gaze lingered too long, but his eyes gave away nothing.

Sarge stayed where he was, curled on the floor, but his ears were alert, as though he were paying attention to every word spoken. Tori wished the fanciful thought of dog eaves-droppers could calm her down.

"Considering everyone seems to have been conspiring to make us spend time together the past few weeks, I have to say I'm surprised. Unless . . ."

"Unless what?" Will replied. Even his voice was devoid of any readable emotion.

What the hell was going on here? Will had always been superficial, so to speak. *She'd* seen beneath all his charm-ing walls back then, or at least most of them, but he always appeared to the world happy and content. He'd never been this mercurial mess.

Had time done that? Divorce?

You?

She blinked at him, trying so hard to see something, any-thing she recognized in this man. Sarge seemed to recognize him. Brandon and Sam seemed to think this was all normal.

Hell, maybe she was crazy and this was all as it should be. Maybe she'd never seen through Will at all. Maybe she'd been a foolish girl with foolish feelings rooted in nothing but fantasy.

She swallowed at the heavy emotion that clogged her throat. She'd considered a lot of things over the past seven years, including her own stupidity. But never that she'd imagined things about him.

He turned to her then, and she'd forgotten whatever they'd been talking about. She'd forgotten anything she might have promised herself this morning as she'd walked up to Mile High.

"Do me a favor," he said, so serious, so rumpled.

She scowled, or at least tried to, skeptically. "What favor?"

"Smile."

"Are you—" He touched the tip of his index finger to her cheek and she batted it away. "What the fuck are you doi—"

"It's right here," he said, tapping her cheek again with just the tip of his index finger before she managed to shove his arm away again. Sarge stepped between them, tense and watchful, and Tori pressed her palm to the dog's head to find some sort of center.

Why was Will *touching* her? She glared at him, waiting for an answer, and he met that glare as if it were nothing.

"Your dimple," he said, staring at the spot on her cheek that now burned from his touch. It shouldn't. He'd tapped her cheek. So what?

"I remember so many odd things about you," he murmured.

"Are you drunk?"

"No."

Then she didn't know what this was, why his simply studying her with this odd look on his face should make the air constrict in her chest. Why her limbs should shake like they had last night in the aftermath of his mouth on hers.

The scrape of his beard, the strength of his hands on her arms and then around her. Enveloped by him. Drowning in him.

She couldn't let herself drown. Not this time. She had to fight. Or flee. "I'm going to go take Sarge for a walk before my excursion."

He opened his mouth to say something, but she didn't dare let him. "Follow me, I'll kick you in the balls so hard you won't find them for a month." She stormed past him, something like lightning and thunder swirling inside of her.

She got to the door, realized Sarge hadn't followed her. She looked back to find the dog sitting at Will's feet, panting happily up at him.

Feeling tears she didn't understand prick her eyes, she let out a sharp whistle. "Come on, boy." *He is not for us.*

The dog obeyed, and Tori would take that as the only sign she needed that she was right. Not for her. Not then. Not now. Not ever.

Chapter Twelve

Will had never considered himself a deep thinker. He didn't analyze his actions. He didn't wonder about his motivations or shit like that. He did. He moved forward. He *enjoyed*.

But something about losing control and kissing Tori last night had recalibrated his brain into something he didn't recognize.

He thought about her dimple. The mole she had right inside her left elbow. The way the ends of her braid always curled, and the way the strands of hair that fell out of it were always the faintest, whitest blond, while the braid together was honey gold.

He thought about her laugh, remembered all the different ones he used to know. She used to laugh at him, with him, in spite of him. She used to smile, that dimple winking, and in that twenty-twenty kind of retrospect way, he could see it.

What he'd avoided seeing back then. The way she'd been something special to him, and he to her. It hadn't been the same relationship she'd had with Sam or Brandon, and he'd sort of understood that in college, but he'd also tried not to look under that too deeply.

He tried not to look under anything too deeply, and yet it was all he seemed to be doing today. Wondering why he'd kissed her. Why Lilly's admission she'd wanted him to be jealous of James had cracked something inside of him.

He let out a sigh and scrubbed his hands over his face. He needed to get out of his mood. He needed to stop thinking about Tori Appleby's damn dimple. He needed to shower and change. He didn't have any excursions today since there hadn't been enough rain to keep the river at safe kayaking levels.

There was paperwork. He could always go into town and put up some fliers. He could take a hike by himself and find some damn clarity. But he sat in his office and stared at his index finger.

He was certain he knew exactly where on Tori's cheek the dimple would appear if she'd only smile at him again. A real smile.

He heard a bark and crossed to the little window of the office that looked out over the back of Mile High. A small yard, a stone fire circle with colorful lawn chairs around it, the trailhead to Solace Falls.

Sarge bounded into sight, followed by Brandon and Tori. They carried climbing gear and were clearly cheerfully rehashing the excursion as they walked over to one of the sheds that kept the heavier gear.

It was a weird thing to watch them when they didn't know it. Probably stalker creepy weird, and yet he couldn't force himself to look away.

This was what was supposed to have been, and now here it was.

He'd never had a second chance at something before. Was this some kind of second chance? He didn't know. So he watched Tori find a stick and toss it up in the air. Sarge barked and followed the arc of the stick, catching it in his mouth just before it hit the ground.

Brandon had disappeared now, likely to come inside and file the paperwork for their excursion. But Tori stayed, playing with a joyful Sarge.

Second chance. That kept echoing around in his head. Never had one. Never wanted one. Didn't even know if she *was* one.

What did a man do with a second chance?

"Will?"

He turned at Lilly's voice. She was standing in the doorway to the office as pretty and polished as ever. No one would have ever guessed she'd been out sick for however many days, on bed rest no less.

She had a binder clutched to her chest, which was par for the course for Lilly. Binders and schedules. Organized efficiency. Perfect for Brandon in every way.

She cocked her head. "Are you all right?"

"No." Because he couldn't really lie about it anymore. He wasn't all right, didn't know what it looked or felt like. Hadn't for a long time.

She let out a breath and stepped into the office fully, pulling the door closed behind her. "I owe you an apology," she said grimly.

"No, you don't."

"Yes, I do. I never should've—"

"Butted in and meddled, like you always do?"

She pressed her lips together at that before very purposefully relaxing her shoulders. "Okay, maybe I don't apologize for everything. But I apologize if this time when I did, you got hurt. I didn't ever mean to hurt you."

He looked back out the window at Tori playing with Sarge. It was so disorienting to feel like he should be out there. He should be playing. He should be a part of this.

"Maybe I needed to be hurt," he murmured, half to himself, thinking those words over and over.

Lilly didn't say anything, and when he finally looked

back at her she still had her lips pressed together. As though she was about to smile, but there was also worry etched in her drawn-together eyebrows, in her warm blue eyes.

The thing was, Lilly cared. About people and things and Mile High. About him. Brandon cared, and Sam. Even Hayley. They all cared. The hardest part of the past few months had been watching them all open up to that and do it better.

Do it far better than him.

"You don't need to apologize to me. I've been . . . I was angry last night. But not at you."

"Then at who?"

Will raked a hand through his hair. That was the thing, when he let himself feel anger he aimed it at people, but . . . Last night there'd been no aim except . . . "I guess myself mostly." Which wasn't all that different than any other day, just him admitting it to himself.

He didn't look at Lilly, but could feel her studying him. This polished, empathetic, really good woman who loved his brother. Who was carrying twins. Evans twins.

He took a faltering step toward her, lifting his gaze. His brother's pregnant wife. There would be babies here, soon enough, and he'd sort of kept himself apart from all this. The reality of what Lilly being pregnant meant.

He'd convinced himself it didn't affect him. The babies weren't his, what did it matter to his life? If he let it matter, he'd have to think more about Courtney, and telling Brandon about that had been bad enough.

But he'd convinced himself that was it. He'd told and he'd gone back to . . . What exactly? Pretending he didn't feel anything about it. Ignoring the emotions because she'd had her reasons and it didn't matter.

But it did matter. It would always matter that he hadn't had a chance. He looked at Lilly, who'd put her binder down and was looking at him with concern.

His hand reached out, seemingly of its own accord, a little unsteady. Hell, everything about him was unsteady right now.

"I know . . . I know this is weird, but . . . Could I . . ." He didn't even know how to communicate it. The desire. The painful, needy thing unfurling inside of him.

Lilly smiled and stepped toward him, taking his hand. Without a word or question, she placed his hand over her still-flat stomach.

"Not much to feel yet," she offered. "But the doctor says they're in there."

It felt bigger than it had. Everything right now felt so much bigger than it had, and he knew it was because he was letting it. A little bit against his will, but a little bit with his will. Letting himself feel. Absorb. Think.

He glanced up at her then, meeting those strong steel-blue eyes. She was a good person. Strong and thoughtful, honest and determined. Perfect for Brandon. Perfect for Mile High. *Perfect* for the job of mom of two more human beings in this world.

Who would share his last name, his blood.

"I'll be a really good uncle," he promised.

Her mouth curved. "Of course you will. I never had any doubts."

He did. A million and one doubts. Confusion and insecurity. About everything. He dropped his hand from her stomach and stepped away.

Terrible things lived inside of him, and he had given them credence all his life. Let them win. Let them dictate.

But he wasn't only the son of Phillip Evans anymore. He wasn't a child, and he wasn't a teenager. He wasn't mixed up in a toxic marriage. He'd made mistake after mistake in his life, but he was in charge of it now. Not his father or the Evans name. Not Courtney. Not Brandon or Mile High.

Not Tori.

He'd been drifting for so long and he hadn't realized it clearly until this moment. Until the future was basically staring him in the face.

Tori. Here. In his life for good, supposedly.

Brandon's kids. Growing in Brandon's *wife*.

They weren't kids anymore. There were going to *be* kids around, and he needed . . .

Well, Will Evans needed to grow the fuck up.

After everything that happened last night, Tori had decided to keep her distance from any sort of extracurricular activities with the Mile High crew. She'd work, she'd enjoy it, and then she'd go home to her sunny house down in Gracely and most expressly not get mixed up in any more weird dinners.

So she'd adamantly said no when Hayley had mentioned to her they were having an impromptu get-together around the fire pit that night. Tori was busy, and not interested. They could have hot dogs and s'mores without her.

She'd repeated it to Sam, and to Brandon. Even to Skeet. No, no, no. She was busy.

Then somehow as she'd been about to take off, Lilly had physically wrangled her out back, and a woman couldn't fight a pregnant lady who'd just gotten off bed rest. Then Cora and Micah had shown up, and Micah had started wrestling with Sarge, and Cora and Hayley were talking her ear off about getting dogs.

So here Tori was. Sitting in one of the colorful lawn chairs in back around a little fire in the stone circle. Brandon had put a cooking grate over the fire and was efficiently roasting hot dogs while Lilly set up a s'mores station with Hayley's help.

It was like something out of a movie. A colorful sunset, prettily organized foods, a gorgeous summer evening complete with campfire smell and the faint buzzing of insects. Tori wanted to hate it out of principle, but everything was too nice. She relaxed into the chair against her will.

It was soul-refreshing to sit here with the stars winking to life in the sky above her, Sarge at her feet while Micah snuck him bites of hot dog. People she knew and liked circled around, grabbing food, taking seats, chatting together and laughing.

Some of her relaxed posture faded when Will took the seat next to her. He handed her a plate.

"Mustard and relish, right?"

She blinked down at the perfectly prepared hot dog, willing her stomach not to do that obnoxious thing it used to do when Will did something nice for her, or noticed something about her.

She wouldn't go back there. "Yeah, thanks," she managed, taking the plate. She didn't dare look at him. She focused on the fire and the hot dog, all the people around her who weren't Will.

Truth be told, she liked all of these people. She liked seeing Sam happily infatuated with Hayley, liked Hayley's shy sweetness with everyone. She liked having Micah wrestle around with Sarge, and Brandon easily controlling the food situation. She even liked Skeet, weird old man that he was. He made her laugh with his insights and maniacal cackle.

Lilly, well, Tori was never quite sure how to *be* around Lilly. The woman made her nervous, but it was impossible not to see how perfect she and Brandon suited. Even when they were arguing about the appropriate size of the campfire, it was like watching a choreographed dance.

Tori felt oddly blessed to be witnessing it, to be a part of it. All of it.

Too soft. It'd get her in trouble, but in the darkening night, a hot dog on her plate, maybe she could indulge . . .

"Watch this," Will whispered into her ear, too close, to . . . Will. He pointed at Brandon and Lilly—Brandon scowling, Lilly gesturing with a package of marshmallows. "In five seconds scowling will turn into smiling and then three seconds later, what no one wants to witness."

"What does no one want to witness?" Tori asked in spite of herself, watching as Will counted down, and almost on cue the two grinned at each other.

"Three, two, one," Will said again in her ear, and then Tori realized too late what she should have predicted.

Brandon leaned down and captured Lilly's mouth with his.

Tori blinked and looked down at her hot dog. God, she really didn't want to see other people kissing. Not with Will's voice in her ear and last night flashing in her head. Over and over. The heat of his mouth. The scrape of his beard. His *taste*. She wasn't supposed to know what Will tasted like. She didn't like that knowledge. It sucked.

"Everybody got something to drink?" Brandon asked, apparently done kissing his wife.

Tori shifted uncomfortably in her chair, wondering if Will's mind was now on last night, and then chastising herself for wondering. Her hand closed over the can of pop she'd grabbed earlier and she stared very hard at Brandon, trying to focus on him and whatever he was going to say.

"Then let's have a toast," Brandon offered.

"A toast to what?" Sam asked skeptically. "You already got Lilly pregnant once. I don't think it could have happened again."

"Ha. Ha," Brandon retorted. "I think we should toast the future. We have a full staff we can implicitly trust. We have a full schedule for the fall, Mile High's fifth year anniversary. Cora will have enough coursework under her belt to step in while Lilly's on maternity leave."

"Oh, who is going to force Lilly into maternity leave?"

Will called, sounding relaxed and good-natured. "God himself?"

"She's having twins. Even Lilly will need some time off with twins," Cora offered, beaming at her sister.

"We'll see," Lilly replied primly.

"Anyway, the toast. To the future of Mile High. To the future of us. Everyone raise their glasses, well, cans."

"Here, here," a few voices echoed, and Tori did her best not to look at Will as she bumped cans with him.

There should be no talk of futures and looking in Will's direction at the same time, but hell, she was only human.

Much to her dismay and nerves and a million other things that jangled through her, Will was looking right at her. His hazel eyes glittering in the firelight.

Why hadn't she gone home?

She turned abruptly to Cora and clinked cans with her. Cora would be her saving grace. "I didn't know you'd be taking over for Lilly for a bit. That's great."

Cora shrugged. "I've been taking some office management classes. The publicity stuff is still a little beyond my pay grade, but I guess Brandon and Will have faith in me. Or Lilly's making them anyway."

Cora looked a little unsure, but Tori would be the last one to point that out. She liked Cora, and it'd be nice having someone around Mile High she could relax around, even if it was months away.

Tori took a sip of her pop, feeling edgy all of a sudden. She got to her feet. "I've got to run to the bathroom. Be right back." She patted Cora's arm as she scooted by, gave Micah a little nudge with her knee.

"If he throws up, you're in charge of cleaning it up," she offered to him with a grin.

Micah groaned, but she hoped it would keep him from

sneaking any more bites to Sarge. "Sorry, boy," she murmured before picking her way through the circle and back toward the offices.

She used the bathroom and washed her hands and then just paused. She needed a moment alone to breathe. She was overwhelmed with feeling—all different kinds. Hope and joy. Nerves and anger. Discomfort and happiness.

And the oddest, scariest sense that she finally had what she'd always wanted, and what would happen this time to take it away?

Do you really have everything you want?

She shook her head and pushed out of the bathroom. Only to find Will standing in the hallway.

She'd been angry at him this morning. And last night. She'd been so angry with him for so long, but something about the kiss had twisted that anger into something else. Not just hurt or fury, but fear.

A fear she didn't know how to handle. She couldn't march through it like she did with most of the fears in her life. She'd decided Mile High was her landing point, so she couldn't run away.

Or could you?

"Bathroom's all yours," she managed, trying to skirt around him and past him. His hand curled around her arm—not hard and jerky like last night. This was more of a careful touch. He was, or seemed to be, very purposefully giving her the space to step away from him, if that's what she wanted.

It was definitely what she wanted to do, but for some reason, she didn't.

"I wanted to apologize about last night," he said, his voice low and sincere.

The memory of that kiss, with his hand on her, it was

enough to have her pulling away from his light grasp. "Consider it forgotten."

"That's not what I said I wanted. I said I wanted to apologize."

There was something different about him. Something too soft and too open and she wanted to shrink away from it.

"I was angry and jealous. And I didn't quite know what to do about feeling jealous."

"Jealous of what?" she asked, none of it making sense. Not the apology. Not him touching her. Not the way he was acting. God, couldn't he be *predictable* for damn once?

He stared at her as if that would hold some answer. But she didn't understand what on earth he'd been jealous . . .

He didn't mean . . . But he nodded, as though he could read her thoughts. As though he could read them and answer every question in her head.

"I didn't particularly care for watching you smile at James."

Those twin feelings popped up. Something too close to pleasure, and the usual anger. She held on to anger because that was her. Pleasure was how she got knocked to the ground again. Anger was how she survived.

She was so tired of *surviving*. "You don't have any right to be jealous," she managed to say, sounding very nearly dispassionate.

"No, I don't. I know that. But that doesn't change the emotion."

He hadn't taken his gaze off her in the entire time they'd spoken. He was looking at her so intently, and she didn't know what he was trying to say or do, and she didn't want to figure it out. She just wanted things to be easy. She wanted to be left alone.

She wanted his hand on her arm. She wanted his mouth on hers again, rough and needy.

She walked past him. "Fine. I accept your apology. Whatever. Can we get back?"

"I like having you here."

She stilled since those simple words were like an arrow to the heart. She wanted to say something mean and awful in return, but her voice didn't work.

"I guess I wanted you to know that. That I like having you here, working here, like you were always supposed to. That I was jealous. It's something to think about."

"I won't be thinking about it. Ever," she returned foolishly. She was not going to consider what it meant that he was jealous. What it meant that he liked having her here. No, those were off-limits thoughts, that was for sure.

"I will be." He said it softly like a promise, like he didn't understand it was nothing more than a threat. There was no way to explain it to him though, so she simply walked away.

Back to the group who had welcomed her, and away from the man she didn't know what to do with.

Chapter Thirteen

Two days later, Will walked into the office he shared with Brandon, firmly sure of his plan.

Okay, mostly.

Something had to change, obviously, and maybe it was time for the change to come from him.

"I need you to change the schedule."

Brandon raised an eyebrow as he looked up from the computer where he was checking the invoices. "Okay. I'm not sure why the dramatic entrance, but what do you need changed?"

"I need you to give me your climbing excursion today."

Brandon's mouth firmed. "That's Tori's climbing excursion. I'm just observing her one last time before she gets the all-clear to take people out on her own."

"Let me be the one to observe," Will replied. He knew what he was doing. Kind of. He wouldn't be deterred.

Brandon pinched the bridge of his nose and sighed heavily. "I don't want to be in the middle of whatever this is."

"It isn't anything. Mostly."

"'Mostly' is exactly what scares me," Brandon returned, leaning back in his chair.

"Just trust me. Let me take it."

"I don't think Tori will care for that change," Brandon said, clearly choosing his words carefully.

But Will was a little over being careful. Something was bubbling inside of him. A kind of purpose, maybe. He wanted to act and move forward. "Maybe she'll be pissed at first, but she'll get over it."

"Why, because you're so charming when it comes to her?"

Will ignored his brother's sarcasm. "I need you to let me do this. I need you to give me some time with her."

"Why? Will, things are going well right now. The last thing I want is—"

"That's the point. Making things all right. I'm trying to fix things, and I can't fix things if she won't let me within fifty yards of her without scurrying off."

"Typically, when women scurry away from you, it's a sign they don't actually want anything to do with you."

"I'd point out Lilly did plenty of scurrying away from you, but this isn't like that. Exactly."

"Exactly?"

Will shook his head. He was getting off topic and letting Brandon distract him from the point. "This really isn't a joke. I'm being dead serious. Give me the excursion. I will handle Tori's fallout."

"That's not exactly your area of expertise."

Ouch. True, but ouch.

But Brandon hadn't flat-out said no yet. In fact, he was currently studying Will with that obnoxious older brother glare. Will stood there and took it. He let Brandon glare away—scrutinize, analyze, and figure things out.

As long as it got him a yes.

"I'll do it, on one condition," Brandon said at last.

"What's the condition?" Will asked eagerly.

Brandon hesitated, his condition no doubt something Will wasn't going to like.

"Why don't you tell me, in your own words, what the hell is going on there."

Yeah, Will definitely didn't like that condition. "Look, you don't need to worry—"

"The condition for me allowing you to take the excursion is that you're honest with me and tell me what the hell is going on with you two."

"Well, currently, nothing is going on between us." Mostly.

Brandon's frown deepened. "But you'd like there to be?"

Will took a deep breath. He didn't particularly want to air his feelings when they were still confusing, so he went with the simplest answer, though it was a little more emotional than he wanted it to be. "I want my friend back."

"And that's all, right? You're trying to get things back to the way they used to be. You and Tori as friends. This isn't more than that, right?"

Will hesitated. He shouldn't have, but he couldn't help it. Mostly he wanted his friend back, but there was the kiss to consider.

That kiss had lingered. It stuck there—in his brain, like a loop he couldn't step off. He'd been angry and stupid, and yet he could remember every detail. Every place his fingers had touched on her arm, the depth and breadth of her mouth, the little sigh she'd made as she'd melted into him.

After that, well, he had a hard time remembering any other kiss before it. He wasn't a poetic guy, but it was true. So the fact he couldn't, the fact it lingered there, well, it had to mean . . . something. Maybe.

"Will. Talk to me."

"I don't know what you want me to say."

"I want you to say anything," Brandon returned, leaning forward and resting his elbows on his knees. He linked his hands together, hazel eyes filled with concern.

Will wished he could wipe the concern away. He didn't

want it. He didn't need it. He was fine. Once he figured out things with Tori, he'd be fine.

Probably.

"I want you to talk to me," Brandon said, his voice so damn *careful*. "I want to understand this thing. Every time I turn around, the vibe between you two is completely different and—"

"First of all, you just said 'vibe' so I know you've been listening to Lilly too much. Second, did it ever occur to you that the 'vibe' doesn't matter? That all that matters is the fact Tori and I aren't at each other's throats, and you can trust me to handle things when you're not here."

"I do. I do trust you to handle things when I'm not here. But if you start . . . If you're poking at Tori to be friends again, to go back to how you used to be . . . Can you promise it won't all blow up again?"

Brandon always knew how to focus on the one little part of a problem Will wanted to avoid or sidestep or deal with later. He knew how to use that careful tone, he knew how to use his care like a weapon.

Which wasn't fair, probably, but it's what it felt like. A dismantling. He'd gotten a handle on what he wanted to do, and Bran was poking holes in it. Leave it to him.

"Of course I can't promise you that," Will snapped, irritation and something close to hurt coursing through him.

"Then maybe now is not the time to rehash something that's gone," Brandon said gently.

So fucking gently.

But it was funny that's how Brandon saw it. *Something that's gone.* As much as things popped into his head from back then, as much as Tori tried to bring *then* up, this thing right now wasn't actually about *then*.

It was about the woman who walked into his life *now*. He'd never kissed young Tori. He didn't know what that was like. But he knew what it was like to kiss *this* Tori. He knew what it was like to argue with this Tori and to see the way her eyes changed and . . .

"Things are precarious right now," Brandon continued. "Lilly's off bed rest, but things are still . . . I need her not stressed. I need Mile High staff to stay whole. I need us to be getting along. The campfire night was great. We had a great time. I want to hold on to that good stuff for a while without poking at things. Tell me you understand that."

"Of course I understand." The last few months had been rocky. Good, mostly, but rocky nonetheless, and he didn't want to add to it. He didn't want to add to Brandon's burden, whether it was fair he took all that burden on his shoulders or not.

"Let me be the one to observe Tori on her excursion this afternoon. Okay?"

Will wanted to argue. For a lot of reasons, he wanted to argue, but he didn't. He gave Brandon a nod and backed out of the office.

Maybe Brandon's refusal was right. Whatever friendship reclaiming Will was trying to accomplish shouldn't be fought for on company time.

He'd have to take his battle elsewhere.

Tori parked her car in the little carport next to her house. Her muscles ached like a bitch, but it was a good ache. The kind that told her she'd put in a hard day's work. Work she loved.

No matter what else was going on in her life, she could smile at the fact she had good work. A lot of people weren't so lucky.

Feeling happy and satisfied, Tori popped out of the car and let Sarge out before she shut the door.

"You like it here too, don't you, boy," she murmured,

patting his soft head. He panted happily and trotted up to the front door.

So far, taking him to Mile High every day was working out. Skeet watched him when they were all out on excursions, and he occasionally accompanied Hayley when she took groups to Solace Falls. Sarge was eating up the attention, and the extra treats.

It was a good life they were building here. Regardless of any weirdness, she was happy. Yeah, a few weird Will twinges, but *overall* happy.

"Tori!"

Tori waved over at Cora, who must've just gotten home from school and picking Micah up from basketball camp.

"Still good for movie night? I've got mac and cheese in the oven."

"Yup," Tori returned. She'd been looking forward to this all day. A night in with her friend—an actual female friend—with movies and junk food and *no* crying over Will. "Just give me a chance to shower and I'll be over."

Yeah, a really good life with friends and a good job and a social life.

Why the hell were tears pricking her eyes? Couldn't she just enjoy something without getting all emotional?

She stepped into her house, slamming the door behind her, already stripping as she headed toward the shower.

"I'll get used to it," she told Sarge. She'd get used to the good stuff—the way it made her chest hurt it was so good. The fear it'd all be swept away.

Sarge went straight for his bowl of food and water, though God knew Skeet was sneaking him scraps most of the day.

Tori went into her bathroom and turned the water to hot. She took a quick shower, washing off the dust and grime of rock climbing, and the weird overemotional feelings with it.

She flicked off the shower and dried herself off. She worked through her hair with a towel numerous times, but no matter how long she lingered, it was going to be a wet mass. She'd need to braid it even though her arms ached at the thought.

When a knock sounded at the door, Tori rolled her eyes with a little smile. Cora could be impatient, but it was nice that someone wanted to spend time with her. Someone who didn't have anything to do with the past or complicated feelings. Someone who wouldn't kiss her and she wasn't going to kiss back.

The perfect friend.

"I said I'd be over in a minute," she yelled, heading toward the door as she pulled her shirt on over her head. She padded barefoot to the front door and wrenched it open.

She might have actually gasped. Which was silly and dramatic, but the last person she'd expected to see on her doorstep was Will.

"Hi," he offered as though it was the most normal thing in the world for him to be on her doorstep. "I brought you some dinner. Pizza."

She blinked at him and then the box he held. "I . . . Sorry . . . What?"

"I knew you had a rock climbing excursion, and you know whenever I do the hard ones I never feel much like cooking when I get home. So I thought I'd bring you dinner."

"Without asking me?"

He flashed her a grin, and her stomach did that jiggly, turning thing it wasn't supposed to do with him anymore.

"If I'd asked, you would have said no."

Why some part of her wanted to laugh was beyond her, but she kept her mouth firm. "I have plans." He wasn't going to charm his way into her house. He wasn't going to . . . well, whatever this was.

"Real plans or Will-go-away plans?"

"Real plans. Cora and I have instituted Wednesday night movie nights," she said as loftily as she could manage with the smell of pizza infiltrating her nostrils.

Her stomach rumbled. God, she was hungry.

"Oh, Cora. That's fine. You know what, I'll go grab another pizza. I bet Micah can put away one by himself, so maybe two. Here. I'll be back." He shoved the box of pizza at her and started walking away.

"I'm not inviting you!" she yelled after him.

He kept walking back to his Jeep with a wave. "It's okay. I invited myself."

She stared after him even after his Jeep disappeared down the street. What the hell? What. The. Hell.

Sarge offered a belated bark. Or maybe he was begging for pizza.

"Thanks a lot," she muttered. She glanced once more at where Will's Jeep had disappeared.

He was joking or something. That was all. A peace-offering pizza and a joke. Surely. She shoved her feet into flip-flops and grabbed the box of wine she'd picked up for the occasion. Balancing both the wine and the pizza on top of each other, she pulled out her keys and whistled for Sarge.

Will was joking. He wasn't really bringing pizza. He wasn't.

She took the step onto Cora's stoop and glanced once more at the street. He wasn't coming back. She knocked once, then opened the door and stepped inside.

"In the kitchen," Cora called as Sarge headed for the stairs. Micah must be in his room.

Tori forced her legs to take her to the kitchen where Cora was frowning at a casserole dish full of . . . black bumps?

"I did it just like Lilly told me to do," Cora said, scowling.

"What is it?"

"It *was* mac and cheese. I didn't even make it! I was just reheating it and somehow it still burned. Oh." She glanced up and grinned. "You brought pizza?"

"Um."

"Oh, it's the new place!" Cora took the box of wine and the pizza box out of Tori's hands. "I heard a rumor that the guy who runs it is really hot. I'm going to start jogging by it in the mornings and see if I can fall in front of him or something."

Tori laughed. Cora was always entertaining. But . . . pizza. "So, something weird happened."

"Oh, let me guess," Cora said, pulling paper plates out of a cabinet. "It has to do with Will."

Tori scowled.

"It does, doesn't it?"

"How did you know that?" Tori demanded irritably.

Cora laughed. "I'd love to say because of my innate and amazing intuition, but Micah was yelling down about seeing Will's Jeep park out front, and since he didn't come here, I assume he went to you."

"He wasn't."

"He wasn't what?"

"I mean he was . . . Okay, so he came to my door. With pizza. He brought me dinner, he said. I said I was busy and he . . ." She blew out a breath. "Why am I always coming over talking about him?"

"I don't know, but I love it, nun that I've become. So keep talking, what did he do?"

"I said I was coming over here, and he shoved the pizza at me and said he'd be back with another one. And *I* said I wasn't inviting him, but he just laughed."

Cora poked at the black mass of supposed macaroni and cheese thoughtfully. "He brought you dinner. And when you said you had dinner plans, he said he would go get more and join you."

"Yes! What's wrong with him? He was joking. He had to be joking. Right?"

The doorbell rang and Tori froze.

Cora grinned. "I think we're about to find out."

Chapter Fourteen

Will was greeted at the door by a very curious-looking Cora, a frowning Tori, and the scuttling tap of Sarge's imminent approach.

"I brought two, just in case," he offered, smiling broadly.

"Didn't you just," Cora murmured, staring at him speculatively. "Well, come on in."

"Cora," Tori hissed, but Cora ignored her and walked farther into the house. He followed, but Tori stood by the door looking mutinous.

"Coming?" he asked, still grinning.

"What are you doing?" she demanded.

"Pizza," he replied, bending over to give Sarge a good ear scratch. Micah clattered down the stairs and came into view. "Hey, MJ."

Micah rolled his eyes. "Try LeBron, son."

Will laughed as the boy zeroed in on the pizza. Will had been in the house a few times. He'd helped Brandon move some of Lilly's stuff, and he and Brandon had done a few repairs for Cora.

It was a nice house. Small rooms, but open. Well lived in, the kind of home he hadn't had growing up. He'd had all of the newest *things*, and they'd had a maid to keep the house sparkling. Basketballs had been forbidden in the house.

Love had been forbidden in that house, and it shone through here.

Which was a terribly morbid thought and he didn't particularly want to dwell on it.

"Had a nice chat with the new pizza place owner," Will offered as Cora opened up all the boxes and handed everyone a plate. "He seems determined to make something of it, so maybe we'll actually have somewhere to send people to eat after a hike besides Corbin's lodge."

"Oh, I hope it lasts." Cora bit into a slice of pizza and groaned. "I haven't had fresh take-out pizza in ages. Is the bakery still going?"

"So far." He glanced at Tori, who was still standing at the entrance to the small kitchen, the plate clutched angrily in her hands.

"Going to eat?" he asked cheerfully.

She set her mouth into a firm line, dropping her plate on the edge of the counter before grabbing his arm.

She took his pizza-filled plate out of his hands and set it on top of hers.

"Hey."

Then she was dragging him to the front of the house, and out of it. For a second, he thought she was going to leave him in the front yard, go back inside, and lock the door.

He wasn't entirely sure that wasn't her plan, but if it was, she changed her mind and stepped out onto the grass with him.

"What are you doing?" she demanded, crossing her arms over her chest. Her hair was still down, and she was wearing athletic shorts and a T-shirt, and her feet were bare. She looked . . . soft, almost. Like some woman he didn't know.

An uncomfortable thought, so he smiled. "I was eating pizza until I was so rudely—"

"What are you *doing*?" she repeated, and it was the fact she didn't seem angry, but a little hurt, that had him softening enough to tell her. That would be part of it, he thought. Some straightforward honesty was required to rebuild a friendship.

"I want to be your friend again," he said as earnestly as he could manage without feeling . . . squirmy. Okay, he still felt a little uncomfortable at that much forthrightness, but it was a start.

"By barging into *my* dinner and movie night?" she demanded, changing her stance from arms crossed to hands on her hips.

"Yes." He smiled again, because he was certain he could charm her. "Consider the inevitable chick flick my penance for inviting myself."

"Will." She tangled her hands in her hair in frustration. It was always so distracting when it was down, thick and wavy. It'd be soft, and smell like her shampoo.

"Will!"

"What?"

She looked at him, exasperation and something a little too close to fear. Was she afraid of him? But what exactly about him? He'd been a good friend. Yeah, he'd clumsily shut down the whole love thing, but before that he'd been a good friend.

What was there to be afraid of?

"We're not friends," she said softly. "Not like that. Too much has happened. We can't just . . . be what we were."

"Are you the exact same person you were back then?"

"No, but I am the exact same person you *kissed* the other night. I can't do this whole thing again. This half-and-half shit."

"Okay." He supposed it was his problem he felt a little half-and-half himself. His problem, not hers. He held out his hand, but she only scowled at it.

"Don't be a coward, take my hand."

Her lips firmed and he could tell she was trying to fight her innate reaction to fall into the trap of reverse psychology. Still, they might not be the same people they were, but he knew Tori Appleby. Deep down, regardless of all the other crap, he knew what made her tick.

She slipped her hand into his, gaze wary but determined. He gave it a squeeze.

"I only want to be your friend again. I'm not the same kid I was, and neither are you, which means it won't be the same friendship. It's not the same us. But I don't want to be angry, and I don't want to be tense."

"You can't just decide not to be those things. There's . . . It's there. You can't erase it."

He took a deep breath, but he didn't release her hand. "I don't want to erase it." She tried to tug her hand away, but he held firm. He'd made a decision, for the best of Mile High, and his friends, and himself, he'd made a decision.

Much like deciding to tell Brandon about the things that had happened with Courtney a few months ago, it was a decision he couldn't back off from, because it mattered. It was important.

"I'm not suggesting we pretend it never happened. I'm saying that we're different people. We're adults, and it's been a long time. The kiss the other night . . ." Well, it was certainly something, but he didn't need to figure it out right this second. One step at a time.

"Was a giant mistake," Tori said firmly.

"Yeah." Maybe. "And I think borne in part due to frustration and trying to pretend and trying to rehash and . . . I just want to start over. That doesn't erase anything that's happened between us, it just puts it firmly in the past. Where it belongs."

She inhaled, still staring at him, still kind of pulling away from him though he held her hand firmly. She swallowed. "I don't know how to do that."

"Honestly? I don't know that I know how either, but I figure it's worth a shot. We're building Mile High into something that could change Gracely, you know? You're a part of that now. I don't want it to feel heavy."

His chest ached at the look on her face before she schooled it away, but he'd seen it. Fear and uncertainty. Underneath all that tough façade, all that poking at old wounds, she was just as *scared* as he was.

The problem was, he didn't know what he was afraid of, only that a low-level panic lived in his chest. Was she the same? As in the dark about that clutching thing and its cause as he was?

"So . . ."

"So we go in and have a movie night. Maybe we shuffle the schedule around a bit so we're on some of the same excursions every once in a while. We enjoy each other's company when our friends get together. We agree that we're different people, in a different time. We were kids before. At least, I was. I hadn't grown up yet."

"And now you have?" she asked skeptically.

He smiled self-deprecatingly. "Slowly figuring it out. A failed marriage helps, believe it or not."

It softened her, he could feel it in her hand, he could see it on her face. "Why did it fail?" she asked softly.

He wanted to withdraw *his* hand now, but he didn't. This was the thing you did when you were an adult. This was the thing he'd seen Brandon do, time and time again, no matter how hard.

When someone asked you a difficult question, one that hurt and brought up things you didn't want to face, you answered it anyway. You summoned whatever strength you had, and you looked the discomfort in the eye.

Brandon had never shied away from being an Evans in

this town when it had come to be a curse. He'd marched on, determined to make it mean something else.

So Will would march on, determined to make this strained relationship with Tori something else. Something better.

"I realized how far apart we were, how little we meant to each other, and I reached a point where it wasn't what I wanted for myself anymore." Not every detail, but the truth.

She was still studying him, the colorful sunset behind him reflecting in her eyes. A vibrant, cloudy storm within.

"So you were the one who walked away?"

"I filed for divorce, but we'd both walked away from each other a long time before that. There was no fight. No tears. She said, 'Suit yourself,' and that was it." *She terminated our child.* It was on the tip of his tongue, but it was a pretty summer night and he didn't want that ugliness between him and Tori. Not when he was holding her hand.

"All right," she said, her voice something close to a whisper. She gripped his hand tighter, began to pull him back toward the door. "You're sounding an awful lot like a woman, I think a chick flick will be right up your alley."

It was so Tori, so something she would have said to him years ago, that he smiled and followed.

Thank God for wine. It was the only tangible thought in Tori's mind as she sat on the couch next to Will and watched the romantic comedy Cora had picked out.

Tori seemed to be the only one who thought this was fucking weird. Cora and Will had laughed at different things in the movie, Micah had played video games on a handheld thing, occasionally asking Will for help. As though they were some screwed-up New Age family.

Tori took a long sip of her wine.

Will wanted to be friends. That was fine. She should be

glad. Isn't that what she'd wanted? For them to be able to be comfortable, or comfortable-ish, around each other. That's all she was after. The opportunity to work at Mile High and with him and not feel horribly awkward.

She felt horribly, *horribly* awkward. This was so much worse than fighting. Fighting she knew how to do. Play nice when they weren't working, when he was infiltrating her new life?

This was supposed to be separate. Her house, her friendship with Cora. This was supposed to be the thing he wasn't a part of.

But he'd answered her very personal question about his marriage outside and unfortunately, she knew enough about Will to know that was a step for him. A change. He didn't like to talk about hard things. He never wanted to dig too deep into a problem.

Wasn't that what she'd liked about him? He'd never asked why she ran away from home, and if she gave a sort of half explanation of what happened with her brother, he never pushed for more details. He never demanded more information. He treated everything with the kind of superficiality that appealed to her.

Because God knew she didn't want to delve into that shit with herself let alone anyone else.

Back then it had seemed reasonable to avoid, to pretend, and now . . .

She realized, belatedly, that the credits were rolling and Cora was picking up plates and glasses and hauling them into the kitchen.

Tori let out a sigh of relief. Will would leave now. She could go back to her little house by herself and relax. She could stop feeling like her muscles would never unclench.

She got up off the couch and the world spun a little bit. Will's long fingers curled around her elbow.

He didn't say anything. Just steadied her and then let her go. Very friendly all in all. Not even a joke about her needing help to stand.

She let out a shaky breath and didn't dare look at him. "Come on, Sarge. Bedtime."

"I'll walk with you."

Dammit. She should have waited for him to leave before *she* tried to. Maybe she could still . . . She glanced at Cora who had a look on her face that reminded Tori far too much of Lilly. A sort of calculating certainty.

Sarge happily followed Will toward the door and Tori could only trudge after. She glanced back at Cora once more, hoping for her friend's interference, but Cora only smiled far too widely.

"You're going to pay for this," Tori muttered, not quite knowing how she would make Cora pay.

Cora chuckled. "I'll pay and pay for it, as long as you give me all the details."

"There will be no details," she growled. She glanced at Will, who was opening the door and letting Sarge prance outside to do his business.

Cora shrugged as if she didn't believe her. Well. Tori would prove it. She'd prove to everyone that she was stronger than the Tori of old. She did not have to fall head over heels for Will Evans. She was stronger. She was immune.

That's so why she'd kissed him back the other night. Immunity to his charms.

She squeezed her eyes shut before reopening them and forcing herself to follow Will outside.

The night was cool, the sky heavy with clouds. There was a faint rumble of thunder and a flash to the west.

"I sure hope we get the rain. I think the customers who keep rescheduling are going to give up eventually."

"Oh, they'll be back," Will said with every confidence in the world. "They know we can't control the weather."

"If it stays dry—"

"It won't forever."

And, of course, as though he could control the weather, a fat raindrop landed on her nose and then her cheek. Lightning flashed again in the distance. Sarge quickly trotted over to her house and the little overhang that protected the stoop from rain.

"Smart dog," she muttered still standing stock-still in the middle of Cora's yard. Will's hand curled around hers for the second time today.

"Come on, drunky."

"I am not drunk." But when she took a step, she stumbled a little. "I am elegantly tipsy."

Will snorted as they broke into a jog across the yard and onto her protected stoop.

"Elegant in all things. Especially drunk off box wine."

"Tipsy."

Her hair was wet again, and so was her shirt and her feet in her flip-flops. She couldn't see Will in the dark. She should've left a porch light on, she thought dimly.

Her hand was still in his.

Again, standing in front of her house, too close. Too many thoughts catapulting through her brain. Thoughts of that kiss. Thoughts of his hands. Oh, who was she kidding? She'd always be this way, helpless and hopeless when it came to him.

Yeah, she'd learned not to tell him that. Learned to keep things like that to herself. Her life had been a series of learning to tamp down her feelings. But it never erased those feelings. They were still there. Haunting her.

"Aren't you going to invite me in to wait out the storm?"

He said it too soft. Too silky. And it was far too tempting. To invite him in. To be alone with him. Be unsteady with him with her hand in his.

"That's what a friend would do," he said, his voice too close to her temple, his breath brushing across her forehead.

"I guess we're not friends then, because I am not inviting you in," she said, her voice overloud compared to his.

"Why not?"

She wished she could see him. If she could see his expression, she'd understand his tone better.

Why not? Was he really that clueless? Or was he trying to get her to say something? This was the thing she hated. The thing she couldn't stand. The not knowing how to do it. Not knowing what the other person was after.

"I'll go," he said. "Because we are going to be friends again. I don't want to jeopardize that."

She really didn't know what *that* meant. How was coming inside jeopardizing it? Did he think she couldn't control herself around him?

Was that it? That pissed her off, because she damn well could. Maybe not her emotions or her heart, but definitely her*self*.

She opened her mouth to say just that, but he was talking on in that low, silky voice that made her stomach jump and her heart beat so hard she could barely hear what he had to say.

"Because I think if I came inside, I'd be tempted to kiss you again. And you don't want that."

No, she didn't want that. Couldn't, anyway.

His thumb brushed across her wet knuckles, and then he released her hand. "Good night, Tori. Night, Sarge."

Then he was gone. When Tori could think again, she'd blame her head spinning on the wine.

Chapter Fifteen

It turned out being platonic friends with someone who you were also attracted to, and had kissed once and therefore knew what it was like to kiss them, was hard.

Will hadn't expected that. He'd been down this road before. It wasn't like he hadn't realized Tori was a woman back in the day. But he hadn't known what she'd tasted like. Or what it was like to have her look up at him with a mixture of fear and nervousness in her eyes.

Tori had always been a force. Confident and sure as she blazed through everything and he'd known underneath all of that were some insecurities and some uncertainty. He'd also known she'd never deign to show it.

He supposed that was one of the things he'd liked about her. She never made him feel bad. She never made him feel uncomfortable. She never expected too much, and she never pushed. Not until that night.

Wasn't that why it had been such a shock? That she'd never done anything like that before. Never asked anything of him. Then she'd shoved it all at him like he was supposed to know what to do with it. Love and care.

Now they were here in this place, and she wasn't asking a damn thing of him. But he wanted . . .

He wanted. It was getting harder and harder to ignore.

Weeks in each other's company and working together had solidified a certain foundation. Here they were. Friends again. Comfortable with each other. Well, a kind of comfortable. There was still something that lurked in the shadows, that buzzed underneath the interaction, but it didn't bubble over.

Every time he looked at her, he thought about that kiss from weeks ago now. Thought about what it would be like without the anger fueling it. Thought about what it would be like . . .

He pushed the thought out of his head and focused on what was in front of him. One of the last kayaking trips they'd give this year since the cooler temps would start to make it too dangerous.

He'd move into taking the extra hiking and backpacking excursions that would crop up for the crowded fall season. Winter would be leaner, but he'd stay busy with more administrative tasks. Brandon was making noise about a business co-op or chamber of commerce for Gracely, to keep the businesses that existed here and bring in new ones.

Plans were being made. Plans for the future. Brandon and Lilly were getting ready for the twins. Sam and Hayley were all moved in together and though Will didn't want to think about it too deeply, he wouldn't be shocked if they ended up getting married eventually. It seemed like a foregone conclusion.

Time was marching on. He wasn't getting any younger.

And he couldn't stop thinking about having the one woman he probably shouldn't want to have. She'd made it abundantly clear that she did not want him to want her.

"Hey."

Speak of the devil. "Hey, what's up?" He lined up the waterproof packs he'd carry down to the beach for the kayaking trip.

"Lilly got a meeting with the pizza place guy, and Brandon wanted to attend. Which means I'll be your second this afternoon."

"Sounds good. Do we know any more about the pizza guy? Any connections to Gracely?"

"They didn't seem to think so." She moved to his line of supplies and started packing the second bag.

"Gracely isn't known for its deep and abiding love for Evanses, so maybe it's best if he's just a random outsider," Will mused.

"It's strange how people hold a grudge. Never quite understood it."

"I can't understand it myself," Will agreed, zipping up his pack. "But I've only been on the other end."

"Everyone I knew growing up just blamed God for their troubles. Or Democrats. Or both."

He gave her a sideways glance, because though it was no actual piece of information, she didn't often talk about growing up. Period. "What things were the people you knew growing up blaming God for?"

She shrugged, focusing hard on her supplies and packing them a little too carefully. "My family lost our farm when I was six."

"I'm sorry. What? You grew up on a farm?"

"We left it when I was six, that's hardly growing up on it. But it's Kansas, what did you expect? CEO daddy?"

"You were a little farm girl. Now I'm imagining pigtails and Daisy Dukes and—"

She gave him a shove, but a smile curled her mouth. "I was six, you pervert."

It was hard not to acknowledge moments like this. When it was easy. When it was nice. He always wanted to tell her what it meant, to be friends again. Because it hit him every time. But if he stopped and said he liked it every time he felt that, well, he'd probably drive her away for good.

"Tell me more about the farm."

"I'm not telling you anything about anything. We're going kayaking, and it's sort of my least favorite excursion, so you're going to have to give me some leeway."

"Sam could probably do it. I forgot you hated water."

"Sam's out with Hayley's hike. And it's not water I hate, it's that I can't control it."

"You can't control the rocks you climb either," he pointed out.

"That's where you're wrong. The rock doesn't move. It doesn't do shit. I am the master of it."

He studied her as she shouldered the backpack. She wouldn't like it, but . . . "Tell me about the farm."

It was her turn to send him a sideways glance. "Why?" she asked skeptically.

"I'm intrigued. You don't talk about your childhood much. Or at all."

"You don't talk about yours," she returned.

"You know all about mine. Silver spoon, prince of the town. Even better than the heir apparent because I didn't have to do anything like Brandon did. It was great."

"Funny, you sound awfully bitter when you say it was great."

He didn't know what to say to that. Parts of it had been great. No one had ever called him on his bitterness before. He said things in a joking enough way. People didn't pick up on the undercurrents.

Of course Tori did.

"I loved it, the farm," she said on a sigh. "I loved walking out my door and seeing nothing but sky and fields. My dad used to let me ride in his lap on whatever he was riding. Tractor, combine, whatever. I had chores and even though I was six, I had to do them on my own and right."

"Like what?"

"Collect the eggs. We had a whole coop full of chickens."

"You're shitting me," he said, pulling his own pack onto his back. He couldn't quite picture Tori, such a bundle of intense energy, sweetly collecting eggs as a six-year-old.

"Nope. Collect eggs. Fight off jackass chickens. But that was a kid's perspective. As I got older, I realized it was a lot more than tractor rides and fun with the animals."

"Like what?"

"Bills. Death. Uncertainty. Everything you do dependent on the weather, on prices that you have no control over. How much fertilizer you can buy from month to month. Credit. Creditors. It's funny, we moved to a trailer and Dad would wax poetic about the farm like it was the best thing we'd ever had and we'd never be happy if we didn't get it back. Mom would remind him of the stress and the pain and suffering."

"Doesn't sound very happy," Will offered softly.

"You'd be surprised."

He wanted to push on that. With every fiber of his being did he want to understand that statement. But he could tell by the way she started marching toward the office she regretted saying it. He'd need a lot more than charm to get her to say the rest.

So he followed her, mulling all that over. Though it made his heart beat a little too hard, he felt like he needed to share something back. He needed to prove to her that when she gave him pieces of herself, it wasn't unnoticed. It meant something to him. As a friend.

As a friend. "You know, I was pretty happy when my dad decided to move the mine away."

She stopped for a minute and looked back at him. They were only a few steps from the door. He could just go in and leave it at that, but that wouldn't get him what he wanted.

"I always hated it. Maybe for a while I hated it because

Brandon loved it, or because it was going to be his and not mine. There was a jealousy for a while, but I was over it then. When I wanted it gone. I hated that place, that company, because it didn't . . ."

Shit, why was he laying all this at her feet? What did it really prove?

"Didn't what?" she asked, and it was that soft note to her voice that reminded him it proved something. What he didn't know, but *something*.

"It didn't have a heart. It was this soulless center. We have this beautiful town and all of this natural beauty around us and they just pumped things out of the ground. I know that I wasn't supposed to feel that way, and I know that it's not . . . It just never spoke to me. It always bothered me."

She was looking at him as though he were some strange creature she'd never seen before. Which seemed about right as it was certainly a feeling he'd never ever in his entire life told anyone. Not Brandon. Not his father. No one had ever heard those words uttered from his mouth.

And he'd given them to her.

"Well, you and Bran built something beautiful. Something with a heart and with a soul. So I guess you win."

He smiled wryly. "At the cost of Gracely?"

"Gracely's not dead yet."

With that, she stepped inside and those words twined with all the other words she'd given him over the years. Her words were always shifting things inside of him. Changing things.

It was only now he was beginning to realize it.

"There you are!"

Tori looked around the hood of her car where she'd been pouring oil into the tank. The damn thing was on its last legs, and she basically had to put oil in when she left home, then again when she went back home at night.

Now there was Lilly, looking pretty as a picture pregnant with *twins* and Tori was sure she was sweaty and covered in oily filth.

"Here I am. Did you need something?"

"Yes. I need a favor. Do you have dinner plans?"

"Um . . ."

Lilly smiled and Tori realized it wasn't an unkind smile. Lilly could be intimidating and it stemmed from a sort of certainty, Tori supposed. It wasn't an unkind certainty either, or a predatory one. It was just . . . Lilly. Certain and sure and Tori was going to have to learn to relax around that.

"No ambush, I promise," Lilly said, holding up her hands. "We had that meeting with Shane Malone—the pizza guy—and we want to prove Gracely will bring in some revenue. So we're getting as many of us as possible to go to dinner tonight. If you can't come, it's not a big deal, but we'd certainly love you to."

"Oh well, sure, I can come." What excuse was there not to go?

Lilly gave Tori's arm a squeeze. "Perfect. Everything with your car all right? I'm sure someone could give you a ride."

"It'll get me there and back. What time?"

"I think we'll all meet down at the restaurant around six-thirty. That'll give Sam and Hayley enough time to clean up after their excursions."

"Sounds good."

Lilly nodded and marched back to Mile High like the general she was. Tori couldn't help but wonder what it would be like to be so in charge of your life. She couldn't begin to imagine what it would be like to march around on heels while pregnant with twins, but that probably wasn't something she'd ever need to worry about.

She ignored the little pang as she always did at the thought of kids. But seriously, what would she do with a baby? She could barely take care of Sarge and herself.

She closed the hood of the car and then whistled for Sarge, who bounded around the corner of the office cabin.

She opened the driver's-side door and Sarge hopped right in, moving over into the passenger seat with ease. Tori slid inside. It was five, so she had a little time to clean herself up.

She hadn't had pizza from the new place since that night at Cora's, and her stomach rumbled at the thought. It was damn good pizza.

She stuck her key in the ignition and turned it. Her stomach sank at the *click click click* sound. No engine noises, no signs of life. Just *click, click, click.*

Oh, ugh, she needed this car to last just a little bit longer. She'd somewhat foolishly sent her entire last check to Mom. Will had made her all nostalgic about the farm the other day and she'd just needed to make a connection, even if it was only money.

Damn that man.

She sighed and got back out of the car. More oil wasn't going to fix *click click click*. Tori didn't know a whole lot about cars, but she knew that much.

"Doesn't sound so good."

She looked back over at Will, who had come out onto the porch at some point.

"No, it doesn't. Learned anything about cars in the past seven years?"

"Not a thing."

"Know any mechanics?"

He shook his head. "Not in Gracely."

"Fantastic," she muttered. She popped the hood—if she looked hard enough maybe it'd whisper the fix to her.

"I'll get Sam," Will called. "Car engines aren't his specialty, but considering what he's rigged up at that cabin, maybe he'll be able to figure something out."

"Thanks."

Will disappeared and then reappeared with Sam. They both clucked over the car engine as though they knew a damn thing when she was quite certain they didn't. But she played fetch with Sarge while they pretended like they were doing something important. That was friendship, right? Letting the other person think they were lending a hand.

She smiled wryly at herself as Brandon and Lilly exited the office.

"No luck?" Lilly asked.

"No luck," Sam said. "I think we're going to need to find a mechanic who'll come up here. Paying for a tow truck to brave these mountain roads gets costly."

"As long as it's okay with Tori, why don't we table the situation for today. We'll go eat pizza, someone will drive you and then pick you up for work in the morning. Tomorrow we can work on finding a mechanic who'll make a car call. Sound good?"

Tori wanted to argue. She wasn't used to someone swooping in and telling her what to do or how to do it, but Lilly gave her a little arm squeeze as though they were the best of friends who just touched each other. "You can say no. I won't be offended. I just thought it might be the most reasonable course of action. But I tend to overstep."

"But you do it so thoughtfully," Will said, smiling at Lilly.

Which made Tori feel like a jerk for being irritated. "No, that's fine. It's no big deal. Hate to put someone out with the extra driving, but—"

"You can't 'put out' a friend. It's a favor, not a deficit."

"Right." Tori tried to smile even though she felt extraordinarily uncomfortable. Even when she'd been friends with the guys back in college she'd always been the one who did the favors. She was the one who swept in with the plans. She was the one who handled things.

The boys drank and partied and occasionally bought her a meal against her will. But she wasn't used to being . . .

"It's okay to let friends take care of you," Will's voice said far too close to her ear. So close she doubted anyone else heard the murmured words. She glanced up at him. He was too close, bending his neck, his beard all but brushing her temple.

"Well, favor or friendship or whatever, thank you for offering. I'll . . . take the help," Tori said with as much cheer as she could muster. Because it was hard to muster cheer when you were panicking about your loss of control.

And perhaps that was her issue and not anyone else's. *Yeah, perhaps.*

"Well then, we better get going. Brandon and I want to get a little talk in with Shane before dinner, but Will or Hayley can take you by your place to drop off Sarge and so forth."

"We'll take my Jeep," Will said, awfully high-handedly in Tori's opinion.

But she gritted her teeth and didn't say anything as people dispersed. It made sense. She didn't want Sarge to mess up Hayley's car, and Will was offering and they were *friends.*

"You're vibrating like, well, something inappropriate," he offered as the other two couples drove away.

"If you're trying to ease my frustration with a vibrator joke, you fail," she muttered, forcing herself to unclench and move.

He grinned and fell into step next to her. "I don't know if I'd say I failed. You did recognize it as a vibrator joke."

She glared at him, but damn it, a smile was tugging at her lips. "I don't like people planning things for me."

"I know you don't. But that doesn't mean you can't occasionally let somebody."

It was even more irritating that he was right. "I just . . . I've been taking care of myself for a long damn time, you know."

"Yeah, I know. And everyone else who came into your orbit too."

She thought of Toby. "Not exactly," she muttered.

She'd been happy to let Toby take care of her and because she hadn't been in love with him, she'd figured it'd be fine. As long as she wasn't trying to love someone, things were fine. But somehow relying on him, even without love, had ended up blowing up in her face.

Will tapped a fingertip to her forehead, then the bastard followed the line she knew must have been dug in there from her frowning.

It was a friendly touch. It was. It didn't shudder through her. It didn't remind her of kisses or yearning. It was just a touch.

"We're helping you out because we care about you."

As if that would make the fear and anger go away. That just made everything worse. "Care doesn't always help," she said, and she shouldn't have. He was going to push that, but she needed some space first, so she whistled for Sarge and got into the Jeep without saying another word, or letting him.

Chapter Sixteen

Will drove the Jeep down the mountain and to Tori's house. He let her have her little sulk because he knew that's what she needed.

He hadn't been surprised Tori had been so off put by people stepping in to help her out, but he was a little surprised at the vehemence behind it. He'd always known Tori was a bit of a control freak, but she'd also known when to relax back in the day.

So he made himself be quiet. He let her scowl in the passenger seat while Sarge happily panted from the back, his head stuck in between their shoulders.

Will pulled up outside of her house and she got out without a word, only whistling for Sarge. The dog gave one little whine before following after her. Will stayed in the Jeep at first.

He should give her some space. Let her get Sarge settled, come back out, then they could go have pizza and pretend.

Pretend. He was so tired of pretending.

So he got out of the car. He walked across the yard and into her house without knocking. Sarge was standing in the kitchen drinking out of a dog bowl. Tori was pacing.

"I didn't invite you in," she snarled.

"I know."

"Look," she began, and he could see all the ways she was trying to unclench. "I know I was a little uptight about it, and I still am. Help freaks me out, okay? I just need . . . Just give me some space."

"I'm not so sure space is what you need."

She whirled on him, a million storms in those ocean eyes. "You will not even begin to pretend like you can tell me what I need."

"It occurs to me that we're an awful lot alike."

She snorted. "Yes, we are exactly alike."

"We bury it. All of the things we don't want. We bury them."

She stilled then, and he knew he'd hit a point. So he kept going. "I'm not telling you to not feel like you feel. I'm just saying that maybe the function of friends is that when you do feel those things, you let it out. You talk to them about it, and then, because you talked to someone who cares about you and wants the best for you, you figure it out."

"Is that what friendship is?"

He thought maybe she meant for it to be sarcastic, but it didn't quite hit the mark.

"You know, I actually helped Lilly and Brandon get together."

"You did not. She swept in, he fell head over heels. That is the only possible story."

"Oh no. We hired Lilly, against Brandon's wishes, but regardless that made her off-limits in Brandon's head, of course. So they fought, and argued, and fought, and then they had sex and Lilly got pregnant. For a variety of reasons, she was ready to have nothing to do with Brandon."

"You're lying." But she was paying attention, and she was relaxing.

"In the beginning, when she was trying to cut Brandon out, I think it was her own fear, her own insecurities—they do exist, believe it or not. But Brandon was really struggling with how to deal with that. How to handle it. Because she'd hurt him. You know Brandon and how much it would hurt if someone told him that his responsibility wasn't his to take care of."

"It'd kill him," she said softly.

"Exactly. And I got in there, and I told him some things about my marriage that made him realize he needed to fight, and he was probably not seeing things any more clearly than she was. Then they made up. Happily ever after."

Tori cocked her head and studied him. "What things in your marriage?"

It was always amazing how any hint at having to talk about *those things* could freeze his insides into sharp shards of ice. He'd prepared himself for this, told himself if she asked, he would tell her. He would tell her because friendship and shit like that. Because he was trying to change.

Still, he froze and everything hurt. Still, it sent a wave of panic through him, to explain it. Discuss it. To have to put his feelings on the matter on display like that, because they weren't ones he was any good at hiding.

"If I tell you," he managed to croak out, "then you have to promise to do the same."

"I've never been married."

"You know what I mean. If I tell you that, then you have to tell me why friends trying to help makes you so angry."

"You said it yourself, you already know why."

"But I want you to tell me."

"That doesn't make any sense."

"Those are my terms, Tori. Tit for tat, so to speak."

She blew out a breath, rolling her eyes, but she was

curling and uncurling her hands into fists and then out. "Fine," she muttered. "Give me your tit." She managed to smirk at him, but something like fear lingered in her eyes.

But she wanted to know. She wanted to know this about him enough to give a piece of herself, and he would take that. He glanced at his watch. They probably had about fifteen minutes before anyone wondered why they weren't at the pizza place.

"Let's sit," he said, nodding toward the living room.

Tori led the way and settled herself on the edge of the dark blue couch. He knew she would've preferred he sit anywhere else, but he took a seat right next to her. Close enough that their hips touched. If he was going to tell her this, he wasn't doing it half a room away. He wasn't going to pretend like it wasn't important. Because telling her this definitely mattered to him.

"A while ago, Courtney was in between modeling jobs, and a little worried she wouldn't find a new one. But we did what we always did. We drank, we partied, we had *fun*. She got irritated I was spending so much time helping Brandon with Mile High, but mostly it was . . . okay."

He clasped his hands together, trying not to get lost in the details. He needed to focus on the facts. The simple story. "Then she got a job, and she happily jetted off to Italy or France or some such. I didn't pay much attention, furthering my excellent husband reputation. But that was . . . That was our marriage. Fun while we were together, pretty much not interested when we weren't."

"That doesn't sound like much of a marriage."

"Yeah, well, exactly. I mean we were . . ." How to explain it? "It never bothered me when she was gone. Every once in a while if I heard something through a friend or saw a guy on her Instagram page or whatever, it was a little infuriating, but mostly I didn't care enough to know. I liked spending time with her. I liked certain aspects of her company, but it was no great love match of the century. It just was what it was."

He kept his gaze on his hands because he wouldn't get through it if he looked at Tori. If he saw sympathy or the lack of it. If he saw anything, he would break. He wouldn't break now.

"Her sister called me out of the blue one day asking why I hadn't come up to Boulder. She tried to cover up her mistake, but I realized Courtney was home and she hadn't come to Gracely or even told me she was with her family."

The problem with telling people about it was that he remembered it. Too clearly, too harshly. The shock and the horror. The pain, and the betrayal, and the realization Courtney hadn't seen it as one, and he couldn't even blame her.

"It came out, as things do, that she'd been pregnant." He squeezed his hands tighter. "She . . . wasn't . . ." He cleared his throat.

"Will."

It was too soft, something like a plea, so he had to spit it out. "She had an abortion. Which, you know, that was her choice to make and all that, but I realized . . . I realized that's not a marriage. When your wife does that without telling you. Without *thinking* of telling you. So I filed for divorce, and when Brandon was uncertain about Lilly, I told him that story and . . . That's that."

"You told him . . . after the fact? You didn't tell him when it was going on?" Tori asked, shock and outrage in her voice.

"I didn't tell anyone."

Tori didn't know how to absorb that. He'd gone through something patently awful, because how did you deal with something so intangible? So detached, and yet so important? But he hadn't told anyone. He'd been in this horrible misery without telling *anyone*. He had a brother who loved him, and a friend in Sam, and he hadn't told anyone.

"Aren't there things you've never told anyone about?" he asked, that kind of deadly calm question that could lead nowhere good.

Maybe if he wasn't staring right at her with those all-too-insightful hazel eyes, she might have been able to sidestep the question. But he'd just told her this horrible thing, and he was staring at her like . . .

She knew better than to fall into this trap. To think she mattered. To think things would be different. She had to claw her way out of it. She had to . . .

"I can't think of anything offhand," she lied. Of course there were things she'd never told anyone. There had been no one to talk to about Toby because she hadn't had any friends outside of his influence. She didn't talk to her family about her personal life. She barely talked to her family at all.

She supposed, if she was being really, really, horribly honest with herself, there were bits and pieces of things Tim had done to her she'd never told anyone in glaring detail. Nothing drastic, just trying to protect her parents. Trying to protect herself.

"Tell me something. Anything. Just open up a little."

She got off the couch. This was too much. She wanted to do whatever it would take to comfort him, tell him whatever he wanted. But she'd been here and done this and gotten clobbered when she'd asked for more.

"We should go. People are waiting on us."

"But it was a deal, Tori. I tell you, you tell me."

"Yes, well, I don't want to make someone wait on . . . whatever this is."

"Why are getting so upset?"

"I am not upset!" she yelled, which of course completely undercut the words. "I just . . . I'm not doing this with you," she said. "I don't do this with anyone." Which was a sad, sad truth, but honest nonetheless. "There are people waiting for us."

"And they'll keep waiting for us. What happens if you tell me? What is it that you're afraid of happening if you tell me?" he demanded, and though his voice was still calm, there was an edge of frustration to it.

Good. But when did he get so insightful? He'd never been like this. Oh, she'd fooled herself into thinking he saw through her back then, but he'd never pushed. Never demanded.

"You didn't used to do this shit," she grumbled.

"Yeah, that's kind of the point. I skated. I kept it all inside and I didn't tell anyone about anything. But it doesn't work anymore. I'm not . . . It doesn't feel the way it's supposed to feel. So I am trying to change."

"You can't force me to change with you." It scared her more than anything that part of her wanted to try.

"But don't you want to?" he asked, his voice soft and full of . . . care. He took her hand, this horrible habit he'd developed, because it was hard to fight something when someone was touching you. When someone was looking at you with earnest eyes and something like care in them.

His big, warm hands covering her small one. She closed her eyes.

"It's scary to change, and it's hard. I've spent the past few months somehow watching Sam and Brandon do it. Open up and get something out of it. Change into someone stronger and sure. And I want that. For both of us."

"What does it matter if I change?"

He blew out a breath, still holding her hand. "It's nice to do it with somebody," he said, his voice low. "I think that makes it maybe not easier but . . . They all did it with somebody. This change."

She bit her cheek so she wouldn't say the things she wanted to say. That Sam had opened up because Hayley had come into his life. That whatever issues Lilly and Brandon had resolved came because they were in a romantic relationship. And that was not her and Will.

This wasn't romantic. It wasn't love, and it couldn't ever be.

She was afraid if she pointed that out, he'd have far too many things to say about it. That would be worse. That would be worse than sharing pieces of herself. Introducing love into a conversation with him.

"My brother tried to kill me once." Which she realized too late was not how you blurted something like that out. "That sounds worse than it was. It was just that he's sick. I can't remember the labels, but mentally ill. So it wasn't like . . . meaningful. He just fixated on me sort of, and toward the end he, uh, locked me in a room. And he told me he was going to sacrifice me. But you know, he didn't, obviously." Oh God, she was babbling. Was this really better than mentioning romantic relationships?

Yup.

"My older brother found me and rescued me, so to speak, and I didn't quite ever . . . tell anyone the whole of what was said to me."

"Why the fuck not?"

The fury in his tone surprised her. Such an old wound, it felt more like an old nightmare than reality with all this space of years and distance between them. "I just . . . They already knew he was sick. He'd been threatening me for years. So . . . Mom and Dad would just say he was sick and didn't mean it." Why was there a lump in her throat? She had never meant to tell Will this. What was he doing to her?

"They'd already chosen him so further details didn't matter," she forced herself to say as dispassionately as she could. She forced herself to look away from his hand clutching hers. "That was when I decided to run away and everything's been fine since then. There. I told you. Can we go now?" She looked at him as defiantly as possible.

He dropped her hands and she breathed a sigh of relief. They could go and forget this whole stupid thing had ever happened.

But then he was pulling her into him, wrapping his strong arms around her and holding her tight against his chest. So tight she couldn't move. One hand stroked her hair as though . . . as though he were offering her some kind of comfort?

"It was a long time ago. It's no big deal," she said muffled into his chest.

"Baby, I don't think so. That's a hell of a thing to go through. Worse when you're a teenager and even worse when your parents don't care."

"It's not that they didn't care. It was just . . . He was sick. And they . . . he was their priority because he was sick. It wasn't his fault. He's sick." What everyone always said.

He jerked her away from him, but he didn't let her go. His hands were tight on her shoulders as he looked her in the eye.

"I get that to an extent, but my God you were threatened. He locked you in a room. How could . . . that isn't care."

Which was possibly the worst thing he could have said because it confirmed all her deepest fears. No one had ever cared about her. Not really. And no one ever would.

"We have to go," she said, her throat too tight, the tears too close to the surface.

"You can cry in front of me," he said with a gentleness that made her bristle.

"Fuck you. I don't cry in front of anybody. Now I'm going, and you can either stay here and do whatever, or you can come with me. We're done here with this."

He studied her for the longest time, his tight grip on her shoulders slowly loosening.

"All right," he said at last. But though his grip had loosened, it hadn't fallen away, and he pulled her to him again. He brushed his mouth against her temple, a sweet, comforting gesture.

"Let's go," he said simply, and took her hand as they walked to the car.

Chapter Seventeen

They drove in silence to The Slice Is Right. There were too many things running around in his head and he needed to get a handle on something before he pushed her further.

That's what it would take. Pushing it, because there was so much here. In both of them—pushed down and hidden.

Maybe if he wasn't the same, he might not have understood it. But he understood her. He pushed away with charm and pretending like things didn't matter, and she pushed away with anger while pretending things didn't matter.

Underneath it all, it was the same. Which meant, deep down, she was hurting the same way he hurt. Was probably, though he was loath to admit it about himself, lonely.

He'd always figured he was supposed to be lonely, or something, but if he thought that, then she thought that and . . .

He couldn't work it all out quite yet, but it was twisting around in his head.

Tori was stiff in the passenger seat, clearly vibrating with repressed energy as they got out of the Jeep and walked into the pizza place. Doing her own version of working through it.

Well, more likely pushing it down, but it wouldn't be that easy. He wouldn't let it be that easy.

As the night went on, and they sat with Sam, Hayley, Brandon, Lilly, Cora, and Micah, Will relaxed. Every time he glanced at Tori, she seemed as though she had too. He saw it in the set of her shoulders and the way she laughed at Cora, or teased Brandon.

This was the thing he'd always taken for granted. Any night he wanted, he could surround himself with people who cared. Tori might not realize that, she might not admit it, but this relaxed her. He had to wonder where she'd been for seven years, and if she'd had any of this.

He doubted it, and it was a little shameful to realize he always had. His parents were shit, sure, but he'd always had Brandon. For so long he'd had friends who could mean something even if he didn't give over his whole self to them. Brandon, then Sam and Lilly and Hayley, were a soft place to land, to heal, to center himself.

Tori wouldn't let him drive her home. She'd go with Cora and Micah as it made the most sense. He should probably give her space anyway. She needed time to deal with telling him about her brother.

She'd never told anybody about that. Not a soul. Her brother had locked her in a room and threatened to kill her, and she hadn't told anyone because she'd been so certain her parents wouldn't take her side.

It was unfathomable. Even if his parents hadn't loved him, Will had never experienced *danger* as a child. He'd been safe. Wholly.

Will glanced around as shuffling began, people standing up and making their good-byes. He didn't miss when Tori shot him a glance, because he'd been watching.

She quickly glanced away, some of that tension returning to her shoulders. He could feel bad about it, but mostly he knew it wasn't as simple as that.

She wasn't angry with him anyway. She was uncomfortable that he'd seen some piece of her she didn't particularly want people to see. She never wanted anyone to see her cry, and he understood it so deeply. He was never comfortable with people seeing him hurt because it showed too much. It hurt to have someone else care because what did you do with sympathy when it only made you feel worse?

So he understood. He got it. The more he understood and the more he got, the more he realized this wasn't so simple as friendship. It wasn't even as simple as friendship with some attraction underneath. Everything about Tori and who she was and who she was to him was complicated, and doing anything with that was only going to be hard. It was only going to be everything he'd shied away from his entire life.

Which was why he was becoming more and more certain he needed to go for it.

He'd talked about changing, and he meant it. He wanted to change, which meant doing hard things. Not half-assed things.

So he walked with everyone to their lineup of cars saying nothing. He watched as Brandon and Lilly got in Brandon's truck, Sam and Hayley drove away in Hayley's car. Tori, Cora, and Micah piled into Cora's.

Will sat in his Jeep and once everyone drove off, he didn't. He started his car and drove, but not to Mile High and not to the cabin. Because that wasn't going to solve anything, and it wasn't going to get him any answers.

He drove around Gracely. Well past nine, most of the town was dark and tucked away in the faintly glowing dusk. He could almost pretend it was as it had been, because even when he'd partied through this town in high school, the town had closed down well before ten.

Back then, the only lights would have been the occasional house and the Evans Mining Company lights up in the mountains. A shining beacon of all the town had to bow down to.

But Evans Mining Company was gone and so was the past. The future and the present were all that mattered.

After meandering around town for a while, giving Tori plenty of time to be dropped off and Cora and Micah to have settled in at their house, Will pulled his Jeep up to the corner of Hope and Aspen.

He parked his car and stepped out. It was a clear night, the stars winking above. The moon was half hidden behind a row of houses on the street, but it would rise soon enough. So many things would rise.

He walked across the yard, glancing once at Cora's house. Everything was dark except for a light upstairs. Which was a good sign.

He stepped onto Tori's stoop and steadied himself before knocking on the door. He knocked, firmly and determined.

It took a few minutes before Tori answered, and based on the wary look on her face, she'd already looked out the window to make sure it was him.

"Hey."

"Hi." She didn't invite him in. In fact, she stood defiantly in front of the door, blocking any sort of entry.

"I thought maybe we should finish our conversation."

"Boy, did you think wrong."

She started closing the door, but he put his hand out to block its progress. "Let me in."

"No. I'm going to bed." She hesitated for a second. "I'd take a ride up to Mile High in the morning though."

He should be gratified she was asking him for a favor. But he knew what it was. A distraction.

"I'll give you a ride in the morning, but that doesn't mean I'm going to leave now."

She sighed heavily. "I don't want to talk about anything."

He stepped closer to her, swallowing against all the panic inside of him. All the things he usually listened to, telling him not to do something. He was good at listening to those voices that insisted nothing would end well if he went after something he wanted. Nothing ended well when he tried to do something for someone.

But this was different. It had to start being different.

"You have two choices," he stated, his voice barely recognizable to his own ears. Low, determined, *sure*.

She scoffed. "Oh, do I?"

He stepped closer still, their toes touching and only the fact that she leaned away—though he noted she didn't step away—kept their bodies from touching.

"You can invite me in to talk . . ."

"Or you can leave. So, bye," she snapped.

"No. *Or* I can come in for this." He didn't grab her like he'd done when he'd kissed her in the yard, he slid his arm around her waist and pulled her against him. He lowered his mouth to hers, but he stopped a breath from touching his lips to hers.

Her eyes were wide and she still leaned away, her back curving over his arm, but she didn't push him. She didn't fight him.

"So which is it going to be?" he asked, looking her right in the eye and keeping her pressed firmly against him. Her compact body trembling in his arms, as she sucked in a breath and then another.

God, he wanted her.

He watched her swallow, her neck moving with it. She moved her hand to his chest, and though she clearly *wanted* to push him away, the strength behind the palm against his heart was minimal at best. It just felt like she was pressing her hand to him.

"We're not doing this." But her voice was shaky and her

eyes were so wide, and she didn't fight him off. She could, too, she could if she wanted to.

"Then what are we doing?" he asked, because he wasn't backing down. Not anymore.

Tori had to say something. *No. Go away.* Anything. Yet none of the words would come out. Everything was all backed up and stuck in her lungs—her breath, her heavy heartbeat, apparently her brain.

He was holding her against him, looming over her like some sort of . . . She didn't know. She didn't know what he was trying to do or prove, and she had to fight it. She had to fight it. She *had* to *fight* it.

She couldn't seem to do anything but stand there and absorb the heat of him, the strength of him. Her hand was on his chest and she could feel his heart beating just as heavily as hers. His eyes never left hers, not for a second, and they were nearly green. Every second was overwhelming.

She couldn't let him kiss her, good Lord. She couldn't let him make her talk. She had to stop this somehow. His mouth was so close to hers, and his breath mingled with hers, and everything felt somehow fated.

You're being ridiculous. She squeezed her eyes shut and forced herself to wiggle out of his grasp. She took a few halting steps away from him, but that only gave him the chance to step inside her house and close the door behind him.

He stood there, tall and broad and bearded and gorgeous and . . .

"What are you doing?" she managed to ask him, breathless and furious. Yes, fury, that was the thing galloping through her chest. "And why?"

"I'm tired of this bullshit. This dancing-around-each-other bullshit. You have to give me something. I gave you something. You have to give me something."

"Because that's how life works, huh? You offer someone some part of yourself and they *have* to give it back."

He sucked in a deep breath, but he didn't yield or back off. He stood there, if anything more certain. What *was* that? Did Gracely just imbue people with it, but not her, because she wasn't certain about shit.

Except that they were standing on some precipice. She knew she had to jump, but there was no sensible jump to take. If only she could find the jump she'd survive, the one she'd be able to climb back up the wall.

But how did she? When it came to people, she always chose that wrong spot. Wanting something or someone was always the wrong spot. Depending on someone else was always the wrong spot. Wanting someone to choose her and her alone was always the wrong thing.

"There's something here," Will said, certain and sure. "Something has to break. Or it just keeps building. If you let it build for long enough, when the break comes it's . . ."

"What happened before," she realized aloud. She'd let things with Will build for years back then, and then she'd convinced herself that he had to feel it back. She'd been crushed when she'd been so very wrong.

But this was only a few weeks in the making, this new thing between them, and maybe . . . Maybe he was right. Maybe if they broke things now, there was the hope of getting over it instead of another crash in six years.

"I'm not having sex with you." Because that would kill her.

His mouth curved, sexy and dangerous. "There's a lot of room between a kiss and sex."

Oh God. "We could talk," she blurted, because that was less scary. Maybe.

He lifted his hands in the air. "I gave you the choice."

She took a few steps away again. She needed space. Time

to think. But he was staring at her with intent in his eyes and sex in his smile. A smile he'd never, ever used on her before.

She wasn't sure she'd ever seen him smile this way before. Edgy and threatening, but somehow kind with it.

She was losing her mind.

"What do you want to talk about?" she asked, still edging to get more space between them. Sarge had trotted in and lay helpfully between them.

"You told me about why you ran away. I want to hear why you came here. Why seven years later, you finally showed up."

Which would require rehashing Toby and all the ways she was pathetic.

Which was worse: letting herself think he was actually sexually attracted to her or rehashing the whole Toby situation? Which had less likelihood of blowing up in her face?

She honestly didn't know.

"You don't actually want to have sex with me, or any of those in-betweens. I am so not your type."

"I hate to break it to you, but men aren't that discerning. Sex with a woman they like is sex. You're gorgeous and you always have been. Huh." He rubbed a hand over his beard as if he was giving something deep consideration. "Isn't it interesting that I always gravitated toward the opposite of you?"

"Yeah, so interesting that you don't like me in that way. No matter how hard up a guy is, he has a type he'd prefer."

"Everything about you is everything I avoided back then. That's worth thinking about."

"No, it isn't."

"But here I am. Thinking about it."

She supposed that was the scariest thing. She couldn't fight what he thought, what idiotic ideas he was spinning in his head.

How did she fight him when he was offering what she'd always wanted?

Will moved behind her, gently putting his hands on her shoulders. It shouldn't comfort her, not when he was the source of all her panic, but something about his easy presence and putting a hand on her shoulder and standing behind her . . .

"I don't want to make things harder on you," he said quietly, close to her ear. Close to her heart. "But I don't know how else we move on from this. I can't pretend I'm not attracted to you, and I can't pretend I don't want to know more about you."

"I can't go down this road again with you," she whispered, staring blindly into her kitchen. *Hers.* She was building her own damn life.

"This isn't the same though, Tori. It's a brand-new road. All those years ago we both hid everything from each other and from ourselves. I'm not content to be that guy anymore. So I'm being straight with you. All you have to do is the same."

His hands tensed on her shoulders just briefly, and she realized then that he wasn't quite so certain. He wasn't quite so sure. This was a step for him, and he was trying to figure things out.

He was using her to figure his shit out. Using her. That was it. Maybe she should be angry about it, but . . . She could also just let him.

And she would use him to feel something again. The comfort of someone to share a bed with or to ask if she was okay.

It was twisted and fucked up, but if she knew going in he was just using her as some sort of pawn in his attempt to figure his life out, well, she wouldn't get hurt this time. She didn't have to give him anything back. She didn't have to be *straight* with him, and she could get some old shit out of her system.

She wouldn't depend on him. She wouldn't love him.

She would use him right back. She just had to find the courage to take that leap.

Chapter Eighteen

Tori still faced away from him, but she didn't move out of the loose hold he had on her shoulders. Something in the way she held herself changed, though without seeing her face, Will couldn't read it.

He wanted to run his hands down the length of her arms. He *wanted* . . . Hell, why not take what he wanted? Wasn't that the point? One way or the other, some piece of this pressure between them had to be let out.

So he let his palms run down the length of her arms, then back up. A little tremor went through her, barely noticeable, but there nonetheless.

She took a deep breath as if stealing herself for . . . something, then she turned to face him. Her eyes weren't wide anymore, and her mouth was set into a determined line.

She jerked her hand up, but then paused, before slowly inhaling and lightly placing her fingers against his face. She traced the edges of his beard down across his cheek, then back up again.

"You didn't have this in Boulder," she muttered, and he

didn't know if it was accusation or some uncomfortable memory or what.

So he went with a joke. "I'd offer to shave it off, but it's like a Mile High cornerstone now. It makes us look very mountain man-y."

Her eyes met his, serious and studying. She clearly found no humor in it, but her fingers were delicately moving across his face. Gently. Tori gentle.

Her gaze drifted to his mouth, and she was still so close he'd only need to shift for their bodies to touch, only need to lean forward to rest his head atop hers.

There was a panicked beat to the way his heart was pounding against his chest, but that was the kind of panic he'd always listened to, always believed in. He was trying to change, not let the worst parts of himself lead.

"Did you make your choice?" he asked, because one way or another . . .

She didn't say anything, but she stepped forward and slowly wound her arm around his neck. It meant getting up on her toes, and it meant her body grazed his as she arched to get the leverage.

She didn't look him in the eye, which bothered him for some reason. That she was holding him, pressing against him, and looking at his nose or mouth or beard or *anything* that wasn't actually . . . him.

He slid his arm around her waist, tipping her upper body back with his chest so she was just a little off-balance. But he held her up, and he would.

Then finally *then* her eyes flicked to his, and he supposed she meant it to be brief, maybe a little censuring, but—featherlight, he pressed his mouth to the corner of hers, gratified when he felt her shaky exhale across his face.

"Not like last time," he said close to her ear, still holding her basically still.

No, this kiss would not start in some angry space, it wouldn't be driven by some wild thing inside him he didn't understand and couldn't control. This would be slow, soft, careful so he could figure it all out.

He brushed a kiss across the soft skin of her cheek, indulging himself in a deep breath of the faint smell of shampoo or soap. Something clean and fresh, simple.

He kissed the underside of her jaw. He lingered there in the smell of her, in the hope of her.

Her breathing was shaky and uneven. Every inhale in, every exhale out, she shuddered with it. But she didn't hold on to him, though her arm was around his neck. She leaned back against that arm holding her up, and she didn't kiss him.

"You want to talk instead?" he asked, scraping his beard purposefully down her neck.

"Oh, shut up," she said, probably not sounding quite as tough as she wanted to, but the arm around his neck tightened and then her mouth was on his—fast and hot, and yeah, a little angry.

He wouldn't fall victim to it. She might have the choices here, but she wasn't leading him where he didn't want to go. Not anymore.

So he used his free hand to tangle into her braid, thus controlling the angle of her head, her mouth, and how much pressure she could wield against his mouth. He nibbled at her lower lip, grinning when she huffed out a breath of irritation.

Tori, something like at his mercy, and wasn't that . . . something. He held her there, head and body tipped back, lips slicked, eyes half closed as she glared at him. And since she was giving him eye contact, he pressed his mouth to hers, eyes wide and right on hers.

He dragged his tongue across her bottom lip, absorbing every little shiver that went through her.

She squeezed her eyes shut trying to press closer, harder, but his fingers were tangled in all that thick hair and he simply wouldn't let this be something she could write off.

"I'm not going to let you forget it's me," he murmured against her mouth, loosening his grip on her enough so he could splay his hand over her back, feel the strength in her slight frame.

She sighed, something exasperated more than the dreamy he would have preferred, and her now open eyes were like cloudy storms. He could all but picture lightning there. "Like that'd even be possible," she muttered.

He grinned again and she rolled her eyes, but her arm hooked around his neck was tight, and her other hand now clutched his shirt.

Yeah, he couldn't say he minded Tori holding on to him, and funnily enough he liked being in the driver's seat. He'd never been one for leadership any more than he'd been one for taking orders, but he liked leading this woman who'd always seemed infinitely un-leadable.

He glanced around the kitchen, wanting more leverage, wanting more *her*, but his gaze landed on Sarge, who was sprawled in the corner of her kitchen, watching them with his head on his paws.

He'd helped her bring Sarge home from some shelter she'd wandered into. Sarge had been part of the team, so to speak. If he'd been looking for a family outside of Brandon, he'd found it in Sam, Tori, and Sarge.

But mostly the two in this kitchen. Tori and Sarge, his peace, his comfort, and he hadn't had it since she'd walked away.

"I guess he's a voyeur," Tori said after he'd been standing there for probably too long.

When his gaze returned to Tori, cheeks flushed and mouth wet from his, she looked . . . speculative.

Of him. Maybe of the position they were in. But speculative wasn't disapproving. Of course, it wasn't eager enthusiasm either, but it was a step.

A step . . . which he needed more of. More steps until he slept with her—something he was beginning to think was definitely an *until*—to make sure he was on the right footing. To make sure he was doing this right and that he *could* change his usual track record when it came to important things.

He'd stepped up for Mile High. He'd stepped up for Brandon, and now he had to right this past wrong. He had to build, and that wasn't done with ultimatum sex with a woman who still looked at him like she wasn't sure if he'd kiss her or slap her across the face.

"I'm not going to have sex with you," he forced himself to say, to believe. "Tonight," he amended.

She made some noise, a laugh, a scoff, some squeak of outrage, he couldn't quite tell. Wasn't sure he wanted to know exactly.

"But I am going to kiss you until we're both stupid," he added, tightening his hold on her hair, tipping her mouth exactly where he wanted it, exploring every inch of her mouth until he had a map of it stamped on his brain, and maybe his heart.

Tori knew she had to get a hand on her whirling brain. She had to think. She had to plan. Hell, she had to protect herself, but he was just . . .

He enveloped her, smothered her, and she couldn't even begin to care. Had she ever felt like the center of a man's universe, even during sex? Not likely.

He smelled like pine trees and the scrape of his beard on

her cheek or neck echoed deep inside her and then back again till she was nothing but a pulsing need.

You don't need him. You won't need him. You need a freaking orgasm.

She arched against his hard body, but he only laughed into her mouth. Like he was Mr. In Charge of Things these days.

The thought of that, him in charge, controlling things, oh so cavalier in how he held her head just how he wanted it to be, it should irritate her, turn her totally off.

All it did was make her that much hotter, and she was here, kissing Will Evans, she damn well needed to follow *hot* until she burned up. Ashes seemed like a better aftermath than jagged, broken pieces of a girl who had to walk away.

Without so much of a warning, or any supreme effort on his part, he lifted her off her feet, took a few steps, then deposited her on her kitchen counter.

Yeesh, he was tall, and so *broad*, and his hands covered her knees, guiding her legs apart so he could step inside the space they made. Which was bad enough, but his hands slid over her jeans, up her thighs. Where they stopped. *Stopped*.

She couldn't get over the way he kissed, like they had nothing but time stretched out in front of them. Slowly, lingering here and there, his mouth finding every little nook that made her squeak unexpectedly. And damn well *yearn* inwardly.

"We could have sex, you know," she said, squeezing his tense shoulders, trying to get his attention off his lazy exploration that was going to make her brain die. "I think I have condoms around here somewhere." She certainly hoped she had some left over from always having them on hand with Toby, and if she didn't . . .

Well, hell, he could run to Benson and get some damn condoms. What kind of man came to a woman's house late at night unprepared?

But Will seemed unfazed by the whole condom comment, because his hands didn't move, just two iron-hot coals branded on her thighs, his mouth continuing its lazy exploration of any expanse of skin she had bared—neck, collarbone, jaw.

"Would you beg me?" he murmured there on the underside of her jaw.

She had to hold herself tense just so he wouldn't be able to read the longing shudder that went through her. "I wouldn't beg . . . I don't know, insert super-hot actor's name here."

"Here?" he asked, mouth curved in that edgy thing that could hardly be counted as a smile. The only descriptor she had was *predatory*.

Which might have been more threatening if his hand wasn't finally moving from the top of her thigh to more of her inner thigh, and far closer to where she would very nearly beg someone to touch her just about now.

This time he didn't stop, his fingers trailed along the center of her, though the jeans she was wearing dulled the touch into not nearly enough. She tried to scoot on the counter so she could press more firmly against him, but he tugged her T-shirt up and off, leaving her in nothing but her bra.

"Aren't you a picture," he murmured.

She bristled, because she highly doubted it. She didn't want his lame playboy words or whatever this was. "You've seen me in a bikini, I don't need the sweet-talking shit."

"I couldn't see your nipples through your bikini. Trust me, I tried." His thumb brushed across one and she realized the fabric was that old and threadbare as to nearly be seethrough.

Which was a thought that flew out of her head the minute his thumb circled her nipple. How was she supposed to have thoughts when pleasure arrowed through her, sharp and overwhelming.

She didn't even realize he'd reached back and unsnapped

it until it fell off her shoulders. He gave the sad thing a tug and then tossed it on the floor. She had the fleeting thought of wanting to cover herself up. Ratty bra, tiny breasts. The guy had been *married* to a lingerie model. He was probably used to lace and an overflowing bounty.

But he palmed her breasts as if they had the answers to the world, and maybe men were really that simple.

She could use that, because she wanted some simple. She undid the buttons on his shirt as he kissed her again, something a little bit wilder and more insistent this time, and she might have felt a pang of satisfaction if his rough hands weren't moving across her nipples, causing her fingers to fumble.

She groaned, couldn't help it, and she settled for half-unbuttoned shirt before she shoved her hands inside the fabric, letting her own palms discover the curves and ridges of his too perfectly formed torso.

His hands slid down her abdomen, and she could feel every callus, every scrape, somehow setting brand-new fires of want deep inside her. He undid her button, pulled down the zipper of her jeans and then, eyes on hers, he tugged them right off her, using only his own strength to leverage her up enough to get them out from under her.

She was on her kitchen counter in nothing but her underwear. With Will. Who was looking at her like she was some mystical unicorn he'd captured all for himself.

But, thank God, he'd changed his mind and they were going to have sex if she was nearly naked. They could get that over with and then move on somehow. This might be the hottest foreplay she'd ever had, but it wasn't like sex was some magical thing she'd ever want to repeat with him.

Maybe it'd be better than Toby and a few other guys who'd come before, but she wasn't the kind of girl who got super into sex. She could go years without it.

But it would be nice to have it, to know for certain it

wasn't anything special, because then it wouldn't be this tempting unknown.

He didn't take her underwear off though, and when his hand settled at the apex of her thighs, it was over the fabric. Which caused her to blink.

"Aren't you going to touch me?" she asked, breathlessly as his finger stroked her through the fabric.

His gaze swept up her body, then held, the greenish color taking over the brown. "No, I don't think so," he said thoughtfully. "Not yet."

Somehow his skilled fingers stroked through the cotton, drawing her closer and closer to something a whole lot bigger than she'd ever felt. Maybe it was his gaze still on hers, or one hand clamping at her hip, angling her exactly how he wanted.

Maybe it was not being in a bed, or being with a man who was as complicated as she was with a past between them, or . . .

Hell, she didn't know, but even as a teenager a guy had never made her feel like she was splintering apart *over* clothes. Or under, for that matter, but Will's touch was like magic and when the orgasm swept through her, he pulled her to him enveloping the gasp and the aftermath as if it's what he'd been waiting for.

It took her a few minutes to wrap her head around all that, and to find the strength to pull away. She'd give him high marks for all that, really high marks, but heavy petting was hardly what she was after.

He stepped back from the counter, eyeing her with a self-satisfied smirk. Then he did the most incomprehensible thing. He started buttoning *up* his shirt.

"What are you doing?"

He bent over and grabbed her discarded shirt and then stepped to her. He pulled it over her head as she stuttered out a protest.

"Will."

He brushed a kiss over her forehead. "Good night, Tori."

"But . . . What?"

He didn't answer though, he started walking out of the kitchen, Sarge trotting behind him.

"Will . . . what the hell?" She shoved her arms into the armholes and jumped off the counter, stalking after him.

"Will!"

He glanced over his shoulder at her, an odd smile on his face, his hand poised on the doorknob, and she wasn't totally nuts because there was the *clear* outline of a very impressive erection in his jeans.

"You didn't . . ." She gestured helplessly. What was he doing? Was this some weird . . . game? Was she supposed to beg? Ha! She wouldn't.

Probably.

"There'll be time for all that yet," he said carefully. "Let's let that one settle."

She could only blink stupidly at him as he stepped out into the night, her orgasm still pulsing through her and him . . .

Gone.

A game. It was all some warped game. It was the only thing that made sense. Too bad for Will that when it came to *games,* Tori always made sure to win.

Chapter Nineteen

Will knew that last night had made things complicated. Tori's texting him that Cora would drop her off this morning was part of that. The uncomfortable erection that followed her entry into Mile High this morning was *also* complicated.

Taking it step-by-step was a patient man's job, and while his *brain* could be patient, his dick was offering a few arguments.

Worth it, he supposed, as Tori's cheeks went a little pink the minute she made eye contact with him.

He wasn't a man prone to blushing himself, but he certainly shifted a little bit at the fact his brother was there, staring at them both alternately, like he could read last night's deeds on their faces.

"Morning," Brandon offered into what Will realized belatedly was the odd silence of the room.

"Morning," Tori replied, fiddling with something on Sarge's collar Will was pretty sure didn't exist.

"Neither of you have excursions until this afternoon, right?"

"Um, well, I don't know Will's schedule. I've got the

rock climbing group at two, but I wanted to get my car situation figured out."

"Right. Lilly was actually on the phone with a shop in Benson. I'm sure she'll come out once she's got it handled." Brandon glanced at Will, apparently expecting some explanation for his being here.

Will shrugged. "Yeah, my morning is free, but I basically live here."

Brandon looked at him, and then at Tori, then back at Will. He seemed to be putting things together, but surely Brandon couldn't read between the lines *that* easily.

"Then we can have our meeting. In our office," Brandon said stiffly, gesturing toward the hallway. "Yeah?"

Will did not like the sound of that, or the speculative look Brandon was giving him and Tori, but Will was being paranoid, and what did it matter if Brandon *could* guess what had happened last night?

Will had woken up not at all sure it was even real. But when he glanced her way, and she jerked her gaze in the opposite direction, it steadied him a little bit.

Real. Happening.

Maybe it was wrong to get a little kick out of making her . . . he didn't think *nervous* was the right word. But uncertain. Off-balance. The fact of the matter was, she had always had the upper hand before. She'd always been the one who knew what they were doing and feeling.

Maybe if he'd paid more attention back then, he might have been able to predict her feelings, but mostly he was pretty sure she kept a low profile because she controlled her shit. He'd straight up avoided his.

Now she wasn't, and he wasn't. That was something to celebrate. Because if last night had proven anything to him, it was that there was something . . . something worth exploring there. Something worth building to.

Even if he didn't know how. Even if it was uncomfortable. Build, build, build. Like they'd done with Mile High.

He stepped into the office that had really become more of his bedroom than anything else. He plopped himself on the edge of the bed, waited for Brandon to unload whatever was on his mind.

"What's going on?" Brandon asked, dark eyebrows drawn together, arms crossed over his chest like the benevolent ruler of the world. Will had always been content to let him take that role. When Evans Mining had existed, when Mile High had started. Brandon was the leader.

Will didn't want to take over, per se, but it was time to exert some of his own control. It wouldn't be easy to convince Brandon he'd changed or was at least in the process of changing himself. Quite honestly the prospect of proving his change was daunting.

He wouldn't turn away from daunting anymore, though. Every daunting thing he was going full throttle for.

"What do you mean, what's going on?" he asked patiently.

"You and Tori. There's something weird there. You're not fighting again, are you?"

"No." Definitely not fighting. "I told you you can count on me. The past is, well, I'm not sure 'forgotten' is the right word, but we're dealing with it. I'm handling it."

"I want to believe you," Brandon said with a sigh.

Will tamped down his initial irritation. All in all, it was fair that Brandon had his doubts. Even if it hurt Will's feelings.

"We've been fine. I don't really know how to prove it to you other than the fact there was no yelling at dinner last night, and I haven't sported even one black eye."

Brandon gave a little chuckle at that. "Fair enough. I don't want to be skeptical, and I wasn't last night. But out there just now . . . Weird." Brandon continued to study him carefully.

"But not antagonistic," Will pointed out, staring right back at his brother instead of cracking a joke and leaving the room. "Tori and I will always have our issues. But they aren't all fatal or bad."

"Yeah, you're right. It's just . . ." Brandon drifted off and shifted on his feet. It was odd to see his brother seem uncertain almost. Unsure. Then it dawned on Will.

"Everything is going well and that freaks you out."

Brandon scoffed. "Of course not. The point is for things to go well."

But Will wasn't nearly as blind as he'd always pretended to be. "Sure, but it's been months of hard shit and change. Lilly, then there was baby, then Hayley, then *babies*, and bed rest, and et cetera. But it's been quiet for weeks now. You can't enjoy it without a problem to troubleshoot."

"Gracely is still struggling, and as far as I'm concerned, that means nothing is perfect," Brandon returned piously.

"Sure, but that's not what you're worried about. You've got a million ideas up your sleeve to deal with that."

Brandon narrowed his eyes at Will. "Are you trying to be perceptive?"

Will crossed his arms behind his head. "Something I'm trying out."

"Why?"

"Huh?"

"Why, after a lifetime of choosing to not be perceptive, in fact avoiding anything that might require you to be perceptive, with a few rare exceptions, suddenly you're being all . . . open. What changed?" Brandon didn't ask it as if he was confused, he asked it with a damn smug smile.

"I made the decision to change. Isn't that what you've been telling me I had to do to do it?"

"You make a decision after years of not deciding it,

there's got to be a catalyst. And it wasn't me telling you to do shit. Care to share with the class what it might be?"

He was tempted to play it off, because even though he was trying to be more open and honest, he didn't really want Brandon's disapproval or ridicule.

But that was kind of the whole thing about opening up. You had to make yourself open to even the bad shit, or uncomfortable shit. It couldn't all be Tori almost naked and in his arms. So . . .

"Maybe it has something to do with Tori," he offered carefully.

Though Will was pretty sure that was what Brandon expected, he still didn't speak for a few beats.

"Are you sure you know what you're getting yourself into there?"

Again, Will tried not to bristle or get his nose out of joint. "I think the point is that I don't. I'm going to make it work anyway. So what? You're going to give me some speech about how I can't complicate Mile High or make things harder for you or Tori?"

Bran was silent for a few more beats. "No. Though I reserve the right to in the future. Thing is, I don't know what happened back then between you and Tori. So I can't make any grand proclamations about what you should do. Because I don't know. So I'll just say I want you to be careful. For yourself. For her. And . . ." He cleared his throat, shifting again. "You know, I'm here, or whatever."

"You're . . . here?"

Brandon sighed heavily. "Here. Like if you need advice or shit. You know. I exist here and could give it, if you're looking or need it. If you want to *talk*."

It finally dawned on Will what Brandon was trying to say, to do. To make these changes not just in themselves, but between each other. To solidify the relationships they'd built, to not just silently stand by each other, but to hold out a hand too.

"Thanks," Will managed. "I appreciate that."

Brandon shrugged. "Anyway, I'm going to go chop wood or something. Lilly's been a little off this morning. Let me know if you notice anything. She's been more careful since the bed rest, but . . ."

"I'll keep an eye out."

Brandon gave a sharp nod, then turned to go, but he stopped before he opened the door. "Is this the kind of shit we have to hug on?"

"Hell, no. Hugs are only required on deathbeds."

"Well, that settles it," Brandon said, turning around. "Come here, little brother."

"Touch me, I'll kill you," Will threatened as Brandon walked toward him, arms outstretched.

"Hug it out, bro," Brandon said, making a lunge that Will dodged.

"Stop it right now or I'm going to tell Lilly to have you committed." But Brandon made another lunge and on a laugh Will dodged, but Brandon had faked him out and grabbed him around the waist.

They fell to the floor, wrestling like seven-year-olds on the playground, and laughing just as hard. Will got an elbow into Brandon's stomach, but then Brandon secured him in a headlock.

At a noise, Will and Brandon both paused, looking up at the door. Tori and Lilly stood there, staring at them with cocked heads and wide eyes.

"They seem to be laughing," Tori offered. "Though the touching is weird under any circumstances."

"It is, indeed."

"We were just . . ." Will pushed himself to his feet as Brandon's grip on his neck loosened. He helped Brandon up. "Talking."

"That sounds about as plausible as anything," Lilly murmured. "We've got someone coming tomorrow to look at Tori's car. I trust you've got ample time to play chauffeur, Will?"

Will grinned at Tori. "Ample."

"Good. Bran . . ." Lilly shook her head. "We have some paperwork to go over, but I'm a little afraid of your current mental state."

Brandon walked over to his wife and slid his arm around her waist, leading her out of the office. "I'll tell you all about it," he said as they disappeared out of the office.

Leaving Will and Tori alone in it.

He flashed a grin. "A morning free. Together. With you at my vehicle mercy. I like this."

"I think Sarge and I will go for a walk. You're only invited if I get the scoop on the creepy adult wrestling."

"How about a swim instead?"

Her mouth twitched. "I didn't bring my bikini."

His grin turned sly, and though she firmed her lips together, they curved.

"Won't the water be awfully cold?"

"Afraid?"

She scowled. "Don't try to goad me into it."

"But it always works." Copying Brandon's move, he walked over to her and slid his arm around her waist, leading her out of the office. "Besides, I'll tell you exactly how Brandon and I ended up wrestling. You can't resist a good story."

"As long as in this version of the story you're both shirtless."

Will recoiled, dropping his hand from her waist. "Gross."

Tori laughed, and funny how something as simple as her genuine laugh could wind up in his chest, tight and uncomfortable, a weird longing feeling he didn't know how to label settling there.

She whistled for Sarge, and the dog tagged along as they stepped out onto the porch. "If you're expecting me to skinny-dip, know I won't be cock blocked again."

"I think only guys can be cock blocked, Tori."

"You blocked me from your cock. I think that counts."

"You're awfully cavalier about my—" Will nearly tripped over her because apparently she'd stopped at the bottom of the stairs.

"Well, this is awkward," Hayley said a little too cheerfully as she stood right in front of Tori, apparently on her way into Mile High.

And Will had been a little wrapped up in cock talk to notice. Apparently, Tori had too.

"Um. Well." Hayley pushed a curl behind her ear, offering a bright smile. "I have an excursion to get ready for. You two have . . . fun." She scampered past them and inside Mile High.

Tori didn't move, and Will didn't know quite what to offer into the silence. His half sister had heard him talking about cock. His, in particular. And the blocking of it in regard to Tori.

"Well."

"Yeah, well. Hope you weren't planning on keeping this a secret, because I don't know Hayley that well, but I don't think secrets are her strong suit."

"Were you?"

"Was I what?" she returned, starting to stride toward his Jeep, and though she was acting awfully casual about it all, the lightness and ease had gone out of her posture.

"Hoping to keep it a secret?"

"I don't even know what it is." She looked at him warily. "As far as I'm concerned we're just fooling around."

There was something of a test in those words, and Will decided that if that's what she wanted to think, it was fine.

Maybe she even had to think it to let her guard down a little bit, but he'd sneak under her guard.

And then, it wouldn't be *fooling around*.

So he smiled. "Then that's what you can tell whoever asks. Hop in, I already threw some towels and sunscreen in the Jeep earlier."

He opened the driver's door, waved Sarge in, then took his seat. He waited for a minute, and then another. Tori didn't get in the passenger seat, and he thought briefly of being completely straight with her.

But the passenger door opened and she slid in, buckling herself as she looked straight ahead.

He would be straight with her, eventually, he just needed to lay some groundwork first. Last night was a start, and swimming would be another layer. Then . . . Well, then they'd see.

Tori stood on the rocky beach of a secluded lake while Will pulled out a bag of supplies from the back of the Jeep. Pine trees surrounded the entire beach, the impressive peaks of the Rockies reflecting along with the trees in the clear, still water.

It was beautiful, the late summer sun bright and warm above them. It didn't mean the water would be warm, but she was no coward.

Hell, maybe a freezing cold dip would knock some sense into her. She could tell herself Hayley overhearing their silly conversation didn't bother her, didn't matter, but of course it did.

Now, more than even before, everyone at Mile High would be watching. And waiting. Which meant fooling around got a hell of a lot more complicated.

She hadn't stuck around before when things had gone

bad, but then again she'd been in *love* before, and she knew better than to do that again.

So what is this?

She didn't know. She only knew it felt inevitable. Like something she had to do to fully excise the past. If that didn't make sense to the outside world, did it matter? This was her life. Hers was the only opinion that mattered in it.

Sarge happily bounded across rocks chasing a chipmunk, and Will plopped two beach towels, an extra T-shirt, and a tub of sunscreen on the space next to her feet.

Without a word, he peeled off his shirt and dropped it to the ground. It didn't hurt to sigh over that, the way his muscles bunched and moved, the clearly defined lines of *six-pack*.

She sighed, too many images of last night flashing in her head. Too much wondering if it would be even better if *he* was undressed.

"Gonna skinny-dip?" she asked, maybe a little too hopefully.

"No, darling, I'll leave that to you." He picked up the sunscreen. "But you can rub my back, if you'd like. I'll return the favor." He grinned and winked, and she wanted it to be fun.

But grinning and winking was so patently Will Evans, Charm the Pants Off Anybody, she couldn't smile back. Getting sucked up into that old charm, into . . . whatever this was . . .

"What's wrong?"

"Nothing," she muttered, stripping her T-shirt off, then wiggling out of her cargo shorts. Because the only thing worse than Old Will was New Will—the kind who didn't just *notice* her mind had gone somewhere else, but called her on it.

Hard pass.

She walked to the lake, the rocks cool and smooth under

her feet. It wasn't the perfect swimming place, being so rocky and made up of snowmelt runoff from the mountains, but it was gorgeous. Open and vast, pristine and untouched.

She felt invincible here, and Lord knew this girl could use some invincible. She stood with her toes barely touching the icy water of the lake, and Will came to stand next to her.

"You gotta just dive in, right?" she asked, sending him a sideways look.

"I'm learning that's the best method," he said a little too seriously.

His seriousness drove her in. She took a few quick strides into the lake, then forced herself into a superman leap into the icy water. When she surfaced, teeth chattering and full-body shivering, she searched first for Will.

Won't that always be your first instinct?

Her feet could touch, but she kept her knees bent and treaded water anyway to keep herself from freezing to death. Will surfaced, wet and perfect, right in front of her.

Water slid down his sharp cheekbones, stuck in his dark eyelashes, dripped off the ends of his beard. Too damn beautiful for his own good.

"You could talk to me, you know, instead of diving into icy water to avoid it." His hands clasped around her arms, pulling her farther out.

The sun was such an odd contrast to the chill of the water, warm and vibrant above, cold and dark below. She didn't know which to look at, but she knew not to look at him.

"I know that talking about how we feel can be scary," he said, his hands rubbing up and down her arms again, much like they had last night. Much like last night she was losing her footing as he drew her deeper into the lake where she had to tread water to stay above it.

Except he's holding you. Above the water. Up and safe.

"But I'm beginning to think it's the only way you ever get to heal or move forward," he said in that measured tone that made her think he was exploring all this for the first time. "If instead of running away, we stood firm. We explore. We walk right through the underbrush and if there's a bear there, you figure out what to do about it."

"Sometimes you also shit your pants."

"You don't run away, though," he said, squeezing her arms, ignoring her joke completely. "Not away to someone else, not into an icy lake. You man up and face it."

"How about this?" she said, her temper bubbling that he was comparing him then to her now. Defiance just her natural default, her protection. "You tell me what the hell it is you want from me, and we'll go from there. Because if you remember a few years ago I told you exactly what I wanted from you and I got jack shit."

"That's the point. I'm deciding that instead of fighting against and running away from things that scare me, I'll wade into them and figure them out."

She stared at him then. "I *scared* you?"

"Of course you fucking scared me. Hell, Tori, you were . . . Look, I broke a lot of things in my day. Hurt a lot of people. I didn't want to do that to you, and it was the scariest damn thing that you'd given me the power to."

"So you hurt me . . . preemptively?" She shouldn't be asking him this. She shouldn't be delving into the old stuff, not with sex on the table. Not in the middle of a lake, alone.

She'd scared him? What sense did that make?

"I know we ran away from each other, and I get I started that domino, but it doesn't delete all of the things we felt."

"*We?* We felt? I don't . . . You made it very clear you felt nothing. You made it crystal you never would. I . . ." She didn't want to go back to those memories, that place, not like this.

In her anger, she could make it seem like war and power, back when she'd been pushing him for answers because he didn't want to give them.

Now he was giving them, but she had no anger, no armor. She only had painful memories, wrapped up in Will's kisses from last night, the heat his body was currently giving her as he held her in the middle of a perfect lake.

"Think about it, Tori. For five seconds think about it. Do you really think I didn't feel anything?"

She hadn't at first, but he'd whisked Courtney off to Europe, by way of Las Vegas, and . . . She'd forced herself to believe he was right. Made sure every second of running away from all her friendships and foundations she'd built after leaving home had been with the belief, the knowledge, the *certainty* he hadn't felt a thing back.

He'd married someone else, hadn't that been proof enough?

But in this moment, in his words, she saw a truth she never wanted to believe.

Chapter Twenty

Tori was gaping at him like he was telling a kid Santa Claus didn't exist. Instead of an honest truth he figured she'd known, at least a little, underneath all the ways he'd hurt her.

How could you know how to hurt someone if you didn't care about them?

Wasn't that the appeal of Courtney for so many years? They didn't even care enough about each other *to* hurt each other, or at least for a time that had been the case.

"I need you to let me go," Tori said carefully. He didn't know whether to attribute the translucent quality of her skin right now to water or shock or even anger maybe.

But she didn't seem angry. She was unnaturally still, so much so that if he did let her go, he was sure she'd sink.

"Tori."

She moved then, wiggling out of his grasp, swimming back toward where her feet could touch without water covering her head. She didn't stop there though, she kept going all the way up the rocky beach and to their pile of stuff.

Sarge trotted over to her and she plopped herself onto a towel. After a second there, her pale skin glistening with water droplets in the bright sun, she grabbed one of his shirts from the pile and pulled it over her head, holding her arms around herself as if to get warm.

He couldn't help but wonder if warm was what she was really after.

Slowly, giving her a few seconds of space, Will made his way back to shore. Sarge pranced up to greet him, then back to Tori, clearly enjoying his morning at the beach.

The sun was warm, as were the rocks under his feet. Still, the wet shorts weren't exactly comfortable. It was a secluded spot and he wasn't about to play shy when that wasn't, long range, what he was after.

So he walked over to his towel, stripped the wet shorts off, and grinned as Tori studied him. A guy still had an ego, after all.

"Don't be ashamed if it keeps you up at night," he offered, grabbing the extra clothes he'd brought.

She raised an eyebrow at him, unreadable except in sarcasm. "You think your penis is going to haunt me?"

"A guy can dream."

She shook her head, but her lips curved a little. She could be so . . . impenetrable. The rock you couldn't get a hand or foothold in to climb. A sheer wall of nothing but hard, stubborn matter.

It was somehow the most frustrating thing about her, and one of the things he admired most about her, all at the same time.

He pulled on the dry shorts, a dry shirt, spread out his towel on the least rocky space next to her he could find. He took a seat and let the warmth of the sun chase the cold of the water away.

It was a good feeling, something like baptism, rebirth and renewal. A new start, not one that erased the past, but accepted it. Forgave it.

He glanced at the woman it all centered around. She had her eyes closed and her face tipped to the sun. Water droplets clung to the slope of her neck and ends of her braid. She had goose bumps on her arms and legs, and it was impossible not to note her nipples poking at her shirt.

It was the perfect summer picture, and he couldn't resist the desire to touch it. He traced the wave of a stray lock of wet hair, grazing his fingers across her cheek as he pushed it behind her ear.

On a sigh she opened her eyes and turned her head to face him. The blue in her eyes stood out today in the sunlight and the reflection of the smooth rocks. She pulled her knees to her chest, then leaned her cheek against them, still studying him.

"I don't know what to do with all that," she said quietly. "Honestly, there isn't anything to do with it. It doesn't change jack shit. What happened still happened."

He wasn't so sure he agreed with that, but arguing with her would only make her more certain. She'd dig in harder, and he needed her to realize, at some point, it didn't change things, no, but it mattered.

It would always matter.

"But now it's rehashed and we can move on." Her gaze dropped from his and she moved her head so her chin rested on her knees and she looked out at the sparkling, reflective lake.

"Move on to where, exactly?"

She shrugged. "Friends. Coworkers. Maybe we do the sex thing just to answer any lingering questions, but mostly we're just going forward."

He wanted forward too, but inwardly he wondered if forward in Tori language wasn't a little too close to running away.

"Brandon and I were talking about . . . well, I guess you'd call it opening up. Leaning on each other. I mean, I'm pretty sure Brandon would call it 'family shit or whatever,' but that's why we were horsing around like kids."

"Because family shit?" She spread out the towel behind her and moved a few of the more jagged rocks before stretching out on her back.

Will watched her, in nothing but one of his old T-shirts, a ratty, baggy thing on her, the hem of it landing somewhere mid-thigh. She closed her eyes against the sun beating down on them, and he'd give her a few minutes before he dumped sunscreen on her.

He rearranged his towel too, and the rocks underneath him, lying out on his side so he could still watch her. "There was the threat of a hug. I had to defend my manliness."

She laughed, her chest moving with it, and he had to touch her again. If only lightly. He pressed his fingertips to the random droplets of water stubbornly holding on to her arm.

"I always figured you and Brandon shared all your secrets when the rest of us weren't around. Or had some weird twin intuition."

"If I had any intuition I would never have paid it any mind. As for telling each other everything . . . not so much. Evanses aren't big on *talking*."

She opened one eye to study him with. "But you always liked each other. Got along."

"Mostly. He's my brother. Even when I want to punch him in the face, I love him. Unreservedly. But it's a strange thing to grow up in a world where everything is about how you look or are perceived, and nothing about what you actually are."

"Because of the town?"

"Because of Gracely. Because of my father. Because of history and because life is weird and fucked up in the best of circumstances."

She laughed a little at that, her eyes drifting closed again. He wanted to touch more of her, know more of her, and she kept it all locked away. It seemed no matter how much he offered over to her, she'd hold more back.

It wasn't so much irritation that clawed through him as a panicky kind of futility. The kind he knew so well. If he listened to that voice it would tell him he'd never get through to her, so why try? If he accepted what he always accepted, he'd convince himself he just wasn't good enough to be the one who did.

He didn't think he could live with himself anymore if that part of himself kept winning. Kept turning him into someone he didn't want to be.

"Why'd you come here, Tori?" It had to matter, the impetus for her reappearance. There had to be some reason she'd finally decided to come back after seven years.

"I was lied to about the availability of cock."

But he wasn't in the mood for humor or jokes. "I'm serious."

"That's always what scares me," she muttered.

A joke, but not. "I'm starting to think nefarious reasons are at work. Are you an on-the-run ax murderer these days?"

"I wish," she said under her breath, but he caught it, and the heavy sigh that followed, which meant she was weakening.

Tori didn't want to tell him about Toby. The truth was, she could lie. Hadn't she come up with a million lies before she'd set foot in Gracely?

But he'd made her soft, bringing her to this beautiful place, talking about *feelings*. Making it impossible not to believe him.

Which made it all worse. The past. The choices they'd both made. It swirled inside of her, a whirlwind of regret and bitterness, and she didn't want to go back to the place where that ruled her life.

Life could only be made by moving forward, by stepping away from the bitterness and regret, and accepting it as your damn lot in life.

But how many times had he asked her now? He wasn't letting her move on from that until she told him something.

"It was a guy, because isn't it always?" she offered, as flippantly as she could manage, forcing herself to turn her head and look at him straight on. Regardless of what she told him, she couldn't let on how much it all hurt.

His jaw tensed at the mention of a guy, and maybe it was a foolish thing to be soothed by that somehow.

"Yeah, what about a guy?" he demanded, his voice suddenly different than it had been all day. Not soft, not easygoing or charming. Not reminiscent or pained or any of the things it had been out in the lake. Just flat growl.

Yeah, this really shouldn't make her feel better, but it did somehow.

"I was seeing him. Working at this posh ski resort. I taught classes or did one-on-one stuff. Skiing and rock climbing." She looked up at the sky through squinted eyes. She missed it, sometimes, the job itself. She liked guiding, but she missed the teaching. Watching someone develop a skill and learn to do it on their own.

"You taught people how to ski?"

"And rock climb. I was a damn fine teacher, I'll have you know. Kids especially. They loved me."

"Did they now?" But any skepticism that had been in his voice at first had changed over to wonder.

She didn't know why that made her more uncomfortable than the initial skepticism, or why this discomfort felt like a warm wave of satisfaction wrapped in sharp nerves. Pride and the desire to hide away all wrapped up into one confusing-as-hell emotion.

"It was a good job. I liked it a lot. The only drawback was

I couldn't take Sarge many places, but we had a nice little cabin and he did all right."

"The guy, Tori, what about the guy?"

"I'm getting there," she muttered. She didn't want to lay out all her embarrassments in front of Will. She turned her face back up to the sky, the warmth and glow of the sun soaking into her skin. It could almost drug her into complacency.

Luckily, the rocks digging into her back kept her rooted in exactly what she was doing. *Exactly what you are.*

"I did these one-on-one classes, and there was this guy. He was smooth, and charming, and good-looking and we went out. For a while. He was one of those guys who took care of everything. Where we were going to eat, what movie we were going to see. He'd stock my fridge with the groceries he wanted, make the bed, change a lightbulb without my having to ask."

"*That's* your type?" Will asked incredulously.

"I wanted it to be. You live your life always doing all that shit, it's kind of nice when someone swoops in and does it without a second thought." She shrugged, focusing on one rock digging into her shoulder blade, letting that pain be more important than the one in her chest.

"Turns out, he was the son-in-law of a rival ski resort, doing some weird corporate espionage, and I was just . . ." She swallowed at the burning ball of resentment in her esophagus. "Something fun for him to do while he worked."

"So, you left?" There was still a note of surprise and disbelief in his voice, and tears pricked at her eyes when she realized why.

He thought she was strong and kick-ass and wouldn't stand for any of that. Because that was the Tori Appleby image, and boy, what a fiction it had turned out to be.

"Not so easily, no. But when your boss finds out you've

been sleeping with the enemy, because the enemy's wife made sure he knew, well . . . You get to be persona non grata pretty quick."

"The fucker was *married*?"

Again it soothed something that it shouldn't, his clear outrage on her behalf. Oh, she had no doubt he'd get over that and realize *she'd* been the idiot who hadn't read the signs, who let herself get into the mess, but for now, he was outraged on her behalf and that was nice. No one else had been, they'd been too worried about what information Toby might have secreted away to his father-in-law's ski resort.

"Long story slightly less long, my boss made sure every ski resort within . . . well, probably the state of Colorado, knew I wasn't fit to be hired, so . . . I didn't have a job, or a house —because that had been part of my salary—so . . ."

"So you came here."

"I didn't think Brandon would give me a job. I didn't think . . ." Hell, she figured Will would have turned them all against her. She should have known better. Turning them against her would have required telling them what had happened. "I figured he might help me find something though. Him or Sam."

"But not me."

Tori snorted. "Yeah, no, I didn't expect you to be particularly receptive after the last time I'd seen you."

He was quiet for a while, and she noted he'd stopped touching her. No little brushes against her arm or leg. He was keeping his distance now.

She swallowed at the lump in her throat. She'd known it would change his opinion of her. She knew people didn't like that story, because it never quite mattered she had been clueless, people thought it was pretty disgusting when you slept with a married guy trying to take down your place of business.

"Why'd the wife ruin *your* job?" Will asked at last, sounding far away and too contemplative for comfort.

"Huh?"

"The wife. You didn't know he was married, and you didn't even know what he was up to. Why did his wife make sure you got shit for it?"

"I assume because he probably told her it was all my fault, slinky seductress that I am, and she wanted to believe him. I can't blame her for that, exactly. I wouldn't want to realize I'd made that kind of mistake in marriage."

"Men like that always know what they're doing, don't they?" Will said, his voice low and disgusted and . . . something else.

She snuck a glance at him, which she'd been avoiding so as not to see any sort of reflection of his lowered opinion of her on his face. His jaw was set, fine lines digging into his face. He had his hand clutched around a rock and he looked like he wanted to punch something.

Not good-natured wrestling stuff like he'd done with Brandon earlier, but a furious violence to him.

"What do you mean, know what they're doing?"

"They know who to target."

Tori frowned. "I wasn't some victim. I was just an idiot."

Will pushed into a sitting position, angling the top half of his body over hers. "It wasn't you, Tori. Men like that, they know how to find your weaknesses, prey on them, then blame you for anything bad ever happening. It's what they do, time and time again."

She was surprised at his vehemence, at his theory. "What are you talking about?"

"Guys like that, who get their wives to look the other way, who get everyone to blame anyone but themselves for their crap. It isn't by accident. It's by design. They know who to target. They know just how to take advantage of people."

"I don't think we're talking about me anymore," she said carefully, resisting the urge to touch his face, to smooth the lines out, to somehow uncoil the anger that was poised tight within him.

Which wasn't about her. Nothing he was saying was about *her*, and she needed to remember that to keep herself safe, whole. His care was only peripheral to whatever he was talking about.

It wasn't about her, these things never were.

"My father had affairs," he said flatly, but his eyes weren't flat, they were full of so much emotion Tori wanted to look away, but she couldn't.

"And your mother blamed the other party?"

"My mother refused to acknowledge them. Even when . . ."

Don't do it, don't do it, don't do it. But her arm had a life of its own, and she reached up to brush some wet hair off his forehead. "Even when what?"

He let out a sigh, and he took her stupid hand in his, studying her palm before pressing a kiss there. He pulled her up into a sitting position, so that their hips were touching, their chests facing each other.

She wanted to scoot away, but he was holding on to her, and she . . . It was like that cancer analogy she'd used when she'd first arrived here. Caring about him, wanting to soothe him, it was a cancer she couldn't cut out.

"At least one affair resulted in a child."

Some of the dots finally connected, because she'd been so wrapped up in her crap, she hadn't given much thought to anything else. "Hayley."

Will nodded.

"I'm sorry. That has to be hard."

Will dropped her hand, looked away. "I wouldn't be sorry for me. Hayley? Yes. Her mom. Hell yes. Me? I knew about it and didn't tell anyone, well, except my mother. I'm not exactly poor little disillusioned son, in this scenario."

So much anguish there, so much guilt. "Well, I think it's time for some tit for tat. I told you why I'm here, now you explain that."

Chapter Twenty-One

Will needed a few minutes to get his whirling emotions under control. It never would have occurred to him to prepare for all this.

Being livid on her behalf. Remembering too much all the mistakes he'd made. A bitterness over his father he'd thought he'd left behind when the old man keeled over, much deservedly.

But she touched his face again, something gentle and soothing, and he thought he'd crack himself open a million times over to earn that.

"My father had a charm, a way of making you forget all his shortcomings and over-focus on his good qualities. The town treated him like a benevolent king, and everyone loved him or was in awe of him."

"Except you," she said, still studying his face and gently tracing his hairline with her index finger.

He wasn't sure if that was something he'd told her years ago, or just something she put together in the way he spoke, but either way . . . she was the only one. As a kid when he'd thought his father wasn't all the town cracked him up to be, Bran and Mom and whoever else usually figured it was because he was the spoiled youngest. Clearly the favorite.

No one had ever figured it must be true, but Tori, forever his benefit-of-the doubter, even now . . .

It was important. It was something to hold on to. More and more and more.

"I . . . I didn't idolize him the way Bran did. I didn't sweep away him being a dick like my mom or people in town did, but you know what sucks is even when it turned out I was right, that Dad was just a jackass on a power trip who didn't care who he hurt, it didn't matter that I was right, because everyone was suffering. There's no satisfaction in that—being the one who sees through the bullshit, living in the aftermath of it. It all sucks."

Her fingers filtered down over his beard and jaw, that soft look still on her face. He wished he knew how to bring that out without sharing tragedies. He wished he knew how to scale her walls without sympathy.

But if this was all he had right now, then this was all he had, and he'd take it. Because she . . . She was it, and this was his second chance, and nothing was standing in his way.

"But the thing is, once you get some hindsight, you see that men like him chose the people they can manipulate. Whether it's a finely honed skill or some asshole intuition, they seek out the people they can bend to their will without the people ever knowing it."

She withdrew her hand. "I'm not sure I like what you're trying to say if you're drawing some correlation to what I just told you."

He took the hand she withdrew, put it back on his jaw, placing his own hand over it so she had to keep it there. "You're thinking I think that makes you weak, that a man could sneak under your defenses, but it isn't weakness. That's the whole point. Everyone has a vulnerability, and some people excel at stepping all over them. I saw the pattern."

She didn't try to tug her hand away, but the ease in her expression had vanished into skepticism and maybe irritation.

No, Tori did not like any implication she might not be Ms. Strong and Mighty.

He wondered if she held on to that idea of herself as tightly as he'd held on to the idea of frivolous party guy.

"What pattern?" she asked flatly.

"One summer I was . . . The summer before college, actually, I was working at Evans Mining Company. Brandon was at some leadership conference Dad had sent him off to, grooming him to lead, and he stuck me in the mail room because of my lack of drive among other things."

"That doesn't sound very fair."

"It was Evans fair, I suppose. It didn't surprise me and since I didn't want the Evans Mining life, I wasn't too bent out of shape, but I overheard a lot taking mail and packages here and there. The ways my father took advantage of employees—mainly women—who also did not view my father as a shining savior of all that was Gracely holy, but they were women who were alone, who didn't have people or money to fall back on."

"Took advantage of . . . like . . ."

Will squeezed her hand under his harder because what he really wanted to do was make a joke and laugh it off, but that didn't *do* anything. "I'm not sure anyone was ever . . . I don't know details. But I heard whispers, and one day I happened to overhear one woman crying to another that she'd slept with my father."

"Will."

"She was upset about it, for a lot of reasons, and the woman she was telling told her not to be like Vanessa. I didn't know who that was, but . . . Well, it stuck with me. The woman crying. The other woman acting like that was normal. That there was a precedent you had to make sure not to do."

Tori's free hand, which had been curled in her lap, uncurled. She gently placed it on his knee, soft again.

Was it his own kind of manipulation that he was using this? He felt sick at the thought, but only for a second. Tori did fit the mold, alone and a little desperate for money, except . . . She wasn't really alone. She had Brandon and Sam, Lilly wouldn't be content to let her flap in the breeze, and he doubted Cora would either.

It had been a short amount of time, but Tori had people now. People who wouldn't so easily let her run away a second time.

"I . . ." He laughed a little at how crazy it all sounded. "I got the name, figured out she was an old employee, and I saved up my generous allowance to pay a private investigator to figure it all out. He found her, and her daughter, and it didn't take a genius to connect the dots. Dad had gotten his secretary pregnant, then paid her off to disappear and never tell anyone about the child."

Tori's hand tightened on his knee. "Oh my God, Hayley."

"Yeah, Hayley."

"But I thought you guys just met her . . . You didn't tell anyone."

Finally Will let go of the hand on his face. He wasn't sure he actually did want all this touching, for this anyway. But her hand remained firm on his face and on his knee, and maybe anchoring with something—someone—good wasn't such a terrible thing.

"Actually, I told my mother." He sighed. "I don't know what I was thinking. That I'd be hailed as a hero? I guess I had it in my head she'd thank me, or tell me I'd been right all along. Something childish and flat-out stupid."

"What did she say?"

"Nothing at first. She just . . . hit me."

"Hit you?"

"Backhanded me across the face. Definitely not the reaction I was expecting." He tried to laugh, but no sound came out. Except a gasp from Tori.

"Will . . . That's . . . Why on earth would she hit *you*?"

"I don't know that I've ever unwound that. I know she was mad, and hell I was seventeen and a lot bigger than her, so the hitting wasn't such a big deal. I never figured out why she got so angry with *me*, but . . . She told me to never utter words like that again to her, and that if I dared spread that story along she'd make sure I was cut off from Evans, Brandon, and Gracely for good."

Will didn't look at Tori, he stared at the stones, and tried not to remember the rage-filled words his mother had yelled at him. When she'd never yelled before. She'd always been so poised, maybe cool and aloof, but never . . . brokenly furious.

"So, point being, my father knew all along what he was doing. He knew Mom was so wrapped up in the life of being an Evans she wouldn't leave, no matter who he slept with. The women he took advantage of knew they had no recourse because the town loved him. Men like that always know."

"And you never told anyone."

His guilt. His shame. "Couldn't be cut off now, could I?"

"I don't believe that's the whole of it, Will Evans, and you shouldn't either."

"What whole of it would there be? She threatened. I caved. And Hayley suffered the consequences."

"I know I don't know Hayley all that well, but I'd hardly say she suffered, and even if she did, those weren't your consequences. They were your father's. Your mother's. How dare she. How dare she lay a hand on her child because of a truth she didn't want to face."

Will didn't really have an argument for her vehemence, any more than he knew how to explain . . . It had started with his parents, sure, but he'd held on to that legacy, hadn't he?

"You don't blame your child. She had no right to lay the blame on you. Tell me you understand that."

She seemed so vested in his understanding that, he couldn't help but wonder if this was just another way their individual stories poked at something inside of themselves.

"Is that what your parents did when it came to you and your brother?"

"No, they never blamed me," she said, and she didn't look away, or get all defensive, so he had to believe she was telling the truth. Still.

"But they didn't protect you."

"I could protect myself," she said quietly, looking away from him. But she lifted her chin. "Still can. Shit happens, Will, and you learn to move on."

"And what's the difference between moving on and running away?"

Everything in her stilled, and then she withdrew herself completely. Her hands off his person, her hip scooted away from his. He'd hit a nerve, which he'd hoped to hit.

Because hell if he knew the answer to that question, and if she didn't, it meant they had to figure it out together.

Tori knew Will would read too much into her standing up and demanding they leave, but she didn't know how to fight the urge.

The difference between moving on and running away? Who the hell knew. She didn't *want* to know.

She had to get up, no matter what he might read into it. "What is this, group therapy? I think maybe it's time to head back."

"Tori."

"I just don't know what the point is," she said, trying to sound calm and careless instead of what she actually was. Panicked as all get-out.

Because how did you keep yourself separate and not in too deep and *not* falling back in love with someone when you were doing things you'd never done back then? Back then she'd known who he was, even underneath all his easy fake charm, but she hadn't known what shaped him.

She hadn't wanted to know. Almost as much as she didn't want him to know what shaped her.

"Okay. Okay, we'll let it settle, huh?"

She almost sighed in relief, but after a second she realized those words sounded awfully familiar. Because they were the exact words he'd uttered last night after, well, everything.

"Is this your new tactic? You say we just let things settle and then you wait until I've let my guard down and—"

"Nothing is a tactic, Tori. I'm trying to figure my life out. It's a life that I want you in, and that means learning when to push and when to back off."

She rolled her eyes. "I'm not a ski slope or a rock to climb. You can't figure out when to zig and when to zag."

"Figuring you out isn't the same as mapping out a battle plan. Learning how to be someone who's good for you isn't the same as climbing a fucking rock, believe me, one's a hell of a lot easier. I wanted Mile High, and I worked with Brandon and Sam to build it—making allowances, pushing when I needed to push, yeah, even me. That isn't tactics, it's relationships."

Tori didn't know what to say to that, because she didn't know shit about relationships. She could be the fun-time girl. She could be the quiet, dutiful daughter or the runaway one. She could be a lot of superficial things.

But the connecting thing . . . Well, she'd learned a long time ago that wasn't for her. Plenty of people lived their whole lives alone, didn't it make sense that she was just one of them? Of course it did.

She jerked a little when Will rested his palms on her

shoulders. She'd been so worked up, she hadn't felt him approach. So tempting to lean into that touch, into him. He'd always seemed strong, but now he seemed certain with it. Even when he was blundering through.

But that is what he's doing. Blundering through. Don't be another man's blunder.

"I spent a lot of time running away from what I wanted, Tori. Because I guess I didn't think I deserved it, or that I'd only mess it up, or maybe some combination of that and other shit. But I'm done with that. I want Mile High. And you. That might be the extent of what I know, but I know that much, and I'm not backing off just because that's hard. For me. Or for you."

Yeah, not exactly a surprise. When had anyone ever worried if things were hard for her? "Right." A good reminder, all in all, that this was all about him. For him, about him. She was some sort of prize at best.

And at worst . . . this ended up worse than it had before, because she could tell herself a million times she wouldn't fall for him, but wasn't she here doing just that?

"We ran away last time we had a chance."

We? She wanted to scoff. *He* had run away, if she wanted to believe this revisionist history of his. She had protected herself. Leaving had been necessary.

Maybe it was always necessary.

It hurt, that realization, but it also calmed her. Because that was the answer. Wading through all this emotion, weighing what-ifs, taking chances . . . it was all too hard and too much work.

Leaving, *leaving* was always the answer. You didn't have to work at leaving, or unwind all the complicated things, you just had to do it.

She looked at him, all certain in his change, in making a life with Mile High and her. Regardless of whom it hurt, because *he'd* decided. Well, that was fine and dandy. Maybe it was even necessary for him. He'd run away. He'd dealt with a kind of insecurity about his own worth. She could understand that. She could even empathize with it.

It didn't mean she would stick around to be clobbered by it. Not this time.

And if she had to leave this thing she thought had been permanent and a new start, didn't she deserve a parting gift? A memory instead of what-ifs. Because on this rocky beach in front of this beautiful lake, she knew she wasn't meant for people.

Not people she didn't love, and not the people she did. She'd stayed away from her family for over a decade, and between her staying away and the money she sent home, they kept Tim medicated and home like they wanted.

She just had to stay away. If she'd stayed away from Toby, well, maybe he would have found someone else to betray his wife with, but it wouldn't have been her.

If she'd stayed away from Gracely, Colorado, none of this would hurt all over again. But here she was, not running away, but moving on. It was moving on when you knew you'd only end up hurting.

It was saving yourself. It was being strong.

She forced herself to meet his concerned gaze, and to focus on *her* certainty while she did it. Here was not for her, no matter how beautiful and good. He was not for her, no matter how much she'd probably always love him.

"What is going on in that head of yours?" he asked, as though he wanted to know.

Yeah, she was positive he didn't. Because he wouldn't like it. He'd fight it, and he'd think he was right, and she would be clobbered in the aftermath.

Not this time.

This time she was in charge, and she would take what she wanted, and then she would leave. She would find a place where there was none of this. Where it didn't hurt.

But first . . . First. She pressed her hand to his chest, then slid it up to his shoulder and around his neck. She tugged his mouth to hers, pressed a sun-drenched kiss to it.

"How much time do we have before one of our excursions?" she asked, not letting her gaze drift from his for a second.

Will glanced at his watch. "About an hour."

"Take me home."

He studied her for a few seconds, but she refused to let him see beyond what she wanted him to. Let him see the want, the need, the attraction, and the way they fit.

She would hide the good-bye behind it, but it would be there.

Chapter Twenty-Two

Will loaded up his Jeep, Tori by his side drying off Sarge. He felt weird. Not because she seemed to want sex, and he wanted sex, and they had an hour with which to have the sex.

No, that wasn't weird at all, but something about the way she'd looked at him so seriously left him . . . He didn't have the words for the feeling that tempered whatever excitement beat inside of him.

Like an eerie feeling of something bad about to happen, but that was dumb, so he pushed it away. He focused on the way his T-shirt barely covered her ass as she bent over to finish cleaning off Sarge's paws. He focused on the curve of her shoulders, and the slope of her calves.

He focused on Tori.

Whatever wasn't quite right, they'd fix. Together. They were going to have what he'd been too stupid to try for years ago, he was sure of it, because they were both old enough and mature enough to *try*. To *fix*.

He was almost sure of it.

They got in the Jeep themselves. He drove, the car silent except for Sarge's panting, but he didn't take her home. Gracely was too far away, and if he wasn't going to get her for a whole night to himself—yet—he was damn well going to have some time to take *his* time.

So much between them was about second chances, but this was a first, and that deserved some kind of reverence.

So he turned off before Mile High, before the road down to Gracely, and took the path to the cabin he and Brandon had built into the mountains and woods. He pushed the Jeep into Park and looked over at Tori.

She sat with a certain tenseness he didn't know how to read. She'd made clear she *wanted* this, but he supposed wanting it might not offset nerves and Tori would never willfully admit or show nerves.

She frowned at the cabin. "Isn't this . . . Brandon and Lilly's place?"

"This is Bran and *my* place, that I so graciously stay scarce from to give the lovebirds room."

"Couldn't Lilly or Brandon come by? My house is empty and mine."

"Brandon's got an excursion and Lilly's in town for a meeting. On the off chance either of them would leave their strict schedules to stop in, I'll lock the door. Besides. Condoms."

She didn't smile. She didn't move. She stared at the cabin, some strange expression on her face—a mix of pain and surprise.

"It looks just like . . . That dumb drawing you and Bran did when we signed our drunken pact. It looks just like it."

"And inside, you will find said drunken pact, framed."

She whipped her head to face him. "What?"

"Brandon would have preferred putting it at Mile High, but I wasn't too keen on the idea at the time. I think it's an idea worth revisiting though." He reached over, squeezed her arm, but she didn't react in any way.

"Come on." He pushed out of the Jeep, pushing down

whatever weird feeling was still dogging him. Because
Sarge hopped out and followed him, and Tori did too. She
didn't lose that very nearly shell-shocked look about her,
but she followed him up to the porch.

The dark wood of the cabin mirrored the dark wood of
Mile High offices. Green roof and trim, gabled windows,
and, thanks to Lilly's influence, some bright pots of colorful flowers.

Picture perfect and a place he'd mostly been avoiding,
but it was still his. Still partially his.

And all its existence—from Mile High to this cabin outside of Gracely, Colorado, was *theirs*. A joint idea, and now
Tori was back in the middle of it exactly where she belonged.

He took her hand, because for the woman who'd asked him
to take her home—with the express intent of something—
she was moving awfully slow.

"Are you . . . Do you think Sarge would be okay inside?
I don't know how particular Lilly is and . . ." She looked
back at Sarge, who was sniffing around the bottom of the
porch as Will tugged Tori up the stairs of it.

"He'll be fine. He stays inside at your house, doesn't he?"

"Well, yeah, but I'm not Lilly. I . . ." She blinked, looking from the dog to Will, and then back again. She sucked
in a breath and then let it out, and it was like she was cen-
tering herself, shaking herself off from a blow.

"You're right. He'll behave."

Will dropped Tori's hand to unlock the door and pushed
it open. He waved Tori inside. "Entre."

She took another deep breath, as if stepping inside his
cabin required some feat of strength. It was a little irritating, a little deflating, that he couldn't figure her out, but he
had to believe he would. If he kept working at it, prying her
open, prying himself open to her, they'd get where they
needed to be.

Right now, he needed Tori in his bed.

They both stepped inside. Will whistled for Sarge, who reluctantly left his sniffing post outside. "Lay down, boy," Will murmured, patting the rug by the big stone fireplace that dominated the living room.

The dog sniffed, turned a few times, then complied. When Will looked back at Tori, she was already walking past the living room and the kitchen and into the little hallway that led to the bathroom and bedrooms.

Whatever slowdown she'd had in the car was ramped back up to a focus on one thing—and thank goodness for that.

"Let me guess, this one's yours," she said, pointing at the bedroom at the far end of the hall.

"How did you figure that out without looking inside?" Will asked, coming up behind her.

"This one smells flowery just walking by," she returned, gesturing toward Bran's room. "Unless you've changed cologne and I haven't noticed." She walked to the end of the hall and nudged Will's bedroom door open. She laughed a little. "Yeah, this one's all yours."

Will stepped in and around her. "Yeah, yeah, yeah, give me a minute." He scooped the random debris off his bed. He'd forbidden Lilly from touching anything in his room, for fear she'd clean it and he wouldn't be able to find anything, but he was surprised to find she'd listened.

He dumped the random clothes, hiking gear, and magazines in a pile onto the floor in a corner.

Tori rolled her eyes. "Some things really do never change."

"And some things do. Which I'd say is a very good thing."

Something in her expression changed at that, her eyebrows drawing together, that overly pensive line creasing her forehead. She looked down at her hands, opening one palm to reveal one of the rocks from the beach.

She shook her head and looked around the room before placing it on his dresser. "Don't let me forget that."

"Getting sentimental in your old age?" he teased, but she pulled her shirt off and tossed it onto the floor. The underwear she'd used as a swimsuit had dried, but that didn't make it any less see-through.

She'd probably kill him if he offered to buy her some new underwear, but it was tempting. Tempting to want to take care of her, no matter how well she could take care of herself.

"We going to get this show on the road or what?" She shimmied out of her panties, unclipped her bra, and dropped them both on the floor. With a swing in her hips, she walked over to his bed and lay out on it.

He watched her, enjoying a very naked Tori, in his life, and in his bed. His. Whether she was ready to quite capitulate to that or not, she would.

"Don't move," he muttered, leaving the bedroom and crossing to the bathroom. He fumbled around in the cabinet under the sink until he found a box of condoms and tore one off.

When he returned to his room, he closed the door behind him and locked it for good measure. He placed the condom on the dresser, next to her rock, which she could avoid answering questions about, but was clearly sentimental.

"Lose the clothes, hotshot."

"You always in this big of a hurry?" he asked, peeling his shirt off.

She looked up at the ceiling, her fingertips trailing over his sheets. Tori's small, compact body, naked and perfect, on his sheets. In his bed.

His.

He lost the rest of his clothes and then slid onto the bed next to her. She smelled like sun and lake and he pressed his nose against her neck and inhaled. "Lucky for you, I think I'm in a hurry too."

Sex had always been a purely physical act. A cute guy, the right mood, maybe a few well-placed compliments on their part, but it had never included much in the way of emotion.

Tori had never wanted it to. A girl let her emotions get in the way, and what happened? Nothing good.

But this was Will, and no amount of self-control could eradicate the fact her heart *fluttered* when his big, rough hands slid over her hip. It wasn't just that little thrill of physical contact, of a person finding those centers of pleasure on her body.

It was *Will*, and it was more, and no matter how she tried to wall off her heart, it was deeply involved. Everywhere her body pressed to his, every delicate kiss he placed against her neck, jaw, cheek, every stroke of his hand over her body as if he could memorize each centimeter, her heart twined with it. Soaked it up. Grew too big in her chest.

His mouth whispered across her cheek, sank into her lips, and it was all too much. The physical, the emotional, both together was like a swamp—unbreathable, drowning, dangerous.

Because she couldn't pretend in kissing him back that all those feelings weren't still there. She loved him as deeply and desperately as she had when she'd confessed as much all those years ago.

She had to pull her mouth away from his to breathe, to think, to manage anything that wasn't just soul-crushing pain.

Loved him. Still. Always. She'd convinced herself it had gone away, but of course it hadn't. It had only ever been him.

"You okay?" he asked into her ear, holding her. Just . . . holding her.

For a heartbreaking second she wondered if that mattered, if things might be different. They were older and wiser, and he wanted . . .

Well, *he wanted* was the beginning and end of that. What she wanted would never fully matter, and she couldn't contort herself to accept that kind of existence. She wouldn't.

"I'm fine," she managed, because she would find a way to be. She couldn't protect her heart from Will, it had always belonged to him, but she could protect herself, period. She would have this, and then she would leave.

No matter how the thought cut her to ribbons. It was the right thing, the *strong* thing. The only choice.

"We can stop. There's not really any hurry," he murmured into her ear, holding her tight and close. Naked and warm.

Which was exactly why they *did* need to hurry. Her eyes were wide open, and she knew, with a painful certainty that made tears sting, this was it. She would have to leave after this.

But at least she'd have this. Leaving with something other than bitterness and blame. She'd have a memory, a good one, and it'd get her through.

So she pressed her mouth to his, wrapping her arms around his neck, pulling him closer. She reveled in the heat of his hard body, in the length of the erection pressed to her hip. This was hers.

This moment, which didn't have to be tainted by the past, and didn't have to be heavy with an impossible future. She would erase it all with this kiss. Everything before. Everything after. She would live in this joining, and pretend for this brief period of time that apart wasn't all they could ever be.

She threaded her fingers through his hair, pressed her chest to his. She breathed him in, committing to memory the scrape of his teeth against her lip, the way his large hand encompassed her hip. She inhaled the smell of sun and lake and what she assumed was the laundry detergent used on the sheets and pillow.

Like this moment, like his hands on her naked body, the smell was a once-in-a-lifetime thing that wouldn't be repeated, and it made the moment—all those things she'd never experience again.

She pressed against him and rolled until she was on top of him, straddling his legs, trailing her fingertips down his shoulders, his chest, his abs. He watched with heavy-lidded eyes, his irises somehow a greenish otherworldly gold.

She closed her fingers around the hot, hard length of him, and stroked. He sucked in a breath, but that languid watching never changed. He merely watched her hands.

And then her mouth. He groaned, and she grinned as she took him into her mouth. She wanted everything, and so she would take. The feelings. The taste of him. All of it. Hers.

"Pause," he growled, pulling her up into a sitting position as he lifted himself into one. He reached around her head and tugged the band out of her hair and started weaving his fingers through the wet, straggly strands.

She tried to bat his hands away, but he only grinned and kept unwinding her braid until it was a damp mess around her shoulders. She scowled down at him.

"Now I look like a drowned rat."

"No, you look like a drowned fairy."

She rolled her eyes. "There is nothing remotely fairylike about me." To prove it, she pushed him back and pinned his hands to the mattress, her wet mass of hair brushing his cheeks.

He flashed a grin, which if she'd been thinking straight

instead of about the hard man between her legs, she might have recognized as a warning.

Before she even knew what he was up to, he flipped her underneath him, switching places down to his hands pinning her wrists to the mattress as hers had just done to him.

He looked down at her, eyes blazing, gaze raking over every part of her until her skin began to goose-bump.

"Tonight, I am spending the night with you, and damn I will take my sweet time, but right now, I have got to be inside you." He reached for the condom he'd put on the dresser, and part of her wanted to protest, stop this.

It was irreversible, and going further meant it would be over, and he couldn't come over later and spend the night. He couldn't take his time. It couldn't . . . happen.

He rolled the condom on himself then looked down at her. Something passed through his expression, maybe even concern, but she didn't want that. Or rather she did want it, and couldn't trust it. Not here. Not now.

Not ever.

He gathered her to his chest, encompassing everything, sliding slow and deep. Her name a rough exhale from his mouth. "God, I've needed you for so long," he murmured, pressing a kiss to her jaw, to her mouth.

"Will." Except there was nothing to say with it. Just his name, as he moved into her, with her. Slow and deliberate, adjusting his hold on her, the way he moved, to make her sigh, then moan. Until she was moving with him, chasing that end she needed, and trying to somehow circumvent the end she didn't want.

But it was all crashing down on her, the emotions, the way he kissed her, the physical coil of desire binding so tight its only choice was to crash apart.

And that's exactly what she did. The orgasm was familiar, but all that whirled with it was some new, different world.

Not just the wave of physical release, but the need to hold on to Will desperately as he groaned his way to his own satisfaction.

Her chest was too tight, her heart too big and beating too hard. Everything inside her was *too* much and she wanted to sob against his shoulder.

Which she didn't do only because he would press. He would wheedle all the emotions out of her until there was nothing left, and no armor to save herself.

She couldn't let that happen again.

Chapter Twenty-Three

Will knew somewhere in the recesses of his mind he should roll off Tori. Clean himself up, give her some space to breathe, but there was nowhere he'd rather have her than curled up into his chest, sated and pliant, all his.

It had been a long time since he'd indulged in sex. He'd been faithful in his marriage to Courtney if only because his father hadn't been faithful in his marriage. He'd been celibate afterward if only because the town wasn't exactly crawling with young, available women.

He'd been on one disastrous date a few months ago where he'd been certain he'd seen Sarge.

"When did you first get to town?" he asked absently, wondering if he'd been as off his rocker has he'd thought at the time.

Tori wiggled underneath him and he finally released her, withdrawing from the comfort of her body. She was flushed and tangled, and no matter that she thought she looked like a drowned rat, he thought he liked her best this way. Mussed and flushed. From *him*.

Yeah, he liked that a whole hell of a lot.

"Few weeks before the wedding."

Will rolled off the bed to get rid of the condom. It wasn't

enough time to have gone back to his date with Dr. Frost, so apparently, he really had been losing it a bit.

"Why?"

He shrugged, walking back to the bed, not missing the way her gaze dropped to his dick. He grinned, and when she finally tore her gaze away, she rolled her eyes.

"Oh, so I'm ogling. Don't let it go to your head."

"But that's exactly where it's gone." He crawled back into bed, and though he noted the way she shied away from him, he didn't react to it. Tori was . . . well, she'd hate the comparison but she was a bit like a skittish dog, and she'd been hurt a lot. It would take some time and care to prove he wouldn't cause her harm.

Something sickening flipped in his stomach, that old certainty he wasn't the man for a sensitive job, but he pushed it away. The dipshit he'd been seven years ago couldn't handle this, but the dipshit he was now could, or would.

He wouldn't hurt people out of his own fear anymore, and he wouldn't hurt himself. Something had to change, because Brandon had entrusted him to change.

He crossed his arms behind his head, hoping she'd snuggle up to him, wondering what it would take. If only she was as easy to win over as Sarge had been. A piece of hamburger and the dog had loved him for life.

Love.

He still shied away a bit from that. He needed time to sit with it, work out what that meant for him. For her. It would take time and finesse and making sure he didn't fuck it all up again.

So he changed the subject in his head. "You just let me know when you're up for another go. I haven't had sex in a while, so I'm pretty sure I could manage."

She cocked her head, inching just the tiniest bit closer. She smelled like lake water and fresh air, and it was the perfect scent for his drowned fairy.

"How long is a while?"

He shrugged, not meeting her curious gaze. The more he *didn't* look at her, the more she scooted closer and closer, and eventually she even laid her head on his shoulder.

He curled his arm around her, drawing her in, nuzzling against her tangled hair. "Well, as screwed up as the end of my marriage was, I wasn't going to sleep with someone else."

Silence followed, and after a few seconds of that heavy, considering silence, Tori tilted her head back so she could look at him. "Because of your father?"

Will shrugged. "Guess so."

"But that was months ago, wasn't it? Your divorce."

"That it was."

"And you haven't had sex since . . . *her*?"

Tori was looking at him with such consideration he couldn't help but fidget, and he was not a man prone to fidgeting. "What?"

She shook her head lightly, strands of her hair brushing against his arm. He twined his free hand in one of them, curling it around until it was tight.

When he finally met that shrewd blue-green gaze, she spoke.

"That's noble, I think. Good, anyway."

"I'm not perfect," he replied, because he knew it would earn him a scoff. She hardly thought he was *perfect*.

"No, but you are . . . Well, you're more like Brandon than I think even you'd like to admit."

Will didn't care for that observation. All those moral codes and shit came easy for Brandon. Will had pieced together his moral compass to make sure he wasn't like his father. It wasn't some innate goodness in him, he'd just wanted to be something Phillip Evans wasn't. Decent.

Which is different than Brandon, how?

Not something he wanted to dwell on, all in all, so he

turned to her instead. She was still looking at him with that careful, studying gaze that tumbled through him alarmingly close to worry. But there was nothing to worry about.

He wouldn't fail at this. He'd stick until he convinced her, and then he'd stick some damn more. He tugged the twined piece of hair until her mouth was close enough to his to devour.

The thing that amazed him was not that kissing her was like finding some peaceful, perfect spot in the woods where he could lose himself, his thoughts, his fears, his shitty past; it was that there were so many ways a kiss with Tori could tangle deep inside of him.

Not just attraction. Not some past affinity for each other, something deep in his bones that archaeologists would read civilizations from now. It could be hot, it could be tender, it could be a million things, but it was always *Tori*, and that was always what mattered.

There was a moment, sweet and pure and damn near perfect, where she sank into it, willingly, enthusiastically, not an iota of that thing hiding beneath the surface of her and her attraction to him.

But it was short-lived, and that *thing* was back, something he couldn't read. All he could figure was it was some self-preservation instinct, some hesitancy since he'd hurt her before. Fair, all in all, but he'd prove it wasn't necessary.

She pushed at his chest. "We, uh, have to get back. Excursions. And stuff."

"Uh-huh." He found a spot on her neck that made her squeak and nibbled. "Consider this a precursor for tonight."

"Will. Really. I can't . . ."

He pulled away incrementally. Something in her voice reminded him of panic, and he didn't like that at all. "What's wrong?"

She withdrew from him, drawing herself into a protective

sitting position on the edge of the bed. As far away from him as she could get.

He really, *really* didn't like that.

"I have plans with Cora tonight."

"I can come by after."

She shook her head, twisting her fingers together. "No. I . . . I don't *want* you to come over tonight. I don't . . ."

He reached for her twined fingers but she scooted away, and it was something in that rejection that had him freezing.

"I just need some processing time," she said, not meeting his gaze, not doing anything to ease that frozen fear inside him.

"What does that mean?"

She swallowed. Her eyes were suspiciously shiny, very nearly blue. "Please," she whispered.

It undid him, completely, to see her so vulnerable. So *willingly* vulnerable. Uttering a word like *please* that she'd as likely cut her tongue out as use, at least toward him.

"All right. For today."

She straightened her shoulders and let out a long breath. "Your timetable then, huh?" she asked, lifting her chin, challenging him.

But he wouldn't fall for it. Not here. Not now. "My timetable would be you underneath me for approximately the next seventy-two hours."

"You think too highly of yourself," she replied dryly, but her mouth quirked, amused by him in spite of herself. But that humor died, quickly, and offered a stabbing pain in the center of his chest.

"I hope you know how serious I am about this. About us." He swallowed at his own bolt of panic. Declaring his intentions, being serious about something, it had never worked out for him.

Except Mile High. You built that.

With Brandon. Always Brandon in the background making it right, smoothing things out, because you are the worthless—

He cut off the line of thought when it started to sound too much like his father's voice in his head. Luckily, whatever emotion might have shown on his face Tori couldn't see as she'd wrapped her arms around him, hugging him tight.

He hugged her right back, drew some comfort in her, reminded himself this wouldn't end the same way. Not this time. He wouldn't be the one standing in his own way anymore.

She kissed his cheek. "Thank you," she said so earnestly, so *seriously*.

The reverent way she'd spoken those two words, as though she hadn't meant thank you, but as if she'd been trying to say something else, bothered him the entire time they got dressed, the entire way back to Mile High.

And as they parted ways to go on their separate excursions, she'd looked at him with too-soulful eyes.

"See you later," he offered, trying to figure out the weird post-sex mood she was in.

"Bye, Will," she replied, a smile never gracing her features.

Tori had accepted there was going to be a perpetual lump in her throat until this was all taken care of. Unfortunately, she had to face the second hardest part of this whole thing. The first had been saying good-bye to Will, no matter how oblivious he was to it.

But asking Brandon for help, asking him to keep it from Will, well, that was a whole load of crap in itself.

"It has to be done," she whispered to herself.

She'd hurried through her excursion, desperate to time it so she could get back and talk to Brandon before Will was done with his. She'd been curt with a few question askers, and was probably the new cause of Mile High losing repeat customers.

She pressed a hand to her heart and tried to even her breath and blink back the tears for good, but it was hard to push away all those emotional responses.

She didn't want to do this. She didn't want to leave. She wanted Gracely and Will and the future she'd always planned to have.

Life had taught her better, time and time again. Better to do it on her own terms than let something or someone else clobber her again. She had to remember that.

It was incomprehensible how hard that was when she'd built her whole life on it, but she supposed Will had always been her Achilles' heel. So maybe it made all the sense in the world this was the hardest thing she'd ever done—even harder than leaving home, because as scary as that had been she'd had to do it to survive, to keep herself *safe*.

Now she was only trying to keep her heart safe, and that seemed such a little thing. Maybe she could . . .

She marched forward into the Mile High offices. The longer she procrastinated, the longer she had time to second-guess herself. Did she really want to be the hurt, weak-willed thing she'd been after Will had crushed her the first time?

Hell, no.

Skeet was at the front desk, and he raised an eyebrow as she stormed by, but Tori otherwise ignored him. She had a mission. She had to rip this Band-Aid off.

She went straight to Brandon's office, relieved beyond belief that he was sitting there, alone, a phone cradled to his shoulder as he squinted at a computer screen.

He motioned her inside, and she closed the door behind her. He murmured a few things into the speaker, but he was looking at her speculatively. As though he could see through what she thought was a pretty good calm and certain façade.

"Well, e-mail me the numbers then, and we'll go over it at our next meeting. Yeah. Bye." Brandon pushed End on his phone and smiled blandly at Tori. "What's up?"

"I need you to do me a favor." She swallowed. "A big one."

"All right."

"I'm . . ." Why was this so hard? She knew exactly what she had to say, sweaty palms and sick feeling in her stomach be damned. No one else was going to protect her. She had to do it herself. "I need to . . . I was thinking about getting out of Colorado. I've been here . . . so long."

His eyebrows puzzled together. "I don't follow."

"Would you know of anywhere, kind of like this, out of Colorado, that might be hiring, that you could put in a good word for me?" She was messing it all up, and sounding like an idiot in the process. "The point is, I have to leave."

Brandon's expression went from confused to serious and he pushed out of the chair. "What's happened?"

The demand was so forceful, the truth nearly came tumbling out. A reflex to that no-nonsense tone. Except what happened was none of Brandon's business. "N-nothing."

"Tori. You've been here, hell, not even two months. You can't leave again."

"I . . . I have to."

He crossed his arms over his chest, and she'd forgotten that his natural leadership and innate power didn't just exist inside Mile High or business. Brandon was like that with everything and everyone.

Except maybe Lilly. Would Lilly understand? Maybe Tori should have appealed to her, but it was too late now.

"L-look. So. I . . ." She let out a shaky breath. Hell, she wasn't in the wrong here, she might as well tell him the truth.

Surely he'd see . . . he'd understand. Brandon understood people better than anyone she knew, so he'd get it.

"Will seems to think . . . Well, it's just, he's got it in his head we can . . ."

"He's in love with you."

"No." She said it on more of a gasp than was probably necessary, but the last thing she wanted to hear was that word. "No. Look. No. Things are all . . . No, and I just need to leave. We can't . . . I need you to help me find a job, and if you can't, it doesn't change my mind. I can't stay."

His mouth flattened. "This seems sudden," he said, his voice accusatory at best.

Which was helpful, really, because she'd accuse him right back. "I've thought long and hard about it."

"I see. And what did Will say?"

Tori had to look away. This wasn't going at all like she needed to, and it was her own fault. She was panicking. Not acting rationally. She should have gone home and planned it all out. She should have done everything different.

"Tori," Brandon admonished, his hands falling to his sides.

"Don't tell Will," she said, losing what little pride she had left. "Please."

His mouth went even harder. "You know I can't do that."

"Please? *Please*. Not for me, but for his own good."

Brandon's eyebrows furrowed again, as though she was speaking some foreign language he couldn't work out. "What about yours?"

Her own good? Hell, this was for her survival. "This is for everyone's own good." She knew. She *knew*.

And if you're wrong?

Nothing about this meeting had surprised her so far, but Brandon resting his hands on her shoulders did.

He looked down at her, trying to figure her out, so much

like Will. Same dark, thick hair, same hazel eyes, same beard hiding so much.

But Brandon was her friend, not her heart. She didn't understand him the way she understood Will. She didn't understand anyone the way her soul locked with Will's.

Which was the scariest thought of them all.

"I'm telling you what I would have told him seven years ago, had he asked. I don't know what happened, but I do know running away isn't the answer."

"I don't have a choice," she managed to say, sounding sure. Because it was the truth. Truths were always hard. The right choice was always the hard choice. She'd learned. She knew.

"Of course you do," Brandon returned.

Had he said it in an offhanded, condescending manner she'd heard Brandon employ often, she might have bristled. But he said it in that even, certain way that made her heart waver.

Did she have a choice?

"He's not the same man, and I'd wager you're not the same woman. This isn't the same life any of us had seven years ago. You have a choice, of course you do. Having a choice is the hardest part of the whole thing. You don't want to consider love, fine, but I don't say it lightly when I say he cares about you, in a way he's possibly never cared about anyone else, including himself."

Her heart twisted, painful and scraping. "He thinks he does, but he . . . He doesn't . . . He can't . . ." She couldn't find the words, or maybe she didn't want to give them to Brandon. "Look, it doesn't happen for me, okay? My life is a cruel cosmic joke. I'm saving everyone the trouble."

He squeezed her shoulders, and though she refused to look up at him she could feel that heavy weight of his gaze.

"We get to choose our lives, Tori. What we fight for. What we'll hurt for."

She pushed his hands away and stepped back, finding the strength to meet his concern with her righteous certainty. "I'm done hurting." That was the beginning and end of it. Hurt was shit, and she was done with it. Life was about finding good and happy and easy. It was about being able to take a breath, not going through bloody and broken always wondering when someone would realize what she'd always known . . .

"If you won't help me, that's fine."

"I'll always help you, Tor. Always."

"Then don't tell him!" She swallowed, at the lump, at the rising tide of panic, at all the *emotion* swamping her.

"He's my brother."

"And he means more. Yeah, I get it. Someone always means more," she muttered to herself. There was her certainty. Her reminder.

"If you've got a scorecard locked away in there you'll always lose. Because life is not a win and loss column."

"Well, you're very wise and all, but I've got shit to do."

"I'm not wise," he said, even as she walked away. "But I learned that love will always be scary, and it will always hurt, and sometimes you have to do the thing you think you can't."

Tori closed her eyes briefly, but she didn't stop her retreat. No, not retreat. This was an exit. A good-bye. Inevitable and necessary.

Brandon only thought different because he was married, because he was the type of man who could move mountains if he so chose.

Tori didn't have that kind of power. Never had, and she never would. She marched through the front room of

Mile High again, and though Skeet didn't look up from his desk, he did speak.

"You'll always regret running away. Trust me," he muttered.

She gaped at the old man she barely knew, but he busied himself with papers on his desk, and Tori . . .

She had to get out of here. Clearly, it was some kind of insane asylum. Maybe some screwed-up nightmare.

Either way, it was done, and she had to go home and pack up the life she'd always wanted.

Chapter Twenty-Four

Lilly yawned at her desk. This whole pregnancy-exhaustion thing was really not her favorite, but she supposed anything that assured her the twins were growing as they should be, she would deal with.

She gave her stomach a little pat, something she did only when she was completely alone and no one could see that she was trying to communicate with two tiny fetuses. *Tap, tap, keep growing, little ones.*

She glanced at her watch and frowned. It was at least half an hour after when she had expected Brandon to swoop in with water and snacks and check on her to make sure she wasn't working too hard. He was like clockwork that way, and she couldn't ignore the fact that even though it grated on her nerves when she was really focused on something and he interrupted . . . On the whole, she enjoyed it, felt comforted by it.

So it was especially concerning he hadn't appeared. She pushed out of her chair and shoved her feet back into the heels she'd slipped off earlier. She wasn't going to forgo fashion just because she was pregnant. Though sometimes she *considered* it.

She left her office and went to Brandon's across the hall. The door was open and when she stepped inside, he was standing at the window looking out over the backyard of Mile High.

It was funny that even a surprise baby, a quick wedding, and a million fights in between didn't dull the way her heart could pitch at just the sight of him. So big and handsome and hers.

Lilly took a few more steps toward him and looked out the window herself. She didn't see anything of importance, but when she looked up at Bran his face was grave.

"What's wrong?"

He sighed and rubbed a hand over his beard. "I'm not really sure."

"Elaborate," she demanded, poking his side.

He sighed again, his gaze not leaving the trees that surrounded this side of the cabin. "Tori came in a little bit ago. She told me she wanted to leave. She wanted me to help her find a job out of state."

Lilly frowned. "What did your brother do now?"

"As far as I can tell he didn't do anything. But she wasn't exactly forthcoming."

"Something had to set her off to want to run away."

"I agree. The issue is that I don't have a clue as to what. She asked me not to tell him, so, yeah, it has to do with him."

"Of course, you'll tell him! She can't just disappear."

Bran's mouth curved a fraction and his hazel eyes met hers. "It isn't as if he's never done it to her."

Lilly fisted her hands on her hips. "You think it's revenge then?"

"No, I don't think it's revenge. She was too upset and jittery for that. She seemed . . . panicked. I told her I thought he loved her, and she just . . ." He shook his head, looking back out the window. "I don't know how much of it is my business."

"All of it," Lilly replied resolutely.

"Lilly—"

"We're family, Brandon." She didn't let him lecture her on her busy-bodying. Though she'd vowed to be more careful with it after Will's outburst, it had all worked out, hadn't it? Will and Tori had clearly gotten something out of her interfering.

How could you argue with results? "Will is your brother, and my brother-in-law, and quite frankly anyone who we invite into Mile High has come to be a part of our *family*. It means something more than just a business, this place, and that means the people in it are important to us as people."

"Don't get agitated," he said lightly, already scanning the room no doubt so he could shove her somewhere and hover.

"Then don't argue with me," she replied primly.

"I won't be able to keep it from him. It's not like I'm considering not telling him. I'm just wondering . . . I don't want to get in the middle of this. I think they need to figure out their own shit."

"Because when we were having problems, Will didn't give you any advice or speak to you in any way about it?" she asked sweetly.

Brandon didn't say anything, but his mouth firmed so she knew she'd scored a point.

"Exactly. We have all been pushing each other and into each other's businesses, and it's not always right, and it's not always perfect, but it is what we do. It's what you do when you care about someone. You offer them a shoulder, and you offer them advice, and you're there for them regardless of what outcome they choose. That's love."

"Yes, it is." He wound his arm around her shoulders, pulling her close until she leaned against him, but he was still tense. Worried. "Remember when you weren't too happy with me over looking into Hayley and where she came from?"

Lilly shifted on her feet uncomfortably, afraid she was going to have to acknowledge *him* scoring a point. "Well. Yes."

"And you said that I was using my power to do something against her will."

"I had a little bit of my own baggage in that particular fight."

"I know, but I'm just wondering how much of this is my . . . She seemed scared, and I know she's not scared of Will. I couldn't get out of her what this was all about, and it makes it impossible to know the right course of action."

"Well, if she isn't scared of Will, then it's obvious."

"It is?"

Lilly rolled her eyes. "Love. She's scared of love."

Brandon took a minute to consider that, and she liked that he gave it the weight it deserved—didn't just jump to agree or disagree with her.

"Love is a scary thing," she added. "Some of us feel inclined to . . ." She delicately cleared her throat. "Occasionally run away from it."

Brandon chuckled at that and squeezed her tighter to him. "That they do."

"I just hope Will is smart enough to stand up to that fear." She looked up at the man she'd married, who'd been just that smart, and smiled as she touched her palm to his scruffy jaw. "That would be the right course of action."

"You guys talking about me?"

They both whirled to face Will, who was now standing in the doorway, looking puzzled.

"You're back," Brandon offered lamely.

"Yeah, I'm back. What's going on?"

Lilly looked expectantly at Brandon and he sighed. "Let's go sit down. We'll talk it out."

"How very concerning," Will muttered.

Lilly hooked arms with Will as they walked out to the main room. Sam was coming in the front door as they did, and Hayley was fiddling in the kitchenette.

She knew that some people would find it a gross violation of privacy to air this all out in front of everyone, but when she'd told Brandon they were a family, she meant it.

She wanted to know that when she brought her children into the world, they would have this amazing support. That they would never have to worry like she had. That they would never feel like they were the only person they could count on. She would build that for them, and for herself. For Brandon, for Will. For all these people who hadn't been in her life a few months ago, but she had grown to love and need.

"Why don't we all sit," Lilly said with a wave to the others.

"Okay, now you're just freaking me out. What's wrong?" Will asked, taking a seat on the couch.

"It's not so much that something's wrong," Brandon said evenly as Sam, Hayley, and Skeet gathered.

"Oh, just tell the boy already," Skeet grunted. "Poor girl's running scared. I wouldn't beat around the bush."

"What the hell are you all talking about?" Will demanded.

"Tori came by to see me after her excursion today."

Will's frown deepened and Lilly couldn't fight the urge to take a seat next to him and put her hand on his arm. He looked at her fingers as though they were some offensive thing, but she wanted to offer what support she could.

"She asked me to help her find a job out of state. She said she has to leave. And she asked me not to tell you."

The expression on Will's face didn't change, but Lilly felt his muscles go to steel underneath her fingers.

She had a feeling this was going to be *quite* the situation.

Will figured they all expected him to react in some way. But he couldn't. Much like the freezing he'd done earlier when he'd had that horrible feeling something wasn't right, he couldn't move. Or act.

Brandon's words seemed to sink into his brain, not quite making sense, but slowly clicking into place.

Tori had slept with him, and now she wanted to leave.

He looked around the room at too many concerned faces and tried to smile. "Figures, I guess."

"I don't think it figures at all," Hayley said, so self-righteously he wanted to laugh.

"It doesn't make any sense," Sam added, looking concerned and confused.

But it made perfect sense to Will. Sure, he'd been certain he could fix things with Tori. He'd known he would do whatever it took to have a relationship with Tori.

But what he'd missed in all his certainty was that she'd have to let him.

Why would she let him? He didn't have anything particularly special to offer. Why should she give him the time to prove himself? She didn't have to. She didn't owe him.

So this really made all the sense in the world.

"What are you going to do about it?" Lilly asked, sitting next to him, her fingers resting on his forearm. His force of nature sister-in-law, who thought you could just do things about people, was sitting there asking him what he was going to do.

"Well, aren't you going to tell me?" he asked blandly.

She frowned at him, but she didn't take her fingers

away, and none of that horrible concern choking him left the room.

What was he going to do? He was going to accept that he'd wanted to change, and he'd wanted to love her, and it just wasn't going to happen. People were people, after all. All you could count on was yourself.

His father had branded him useless. His mother had cut him off for telling her the truth. If blood couldn't love him, why would he expect someone he'd hurt to?

"Will."

Will looked up at his brother's voice, and it was there he saw his exception.

Brandon had always been there. His brother. His leader. A million other things, but Brandon had always been *there.*

Mom and Dad had proven that blood didn't mean anything to some people, so it wasn't even because he'd had to be. Brandon wasn't there because they shared blood, because it was some obligation.

He'd been there because that was Brandon.

The frozen thing inside of him started to thaw, and in its wake was not the warm glow of love—brotherly or otherwise.

No, he was hot with anger.

He'd never *deserved* a second chance with Tori, but they both deserved a chance. To learn from their mistakes. To be better and try harder. They deserved a chance at *something*.

And she was going to run away.

No. No, not this time. It wasn't going down like this again. He stood abruptly, jostling Lilly, offering a half-hearted apology as he strode for the door.

A chorus of his name filled the air. He heard Sam tell him to stop, and Hayley ask where he was going. Brandon said his name again in that no-nonsense drill-sergeant way.

"I'll tell you where I'm going, I'm going to tell Tori, if

she wants to disappear, she's damn well going to have to get through me first."

"Don't lead with anger when love is on the line," Skeet's scratchy old voice said, with enough force to make Will stop at the door. "Life doesn't give us very many second chances," he added.

Will could only turn and stare at the old man. Skeet shrugged, not looking any of them in the eye. "You don't get to be old and alone for no reason, or without learning a thing or two. 'Less you want to be like me."

"You're not so bad, old man," Will muttered.

"I'm not so good, either."

Something about that, and the way Skeet finally met his gaze, a lifetime of something Will hadn't a clue about in their bleary blue depths.

But this wasn't the same. Whatever Skeet had gone through, it couldn't be the same as—

"He's right. He's right, you know," Lilly added, always pressing the advantage. "I thought Brandon was going to come after me with ultimatums and demands, and he didn't, and it made all the difference."

"And I took an alternate route because of *you*," Brandon added.

"Fear will always drive people away. It's not sense. It's not reasonable. It's panic. Give her panic time to breathe," Hayley added. "Like you guys did with me."

"Going off half-cocked doesn't get you anywhere. It only puts her back up. You know that," Sam added.

"Why the fuck are you all telling me what to do?" Will demanded, or maybe yelled. He felt like he was being torn into a million shreds of hurt and confusion and damn it, all he wanted was that obnoxious woman who was trying to run away from him.

She could be gone right now, and they were all shouting advice at him?

"Because we're your family, and we care," Lilly said, resolutely and if Will wasn't mistaken with a faint sheen of tears to her eyes.

Oh, hell.

"We want what's best for you," Hayley added.

"We want to help you," came from Sam.

"It isn't as though you haven't stood up and done the very same for us," Brandon continued.

Will took a deep breath. Hell if he didn't want to push it all away, argue it all away. He wanted it to be lies, and he wanted this to be easy, but it . . . It was never going to be that.

It was never going to be easy or simple, not with Tori, not with life. But he somehow, in spite of himself, had this *family*. Built of blood and friendship and mistakes and a million other things.

But mostly love.

He realized somewhere in the middle of all his anger and fear and hurt, that not only were they right, but Tori had never had this. Her family had estranged her rather than protected her. She'd loved him, and he'd run away. There'd been the prick who'd lied to her.

She didn't have people who would stand up and tell her she deserved more, better, that she was loved.

Which meant he had to.

Chapter Twenty-Five

It was strange to realize she hadn't cried this much when Will had walked away from her after she'd told him she loved him some years ago.

That had been a different kind of hurt. Shocked and devastated that her little inkling of fear about herself had always been true. Maybe she wasn't the evil demon her unstable brother had insisted she was, but she certainly wasn't . . . well, worth much.

She let out a little hiccup of a sob, and stumbled down the stoop stair with her last load of crap. Sarge whined from where he sat, shivering and confused, the only thing that had ever loved her with any consistency.

But a dog's love was as temporary as anything else. What was the damn point?

The thought of losing Sarge was too much. No matter how melodramatic, she let herself fall into a sitting position, hugging her overstuffed duffel bag close as she sobbed into it.

Sarge came over and whined again, licking her hair, but it didn't stem the tide of tears. If anything, it made them worse. Why did a damn dog love her? No one else did. Including herself.

She'd never been so dramatic in her whole life and all she could be thankful for was that she didn't have any busybody neighbors to—

"Tori!"

Shit.

Cora's voice and subsequent car door slam was enough to wake her up. She had to stop crying and depressing herself over just-life things that had to be done.

Before Tori even had time to wipe the tears from her cheeks, Cora was kneeling by her side, wrapping her arms around her.

"What's wrong? Are you hurt?" Cora demanded.

"No." Well, maybe a lie, but she wasn't bleeding out or anything. Though it kind of felt like it. She wiped at her cheeks. "Just . . ." The pressure was building again. Usually a good crying jag could make that go away for weeks, but it was just . . .

"Tori, what is it?"

"I have to leave. I have . . ." Her voice squeaked, her throat getting too tight to speak through. She tried to swallow down a sob, but it only exited her mouth like some deranged, keening thing.

Tori heard Cora murmur something to Micah, but she was crying too hard to see or hear. Cora's arms held firm though, and there was some odd comfort in that. She always figured letting someone see her hurt would multiply it. They'd see she was stupid or silly or bad, and then . . .

She took a heaving breath. Well, apparently her brain was a little screwier than she'd given it credit for.

"It'll be okay," Cora murmured, somehow gentle and firm at the same time.

It did what Tori imagined it was supposed to do. Calmed and steadied her. The words, the physical contact, the friendship.

Tori managed to breathe normally again, trying to pull

away to mop herself up, but Cora kept one arm around Tori in a firm grip.

"When you can, you need to tell me what happened."

"It's nothing. I'm overreacting," Tori replied, using her shirt to dry her face.

"That's not an answer, Tori."

As much as Tori didn't want to give one, as much as she imagined standing up and walking away, clean, angry breaks all around, Cora's arm around her was like some kind of drug or spell.

"I don't know. Will thinks . . . I don't know what he thinks. That we've got a chance or something, and I just can't go down that road and have it . . . I just have to leave." Panic was building, that uneven beat in her chest, the pressure against her lungs. She looked at Cora, desperate for some kind of vindication. "You get that, right? When you *have* to do something? Even if it's hard."

Cora studied her for the longest time, and there wasn't a hint in her expression what she was thinking, but she smoothed Tori's hair, a motherly gesture Tori had seen her do to Micah a hundred times.

"Yeah. When I left Micah's father . . . there came a point, and it was a lot later than I'd like to admit, where I finally realized *I* had to do something."

Tori didn't mean to recoil, but it was there. Not because she was horrified at the comparison, but because it put hers into a perspective that made her feel like dirt.

"Oh, not quite the same?" Cora asked with a fake kind of innocence. She took the duffel bag Tori was still clutching and pried it from Tori's grasp.

"I . . ."

"No, give me a second here, let me don my Lilly hat and tell you what to do. Because I have *had* to do hard things, and I've avoided doing hard things, and I've watched people fall in love, build lives together, very much in comparison to what I thought was love and life."

Cora settled them in a more comfortable sitting position on the grass. The sun was setting between the mountains in the distance and the air was cool. Tori took a deep gulp of it, something like calm settling over her for the first time.

She didn't know why.

"The thing is, when you're a mom everything is scary," Cora said, using her free hand to play with a blade of grass even as her other arm stayed wrapped around Tori's shoulders. "I lived in fear of Micah's father, but I also lived in fear of every step Micah took. How a decision I made might hurt him. You put them on the school bus and watch them disappear. You take them to the hospital when they break an arm falling out of a tree, and if you're me you watch your six-year-old bring you an ice pack for your black eye."

"Cora—"

"No, no, I'm getting around to it. See, I liked you from the beginning because you seemed like this fearless person. I like those people. Lilly is like that. On the outside you think she's infallible and fears nothing. But I watched her fall in love, and I've watched you settle in to figuring your Will stuff out and . . ."

Cora turned and studied Tori for a few seconds. Tori didn't know what Cora saw, what she thought, but Tori found more than running away from it, she wanted to hear where Cora was going with all this fear talk.

"I realized sometime this year that no one is fearless, which is weirdly comforting. Because it means I don't always have to be, but it also means sometimes I *can* be. Clearly, you're running because you're afraid."

"I'm running because I know how this ends. It ends with me hurt. It always ends with me hurt. Look, you live a certain kind of life and you learn what you get and what you don't. You . . . see a pattern, and sometimes that pattern is that no one is ever going to fully love you or put you first, and you might as well *accept* it rather than get hurt a million times."

Cora nodded patiently. "So you think you're bad news and he'll eventually see it and leave you?"

Tori hunched her shoulders, looking down at the grass. "Something like that."

"I used to think Micah's father hitting me was love."

"Cora, stop comparing that. It isn't—"

"It isn't the same, but parts of it are. The perceptions we use are. He'd say he just loved me so much and he had a temper and please forgive him and whatnot, and I believed it, because I figured no one had ever wanted me, at least he did. But I had Lilly, and no matter how adamant I was, she didn't let me sink into that. She kept loving me and trying to protect me and finally I realized she was my mirror."

"Mirror?"

Cora squeezed Tori's shoulders. "Sometimes you need someone else to be your mirror. Sometimes you need someone else to be your eyes. To tell you the things you see and think aren't right and they aren't healthy. Our eyes and our brains aren't always on our side."

"And when every person you've ever met has proven what your eyes and brain tell you?"

"You keep searching until you find someone who doesn't. Or, I suppose, if you're an awful, miserable human being, you decide to change. But that isn't you, Tori. I think you're strong and funny and driven. I think you're a good friend. If you asked Brandon or Sam, or Will, what they thought of you, you'd get variations of the same. Maybe you *do* need to change, but I also think there's a lot of good to work with."

Tori took a deep breath, in then out. She watched the orange blaze across the mountains, and she tried to refute

Cora's words. But how did you tell someone who'd believed love was her abusive relationship she was wrong?

"You know the Gracely legend?" Cora asked softly.

"No. Not exactly. Something about people not dying while settling it?"

Cora waved a hand. "Not the lame history stuff. The *legend*. Those who choose Gracely as their home will find the healing their heart desires."

Tori snorted, but Cora didn't so much as smile. "I believe it. Not so much like it's . . . magic, but it's a good place. It's good air, and if you let yourself want to heal, you can. Here."

Tori wanted to scoff again, but she couldn't ignore the goose bumps on her arm, the weird jumpy feeling in her gut.

Then, worst of all, Will's Jeep turning the corner and coming to park in front of her house.

"Oh, shit. No. I . . ." Tori scrambled to her feet. "I'm not ready. Can't you just tell him—"

But Cora stopped her, hands clamping onto her shoulders as her blue eyes looked straight into Tori's.

"I'll be here after, no matter what you decide, but when it comes to this, it only works if it's you standing up to that thing you don't know what to do with. But I'll be here after. Couldn't get rid of me if you tried."

Tori could only stare at this woman who had, yes, become a friend, but she didn't know . . . She didn't know anything about Tori or who she'd been or what she'd done.

Still, there was no doubt she would be there, with wine and a joke, even if Tori told Will to take a flying leap off a cliff.

Cora gave her a hug, then walked to her house, eyeing Will briefly before she disappeared inside.

"Hey, um, clearly you don't want to talk to me, but I have a few things to say."

Tori could only stare at him suspiciously. He didn't seem angry or upset. He seemed . . . subdued.

Her heart sank. He wasn't angry or upset. He was going to say he was glad she was leaving. He was going to tell her she'd misread everything and he'd only had sex with her out of some weird nostalgia and—

"I figure if nothing else you owe me a chance to say I love you before you disappear."

For the second time in not too many minutes, she simply collapsed into a sitting position on her grass, because what in the hell was she supposed to do in the face of that?

Tori looked like hell, and Will had already promised himself to stay calm and soft, but the blotchy skin of her face, the way her hair was tumbling out of its braid, the sheer misery on her face, it helped.

He recognized rock bottom when he saw it. Especially the kind of rock bottom you hit after years of running away from it and pretending it couldn't grab you by the throat and toss you to the ground.

He'd been exactly there not all that long ago. But she had reappeared in his life and given him a breath of hope, of second chances.

God, he wanted to be a second chance for her. Hope and safety and comfort and love, but there was groundwork to lay and he couldn't be afraid of hard work. Of waiting.

"I can't fight right now. I don't have it in me," she said, and the note of desperation in her tone ate at him.

"Okay." He glanced around the yard, the discarded duffel bag, the mussed woman sitting in the middle of it. He picked a spot next to her and lowered himself.

He allowed some space between them, though he didn't want to. He gave himself time to think before he spoke. "I didn't come to fight. I didn't come to change your mind, but I did come to ask you to stay."

She let out a long-suffering sigh, and she looked exhausted.

He could imagine just the kind of circles her brain was going in. The kind of thoughts that made any decision hard. That made the easy way out seem like the only way out.

He knew this, and if he could keep his own hurt at bay, he could keep seeing it and he could fight it. No, not fight, he could *heal* it.

This had never been about a second chance, for either of them, not really. What they would have made seven years ago would not have looked anything like what they'd make from here on out. It wasn't the wrong choice, or the right choice, it had happened. It was over.

The only choice was in the present. The only choice that made any sense was to heal. To believe in the people who'd given him support and love and advice. To believe he could give Tori the same.

"You love this, don't you? Mile High and Gracely and . . . you love it."

She blinked and looked out at all he'd mentioned. The shoved-together old mining-family houses across the street, the streaks of pink and purple across a mountain-dotted sky. Gracely, in all its glory, offering so much.

"It's a great place, and Mile High is great, but . . ."

"I didn't ask if they were great. I know they are. I asked if you *love* it. If it climbed in your bones the minute you set foot in this town. If you can *feel* the magic like blood pumping in your veins, and into your heart."

She cocked her head to study him. "Are you being poetic?"

He glanced away. No matter how determined he was to make this right or give her what she needed, it didn't mean he was particularly comfortable with *poetry*, even if Gracely had always been poetry to him.

Legends and mountains, healing and hope. Home.

"Is it a part of you?" he asked simply, because if it was, like he suspected it was, he didn't need to explain.

"Yes," she whispered, and there was a pain in her voice he wondered if he'd ever fully understand. But then he wondered if understanding mattered when there was love.

"Then don't leave it because of me. You don't love me or don't want to have anything to do with me, fine. You want to go back to being friends? Consider it done. Enemies? I can't promise fireworks, but I'll work at it."

When he glanced at her, her face was blank. Hard. "Because it'd be that easy, wouldn't it?"

"Are you high? It'd be sheer torture."

Her eyebrows drew together, confusion etching into that careful blankness. He could tell her he loved her because she was strong and smart and just . . . *his*, but she wasn't going to believe him. Because she didn't think she was worth it. She actually thought it'd be easy for him to go back.

He closed his eyes, hoping for some kind of divine intervention to find a way to get through to her. He admired that hard-ass head, but boy was it hell trying to break through it.

"I love you. I think I always have. I saw you and my world righted, and I convinced myself I was drunk or dumb, but it was always true from that first moment. It scared me. I ignored it. I ran away from it, but it was always there. The way you carried Sarge around like a damn baby after you adopted him. The way you worked your ass off to be just as good as any of us. Your pride. Your drive. You were something I wanted to *be*, and I could never be all that you are, so it had to be love."

She was gaping at him fully now, as if he'd lost his mind. She would probably find a way to convince herself he had. The only tool he had, the only thing he could fight her with was . . . certainty, space, and time.

All things he didn't particularly care for.

"But that's beside the point for right now."

"It is?" she asked, still gaping.

"Yeah, the point right now is that you stay. Because the most important thing to me right now is that you have this thing you love, that you get this thing you *deserve*. Mile High was made with you and partially for you. Your soul is in it. You belong here, and I won't let you run away from that because I'm here."

"It isn't your choice to make," she returned, back to flat and hard.

"No, it isn't. I'm asking you, Tori. I'm *begging* you to stay because it's where you belong. Look, when Hayley first started with us, she wasn't sure she wanted to have contact with me or Brandon, what with knowing what she knew about our father, and we had her work with Sam so she didn't have to deal with us. You don't want to see me, you don't have to see me. I'll go to part-time. I will do whatever it takes to keep you a part of that, even if it means taking myself out of it."

"Why?" she asked, so baffled and lost, and it validated all his theories on what she was thinking and feeling.

"Because I love you. Because you being happy is the most important thing to me. I'd sacrifice for you, Tori. I'd rake myself over the coals for you, again and again. Maybe the dumbass kid I was seven years ago couldn't or wouldn't, but this dumbass can and will. A million times over. I want you to be happy. I *need* you to be happy for me to be."

She was silent, staring at him, all those gears in her head turning, though he didn't know how or what conclusion they'd come to. So he could only sit there and hope.

Chapter Twenty-Six

Tori had never felt like this before. Like all the pain and certainty and fear was slowly being infused by hope.

By love.

He didn't really love her. He couldn't. All this talk about her happiness . . . She didn't know how to make sense of it. It had to be a game, surely. Some strategy.

Except, even a million years ago when she'd been young and dumb and head over heels in love, Will had never strategized. He'd never manipulated.

So, maybe not a game, but he didn't . . . He didn't get it yet. What was wrong with her. What people always ended up thinking or feeling. Maybe he was the first one to talk about making any kind of sacrifice for her, but . . .

She kept thinking about Cora saying you kept searching until you found someone who didn't reinforce what your brain told you about yourself. But that was Cora. She didn't know. . . .

Tori closed her eyes and tried to get a handle on something. She fisted her fingers in the grass and tried to force herself into action. Into decision.

The thing was, Will had to know he was walking into a

trap here. An inevitable crapshoot. With the crap being shot at her. He was blinded by something when he looked at her.

Or, it's love. It's finding the person.

"You don't want to love me," she blurted.

"Don't I?" he replied blandly. "Because I actually do remember quite well what not wanting to be in love with you felt like. This isn't that."

"You just don't get it. Th-there will come a time . . . I'm collateral damage. Always. People sweep me away in the wreckage, it's just . . . who I am, or whatever." She pulled the blades of grass in her fist until they broke out of the ground. "It's either that or I really am some sort of evil spirit," she muttered.

"You don't think that."

"I don't know. . . ."

He got closer then, his hands cupping her face and forcing her to look at him. She should have fought him. She should end this stupid, pointless conversation. But his rough hands were on her face, and his hazel eyes were blazing with a certainty she envied.

"Tor, you're one of us. You're a part of us. Whatever . . . Look, I had a mother and father who didn't particularly care about my existence, either, I know. But that doesn't make you who *you* are. Something your mentally ill brother said to you isn't something you build your life on."

"I know that," she grumbled, trying to jerk her head away, but he held firm, studying her and seeing too much.

"Do you?" he asked, his voice all concern and bafflement.

She swallowed, but that lump was still there, and growing. She didn't want to cry anymore or hurt anymore like this. Why was everyone *pushing* her?

So yeah, maybe . . . Maybe sometimes she wondered if her brother had the right of things. Sure, he was sick, but maybe that gave him insight no one else had. Maybe he saw the truth. She was the source of evil, of their problems, the thing that needed to be sacrificed. Mom and Dad had let her go without a fight. Maybe . . .

"Look at me." Will said forcefully, so unusually forceful she couldn't think of what else to do but obey. "You are not wrong or evil or bad. You, Tori Appleby, are . . . Hell, you're everything I wanted and was afraid to screw up. I didn't want to hurt you, and I didn't want you to figure out I was as worthless as most people seemed to think I was, so I get that. I get that little voice inside of you whispering only bad things happen, and you must be bad, but it's bullshit."

"I know that. I do. I just . . ."

"You have to do more than know it. You have to believe it."

It was so much worse to want to believe it, to hope it was true, than to just accept it wasn't and deal with the consequences. It was so much more painful to hope for the positive outcome knowing she could fail.

She shoved his hands away and pushed into a standing position. "I can't do this. Whatever this is, I can't do it."

Slowly Will got to his feet, his expression grim, and perhaps it was hurt lurking in his eyes, but Tori looked away.

"Okay. Okay. I didn't come here to fight or . . . I only came here to beg you to stay, and tell you if you want me out of your life, you can have that, too, but you need to stay."

She hugged her arms around herself, wishing she could make herself say terrible, nasty words so he wouldn't want her to stay, but she couldn't make them appear. She couldn't force them out.

"Promise me you'll stay, and I'll leave right now."

Why was he doing this? Why was he sacrificing something for her? It didn't make any sense, and it made her feel . . .

She forced her brain to think *awful*, but it wasn't that at all. It was wonderful. It was a beautiful, amazing thing he was offering. And it was Will, *Will*, and she didn't know how to argue with the fact Will didn't get anything out of her staying, not unless he did . . .

She closed her eyes, so irritated there were more tears to fall, but he was standing there saying he would give her all the space she needed, if only she kept the thing that made her happy, and she didn't know how to deny the fact that was love.

Because against her will and brain and everything else, she loved him wholeheartedly, and she wanted him to be happy. It had been why she'd had to leave all those years ago, because she hadn't been able to face the possibility of his being married to Courtney and being happy, but worse, so much worse, she hadn't been able to stand the thought of him married to her and *unhappy*.

She'd had to leave, to convince herself Courtney would give him everything he was after, and preserve that illusion. It had killed her to do it, but the alternative had been even worse than metaphorical death.

That love had never gone away, no matter how much she'd wanted it to or convinced herself it had, and now Will was offering the same kind of sacrifice—well, *demanding* might have been a better word, but it was still . . . love.

Someone loved her. Truly. Fully. Though the doubts in her head whispered a million terrible things, none of them made any sense. Not in the face of Will's love.

She turned to face him, something like calm settling over her. He loved her. She loved him. They wanted each other to be happy. How . . . how did she run away from that? *That* wouldn't be love—not this time. It would be cowardice and self-protection.

And it wouldn't give them a chance. The chance scared her, so much so she shook even as she made her decision, but much like a dangerous cliff face to climb, with the right tools . . . With the right tools you could do the thing you thought you couldn't.

Brandon's words. A truth that scared her to her bones, but under her bones was her heart, and it beat painfully for the man staring at her with hazel eyes and a grim mouth.

"I'll stay," she said on something like an exhaled whisper. "I'll stay," she said again, stronger this time.

He nodded, once, and she saw him swallow as though he was grappling with some great emotion. Then he turned, just ready to walk away. It should have felt like anything but love, but in this moment, she knew that sometimes, *sometimes* love could mean walking away.

But it didn't *have* to be walking away. Not if *she* was brave enough to stand, to take, to give. Brave enough to hope.

"Will?"

He stopped, and this would be the now or never part of her life she looked back on and wondered about. The way she'd wondered if she should have stayed home instead of running away. The way she'd wondered if she should have never told Will she'd loved him years ago. If she had ignored Toby's advances. Those bright, shining moments of taking the wrong path.

Or were they all right when it led her here? Because this was bigger than all that. Because it wasn't a thing. It wasn't a course. It was Will. It was life.

She'd never been a coward before. A lot of stupid things, yes, but never a coward.

"Don't go."

Will didn't turn at first. He was a little afraid he'd turn around having misread those two simple words. Maybe she wanted him to hash out the details. The hows and whens of avoiding each other.

Which was fine, because as much as he'd wanted the damn woman to fall into his arms and say it was all a mistake, he was prepared for the hard yards. He was prepared for the fact he might have to give her the last thing he wanted to.

But hell, if she was happy, he'd soldier through. The idea of her running off and dealing with everything alone again was too much. He'd sacrifice whatever.

"Will."

Finally he forced himself to turn, and she was standing there, looking at him plaintively.

She drew in a breath, let out one that shuddered and halted. She cleared her throat, dusk enveloping them as the mountains loomed dark and mysterious in the distance, the sun gone behind them.

"I know how to fight a war, but I'm not sure I know how to sign a peace treaty."

Will blinked. "I . . . You lost me."

"I'm using the whole war, collateral damage metaphor," she returned, waving her hand in the air as if that explained a damn thing.

"I'm shit with metaphors, maybe you could just say it plain."

"I don't know how to do this!" She waved her hands between them. "I don't know how to . . . believe it works."

It was his turn to take a deep, shuddery breath because that arrowed hard and deep. Hell if *he* knew how. "I think . . ." He cleared his throat, taking a few steps closer. He wanted to touch her, but he settled for standing close enough to see the swirls of blue and green in her eyes. "I think you decide to keep trying until you do."

"Keep looking," she murmured, almost to herself. "Until you find it."

"Something like that."

She blinked up at him, chewing on her lip before she reached out, hesitantly. He didn't move, though what he really wanted to do was pull her into him and hold her until she got it through her thick skull she was *not* running away. And neither was he. Not ever again.

Finally her fingertips rested on his chest, right above his heart, where it beat a little too hard and fast. She flattened her palm against his shirt, still worrying her bottom lip between her teeth.

Gently, slowly, he brought his hand up and rested it over hers. What he hadn't felt in the light touch was clear now, her hand and entire arm was trembling.

"Christ, you're shaking."

"Well, the last time I told you this, you walked away," she grumbled, still looking at the spot on his chest where their hands touched.

There was only one thing *this* could be, and he was quite certain his heart stuttered to a stop. He'd resigned himself to walking away, keeping his distance, letting her figure out things. He'd resigned to her not being ready for this.

But here she was, always surprising him.

And in that surprise, he could move. He could touch her. He could have her, because they had this.

He crushed his mouth to hers, sinking his fingers into her hair and holding her there as he poured everything he was into kissing her.

"Will," she protested against his mouth, but her body melted into his. "I didn't even say it."

He tipped her head back, looking her right in the eye. "Say it." He swallowed. "Please."

Her mouth actually curved a little at that, even though there were a million worries in her eyes. She took a breath, which only served to press her body closer to his.

"No one's ever cared much whether I was happy," she said, which were not the words he was looking for. "I'm not

sure that's the worst thing, but I think maybe . . . Maybe I never learned *how*. Things don't work out for me, they never have, but . . ." She sighed against him, her fingers tracing the pattern of his shirt. "Somewhere along the line I stopped *trying* to have them work out, and maybe that's as much the problem as anything else."

Will comforted himself over the lack of the words he wanted to hear with his fingers in her hair and his body pressed to hers. With the realization that maybe this was a step, like so many others. "I was pretty sure when you showed up it was some sort of cosmic punishment, or maybe middle finger. Because . . . that's, well, it was what I was looking for. Proof that I sucked."

"Yeah. Yeah."

"But Skeet got to talking at me about second chances, and it wouldn't let me go. That idea that I could have one, but only if I decided to work for it."

"And you decided to work for it?" she asked on a whisper.

"For you. For us."

Her hand slid up his chest and to his face, cupping his bearded jaw as she looked up at him. "I love you, Will."

"I love you, Tori."

But she looked more pained than the thrilled he felt. "I'm so afraid I'll mess it up. That I'm not good enough," she whispered, tears filling her eyes again too.

"Me too."

"That is not comforting!"

He smiled. "Sometimes . . . we screw up. For years. We make the same mistakes over and over again."

"Still not comforting."

He pressed a kiss to her head. "And sometimes you learn from those mistakes, and decide not that you can't ever make them, but that you'll always work hard to fix them. I wouldn't have . . . I wouldn't have decided to kiss you, to

sleep with you, if I hadn't made the decision to make it work, no matter what gets thrown our way."

She blew out a breath, leaning into him. "Okay, that's a little better."

He wasn't sure how long they stood in her yard, arms locked around each other, the night descending rapidly around them. She was letting him hold her, leaning into him, and holding on to him. She *loved* him. He didn't want the moment to end.

"Will?" she murmured into the quiet night.

"Yeah?"

"Come inside."

He shifted so he could look down at her and her mouth curved even more as she unwound herself from him and took his hand with hers.

"What for, exactly?"

She rolled her eyes. "I want you to . . ." She sighed, a rueful smile gracing her sharp mouth as she moved to her tiptoes and wound one arm around his neck so she could tug him closer to her face. "I want you to make love to me, Will Evans."

He pretended to mull it over, even as her eyes narrowed. In a smooth move, if he did say so himself, he scooped her up and off the ground, both arms under her ass so he could have her eye level.

She laughed into his ear as he lifted her off the ground, and he realized only then that he'd still been holding himself tense, still a little afraid it would all evaporate.

But she laughed, and he could finally let that relief course through him, because he'd finally *fixed* something, and now he finally had a chance to *build* something.

She wrapped her legs around him, kissed him as he attempted to walk to the house.

"Where's Sarge?"

"Micah took him."

"Perfect." He managed to hold her up with one arm as he opened the door, then stepped inside and kicked it behind him. He wasted no time striding to her bedroom and then dumping her on the bed.

For a moment he simply took that in. Tori and love and all the opportunities that lay before them.

Her amused expression faded a little, worry edging the corners of her eyes. But it wasn't the kind of concern that undermined his certainty, because he understood it too well. The fear anything good was just that—too good to be true for them.

They both had a ways to go to trust that kind of good, but if they could keep reminding each other, Will had no doubt they'd get there.

"It's real," he said, knowing he'd read her correctly when she blinked at him. He pulled off his shirt and grinned before crawling onto the bed with her and covering her body with his. "And we'll make it work," he whispered into her ear. "Together."

And then he lost himself in a kiss, in Tori, and in a future they'd both work for and believe in, one way or another.

Epilogue

Six months later

"Mr. Evans, don't make me call a guard," a scowling nurse said, glaring at Will from the door of a hospital room.

Will smiled his most charming smile at the nurse. "Not even five more minutes? It's not every day a guy gets to meet his first niece and nephew."

Though the nurse tried to keep her firm expression, Tori knew that telltale pressing of lips together.

Unlike the nurse who shook her head no, Tori was forever falling for Will's charm. Sometimes she tried to be irritated over, but love did funny things to people. So she was learning.

Sam and Hayley had left dutifully at the nurse's first *visiting hours are over* warning. This was now her third, and Tori had no doubt she'd follow through with her threats this time. Will must have finally gotten that through his head, because he sighed and walked over to Brandon.

He handed off the first bundle as smoothly as if he'd had experience with twins himself. When he made an attempt to hand the second baby to Brandon, Lilly—despite her exhaustion—was having none of it.

"If you do not give me one of my babies, you will be barred from this hospital room, Will Evans."

"Mommy's such a meanie," he whispered to the boy, Aiden Skeet—good Lord, Lilly must have really lost her mind—Evans. The girl, Grace Phoebe Evans, was dutifully handed off to Brandon.

The parents stared, rapt, at their little charges, only a few weeks early and in perfect health. Lilly really *was* Wonder Woman.

"We'll be back tomorrow. Text whatever you need me to bring," Will offered, taking Tori's hand in his.

"Don't you have excursions tomorrow?" Lilly demanded.

"Cancelled. Not many are too keen on hiking in the sub-zero temperatures. Looks like you planned the perfect time to have babies, Lil."

The nurse cleared her throat, and Will rolled his eyes, clearly reluctant to leave, but Tori squeezed his hand and led him out if only so the nurse would be kind to them tomorrow when Will would inevitably test her patience, no matter how charmingly.

"Can you believe how small they are?" Will said wonderingly.

"No."

"When do you suppose you'll stop being a coward and hold one?" he asked as they walked out of the hospital.

Something fluttered in her stomach. Though she didn't think he was hinting at something, how could she not . . . go there?

She'd watched him hold two little bundles of life like the precious gifts they were and . . . Well, she'd made a few decisions. Decisions she'd been putting off out of fear for the last six months.

She'd given herself some slack. Learning to love—Will and even herself—was hard work, and the future was a

scary, intimidating thing. One challenge at a time, and all that.

They climbed into Will's Jeep, driving out of the hospital in Benson and back toward Gracely and home.

Her home. Except . . . No matter how often Tori had said no to Will's suggestions of moving in together, her home had become something like theirs. And no matter that she kept rejecting him, she liked it. Him there so often, his things infiltrating their things.

She'd thought she could only trust that in the present, but . . . Well.

"All right," she said, giving a sigh that she hoped sounded exasperated. Even now she was sometimes afraid to give something the weight it deserved. "If you really think moving in together is a good idea, I guess you can move in."

She snuck a glance out of the corner of her eye as he turned onto the corner of Hope and Aspen. Nothing on his face had changed, just that same amazed, peaceful smile he'd had on his face ever since Brandon had introduced him to his niece and nephew.

And it had been that, and seeing him cradle two little newborns, that had unwound a knot in Tori's chest she hadn't realized was still there. She'd been living day to day, trying to trust the moment, trust love.

She'd succeeded, and she'd been happy, but she hadn't been too keen on trusting the future. Not planning for it, not imagining it or what she'd want for it.

When he *still* didn't say anything, just pulled his Jeep behind her car on the little concrete pad next to her house, she frowned a little. "Did you hear me?" she demanded. Maybe he was in some baby fog.

He nodded. "Yup."

"And?" she demanded.

He grinned. "I already did," he offered with a shrug.

"What?"

He didn't explain, just hopped out of the Jeep and started walking to the house. She stared openmouthed after him. He'd been bugging her for almost two months to move in together, and she'd hemmed and hawed and held him off.

How could he have *already* moved in?

She scrambled after him. He opened the door with the key she'd given him as something of a consolation prize one time he'd asked about the whole moving-in thing.

Maybe that's what he meant, that they had all but been living together and *agreeing* didn't really make much of a difference since they rarely spent a night apart.

She frowned, stepping inside as Sarge rushed to greet them. Will patted the dog absently and sauntered into the living room, big and beautiful and so damn perfect that little flutter of fear settled itself.

But he stood by the mantel over the fireplace and grinned at her and it soothed, because he would smile at her. Hold babies like precious cargo. Climb rocks and fling himself down rivers, and he loved her.

No doubts.

"See?" he offered, pointing to the mantel.

She frowned, realizing there was something on it—and as she wasn't much of a decorator it was usually empty.

She stepped closer. It was a rock. Why would . . . Oh. *Oh*. The rock she'd held on to that day at the lake, when she'd decided to make love with him and leave.

The day he'd convinced her to stay.

"You were supposed to give that back," she said, reaching out to touch the smooth, colorful stone.

"Leave it to you to pay attention to the rock-rock and not the metaphorical rock."

She frowned at him and he pointed to another item she hadn't noticed. A velvet box. She blinked at it.

"Well, are you going to *open* it?"

"I . . ." She swallowed. It could only be one thing, and she thought she was ready to give him the answer he'd want in this one thing he hadn't asked her yet, but that didn't mean she wasn't surprised.

Will plucked the box off the mantel, and in his eyes she saw a million things. Certainty and uncertainty, hope and fear, humor and nerves. Love, most of all, *love*.

"Tori," he said, a corner of his mouth quirking as he did the most unimaginable thing she could have predicted, got down on one knee.

She didn't know what to do, so she could only stand, gaping at him like a fish as he opened the lid of the box. A slim, sparkling band was nestled inside, simple and perfect.

"I love you. Wholeheartedly. Unreservedly. Be my wife. Be my family. Make children with me. I know you're scared of planning for the future, but—"

She sank to her knees, covering his hands with hers, realizing there was a tiny tremor there. Always surprising her with ways he was brave even when he was scared or nervous.

"I'm not scared anymore," she said, and it was a truth unlike any other. She wasn't scared anymore. She'd learned, she'd grown on a foundation Will had built for her. Now it was time to grow together, not just build. "I want you. A family with you. A future with you. I want to make a promise with you. A life."

He grinned that charming grin, but emotion laced his words. "Well, then, that settles it." He pulled the ring out of the box, slipped it onto her finger.

She stared at it for a second, surprised at the weight of it, but it was hardly just a ring. It was love, a promise, a future.

"I'm glad you came back," he said when she looked up at him again.

"I came home," she whispered. Then she flung herself at him, and he laughed as they toppled backward, her sprawling across him. Intrigued by the commotion, Sarge came over with a yip, then licked both their faces.

Her little family. Her wonderful future with a man who'd taught her love, and a town that had given her a chance to heal.

Tori Appleby was quite officially the luckiest, and she wouldn't let anyone argue with her on that simple fact.

Don't miss any of Nicole Helm's
Mile High romances:

Brandon's story in *Need You Now*
or Sam's story in *Mess with Me*.

Now on sale in bookstores and online!

Read on for a preview of *Need You Now* . . .

Brandon Evans stood on the porch of his office and stared at the world below him, a kaleidoscope of browns and greens and grays, all the way down the mountain until the rooftops of Gracely, Colorado, dotted into view.

Across the valley, up the other side of jagged stone, the deserted Evans Mining Company buildings stood, like ghosts—haunting him and his name. A glaring reminder of the destruction he'd wrought while trying to do the right thing.

He wished it were a cloudy day so he couldn't see the damn things, but he'd built the headquarters of *his* company in view simply so he could remind himself what he was fighting for. What was right.

"Are you over there being broody?"

Brandon looked down at his mug of coffee balanced on the porch railing, not bothering to glance at his brother. He *was* brooding. They were outvoting him and he didn't like it. He took a sip of coffee, now cool from the chilled spring air.

He leveled a gaze at his brother, Will, and their business partner, Sam. This was his best *I'm a leader* look, and it usually worked.

Why the hell wasn't it working today?

"Hiring a PR consultant goes against everything we're trying to do." Of course, he'd already explained that and he'd still been outvoted.

"We need help. The town isn't going to grow to forgive us. We can do all the good in the world, but without someone actually making inroads—we're not getting anywhere. We can't even find a receptionist from Gracely. No one will acknowledge we *exist*."

"We have Skeet."

"Skeet is not a receptionist. He's a . . . a . . . Help me out here, Sam?"

"His name is *Skeet*," Sam replied, as if that explained everything.

The grizzled old man who answered their phones for their outdoor adventure excursion company and refused to use a computer *was* a bit of a problem, but he worked for cheap and he was a local. Brandon had been adamant about hiring only locals.

Of course, Skeet was a local that everyone shunned, and he seemed to only speak in grunts, but they'd yet to lose an interested customer.

That they knew of, Will liked to point out.

Brandon set the offensive cold coffee down on the railing of the deck. He needed to do something with his hands. He couldn't sit still—he was too frustrated that they were standing around arguing instead of Sam and Will jumping to do his bidding.

Why had he thought to make them all equal partners?

"She's local. Great experience with a firm in Denver. She can be the bridge we need to turn the tide." Will ticked off the points they'd already been over, patient as ever.

"She's recently local—not native—and she can't change our last name."

"Well, even lifer townies working every second at Mile High can't do that."

"Can we cut the circuitous bullshit?" Sam interrupted with a mutter. "You were outvoted, Brandon. She's hired. Now, I've got to go."

"You don't have a group to guide until two."

Sam was already inside the cabin that acted as their office, the words probably never reaching him. Apparently his time-around-other-humans allotment was up for the morning. Not that shocking. The fact they'd lured him from his hermit mountain cabin before a guided hike was unusual.

Brandon turned his stare to his brother. They were twins. Born five minutes apart, but the five minutes had always felt like years. He'd been George Bailey born-older, and any time Sam sided with Will, Brandon couldn't help but get his nose a little out of joint.

He was the responsible, business-minded one, not the in-for-a-good-time playboy. They should listen to him regardless, not Will. Brandon had spearheaded Mile High. It was his baby, his penance, his hope of offering Gracely some healing in the wake of his father's mess of an impact. The fact that Will and Sam sometimes disagreed with him about the best way to do that filled him with a dark energy, and he'd need to do something physical to burn it off.

"Go chop some wood. Build a birdhouse. Climb a mountain for all I care. She'll be here at ten. Be back by then," Will ordered.

"You know I'd as soon throat punch you as do what you tell me to do."

Will grinned. "Oh, brother, if I kept my mouth shut every time you wanted to throat punch me, I'd never speak."

"Uh-huh."

Will's expression went grave, which was always a bad sign. They both dealt with weighty things and emotion

differently—Brandon acted like a dick and Will acted like nothing mattered. If Will was acting like something was important . . .

Well, shit.

"Don't think we don't take it seriously," Will said, far too quietly for Brandon's comfort. "Trust, every once in a while, we know as well or better than you."

"My ass," Brandon grumbled, feeling at least a little shamed.

"She'll be here at ten. I have that spring break group at ten-thirty, and you, lucky man, don't have anything on your plate today. Which means, you get to be in charge of paper—"

"Don't say it."

"—work and orientation!" Will concluded all too jovially.

"I could probably throw you off the mountain and no one would ask any questions."

"Ah, but then who would take the bachelorette party guides since you and Sam refuse?" Will clapped him on the shoulder. "You'll like her. She's got that business-tunnel-vision thing down that you do so well."

Brandon took a page out of Skeet's book and merely grunted, which Will—thank Christ—took as a cue to leave.

Regardless of whether he'd like this Lilly Preston, Brandon didn't see the usefulness or point in hiring a PR consultant. What was that going to accomplish when the town already hated them?

If even Will's personality couldn't win people over, they were toast in that department. The only thing that was going to sway people's minds was an economically booming town. Mile High had a long way to go to make Gracely that. And they needed Gracely's help.

Hiring someone who had only cursory knowledge of Gracely lore, who couldn't possibly understand what they

were trying to do, wasn't the answer. Worse, it reeked of something his father would have done when he was trying to hide all the shady business practices he'd instituted at Evans Mining.

Brandon glanced back over at the empty buildings. If he wanted to, he could will away the memories, the images in his mind. The pristine hallways, the steady buzz of phones and conversation. How much he'd wanted that to be *his* one day.

But then he'd told his father he knew what was going on, and if Dad didn't change, Brandon would have no choice but to go to the authorities.

The fallout had been the Evans Mining headquarters leaving Gracely after over a century of being the heart of the town, his father's subsequent heart attack and death, Mom shutting them out, and everything about his life as the golden child and heir apparent to the corporation imploding before his very eyes.

A lot of consequences for one tiny little domino he'd flicked when his conscience couldn't take the possible outcomes of his father's shady practices.

So much work to do to make it right. He forced his gaze away from those buildings into the mountains all around him. He took a deep breath of the thin air scented with heavy pine. He rubbed his palms over the rough wood of the porch railing.

It was the center—these mountains, this place. He believed he could bring this town back to life not just because he owed it to the residents who'd treated him like a king growing up, but because there was something . . . elemental about these mountains, this sky, the river tributaries, and the animals that lived within it all.

Untouched, ethereal, and while he didn't exactly believe in magic and ghostly legends of Gracely's healing power, he did believe in these mountains and this air. He was going to

give his all to fix the damage he'd caused, and he was going to give his all to making Mile High Adventures everything it could be.

So, he'd put up with this unwanted PR woman for the few weeks it would take to prove that Will and Sam were wrong. Once they admitted he was right, they could move on to the next thing, and the next thing, until they got exactly what they wanted.

Lilly took a deep, cleansing breath of the mountain air. The altitude was much higher up here than in the little valley Gracely was nestled into, but even aside from that, the office of Mile High Adventures was breathtaking.

It was like something out of a brochure—which would make her job rather easy. A cabin nestled into the side of a mountain. All dark logs and green-trimmed roof, with a snow-peaked top of a mountain settled right behind to complete the look of cozy mountain getaway. The porches were almost as big as the cabin itself. She'd suggest some colorful deck chairs, a few fire pits to complete the look, but it took no imagination at all to picture groups of people and mugs of hot chocolate and colorful plaid blankets.

The sign next to the door that read MILE HIGH ADVENTURES was carved into a wood plank that matched the logs of the cabin.

If it weren't for the men who ran this company, she'd be crying with relief and excitement. She needed a job that would allow her to stay in Gracely, and this one would pay enough that she could still support her sister and nephew even with Cora's dwindling waitress hours and low tips.

Cora and Micah were doing so well, finally moving on from the abusive nightmare that had been Stephen. Lilly couldn't uproot them, and she couldn't leave them. They needed her, but her Denver-based PR company had refused

to let her continue to work remotely when they'd merged with another company and kept only those willing to relocate to Denver.

So, here she was, about to agree to work for the kind of men she couldn't stand. Rich, entitled, charming. The kind of men who'd hurt her mother, her sister, her nephew.

Lilly forced her feet forward. This was work, not romance, so it didn't matter. She'd do her job, take their money, do her best to improve the light in which their business was seen in Gracely, and not let any of these rich and powerful men touch her.

Shoulders back, she walked up the stairs of the porch. There was a sign on the door, hung from a nail and string. It read *Come On In!* in flowing script. She imagined if she flipped the sign there'd be some kind of WE'RE CLOSED phrase on the back.

Impressive detail for a group of three, from what she could tell, burly mountain men hated by the town at large.

Her stomach jittered, cramped. She really didn't want to do this. She *loved* Gracely. Even for all its problems, it was charming and . . . calming. She felt cozy and comfortable here. More than she'd ever felt in Denver, where she'd grown up.

Working for Mile High would keep her here, but would it still be cozy and comfortable if the town looked at her with contempt? If they considered her tainted by association with these men she'd never heard a good word about?

Well, as long as Cora and Micah still needed her, it didn't matter. Couldn't.

She blew out a breath and lifted a steady hand. She opened the door. Will *had* instructed her to come on in, and the sign said as much.

Upon stepping into what was an open area that seemed designed as both lobby and living room, she wasn't surprised to find more wood, a crackling fire in the fireplace, warm

and worn brown leather couches pushed around the hearth.
The walls were mostly bare, but there was a deer head over
the mantel, a few framed graphics with quotes about going
to the mountains and the wilderness.

A grunt caused Lilly to jerk her attention to the big desk
opposite the entryway. She wasn't sure what she'd expected
of the other employees of Mile High, but she'd assumed they'd
all be like Will. Young, athletic, charming, and handsome.

The man sitting behind the desk was *none* of those
things. He was small and old with a white beard and a white
ponytail. A bit of a Willie Nelson/*Dirty Santa*-looking character in a stained Marine Corps sweatshirt.

Not what she expected of a receptionist . . . anywhere.

"Hello. My name is Lilly Preston. I'm supposed to be
meeting Will Evans and his broth—"

The man grunted again, a sound that was a gravelly huff
and seemed to shake his entire small frame.

What on earth was happening?

"Ah, Lilly!" Will appeared from some hallway in the
back. "Skeet, you're not scaring off our newest employee,
are you?"

The man—Skeet, good Lord—grunted again. Maybe
he was their . . . grandfather or something.

She returned her attention and polite business smile to
Will and the man behind him. It wasn't any stretch to realize this was Will's brother, Brandon Evans. There were a lot
of similarities in their height, the dark brown hair—though
Brandon's was short and Will's was long enough to have a
bit of a wave to it. They both sported varying levels of
beard, hazel eyes, and the kind of angular, masculine face
one would definitely associate with men who climbed
mountains and kayaked rivers.

There were some key differences—mainly, Will was
smiling, all straight white teeth. Brandon's mouth was formed
in something a half inch away from a scowl.

Well. She forced her smile to go wider and more pleasant. She wasn't a novice at dealing with cranky or difficult men. About seventy-five percent of her career thus far had included dealing with obstinate and opinionated business owners. The Evans brothers might be different, but they weren't unique.

"You have an absolutely lovely office. I'm so impressed."

Will gestured her toward the couches around the fireplace. There were rugs over the hardwood floor, patterns of dark red and green and brown. It was no lie, she *was* impressed.

"Have a seat, Lilly. I have a group to guide rock climbing shortly, so Brandon will conduct most of your orientation. We've got the necessary paperwork." He placed a stack of papers on the rough-hewn wood coffee table. It looked like it had probably come from Annie's—the furniture shop in Gracely. Furnishing and decorating from local vendors would be smart.

Smart, rich men with charming smiles and handsome scowls. It didn't get much more dangerous than that, but Lilly never let her smile falter.

"Once we've done that, Brandon will show you around, show you your desk, and you can ask any questions."

"Of course." She leaned forward to take the paperwork, but Brandon's hand all but slapped on top of the stack.

"One thing first."

Will muttered something that sounded like an expletive.

The stomach jittering/cramping combo was back, but she refused to let it show on her face. Nerves were normal, and the way she always dealt was to ignore them through the pleasantest smiles and friendliest chitchat she could manage until they went away.

"I'm at your disposal, Mr. Evans," she said, letting her hand fall away from the papers as she settled comfortably

into the couch. At least she hoped she was exuding the appearance of comfort.

His expression, which hadn't been all that friendly or welcoming, darkened even further. "You will call me Brandon. You will call him Will. There are no misters here."

Ah, so he was one of those. Determined to be an everyman. She resisted an eye roll.

He leaned forward, hazel eyes blazing into hers. "Do you believe in the legend, Ms. Preston?"

"The . . . legend?" This was not what she'd expected. At all. She quickly glanced at the door in her periphery. Maybe she should bolt.

"You've lived here how long? Surely you've heard the legend of Gracely."

"You mean . . ." She hesitated because she didn't know where he was trying to lead her, and she didn't like going into unchartered territory. But, he seemed adamant, so she continued. "The one about those who choose Gracely as their home will find the healing their heart desires?"

"Are there others?"

Lilly had to tense to keep the pleasant smile on her face. She didn't like the way this Evans brother spoke to her. Like he was an interrogating detective. Like she'd done something wrong, when Will had been the one to convince her to take this job.

Because working with the Evanses was going to put a big red X on her back in town, and she didn't trust men like them with their centuries of good name and money.

But she needed a job. She needed to stay in Gracely. So, she had to ignore the way his tone put her back up and smile pleasantly and pretend he wasn't a giant asshat.

"So, Ms. Preston." Oh she hated the way he *drawled* her name. "The question is: do you believe in the legend?"

This was a test, a blatant one at that, and yet . . . she didn't know the right answer. Would he ridicule her for

believing in fairy tales if she said she believed the first settlers of Gracely were magically healed when they settled here and all the stories that had been built up into legend since? Would he take issue with her being cynical and hard if she said there was no way?

The biggest problem was her answer existed somewhere in between the two. Half of her thought it was foolishness. Losing her job and having to take this one hardly seemed like healing or good luck, but her sister and nephew had flourished here in the past year and, well, healing was possible. Magic? Maybe—maybe not. But possible.

So, maybe it was best to focus on the good, the possibility. "Yes." She met his penetrating hazel gaze, keeping her expression the picture-perfect blank slate of professional politeness.

"And what do you think is the source of that legend? What makes it true?"

"True?" She looked at Will, tried to catch his gaze, but he looked at the ceiling. She might not trust Will, but at least he was polite. Apparently also a giant coward.

"Yes, if you believe Gracely can heal, what do you believe *causes* that ability?"

She flicked her gaze back to his. It had never wavered. There was a fierceness to his expression that made her nervous. He was a big man. Tall, broad. Though he wore a thick sweater and heavy work pants and boots, it was fairly obvious beneath all those layers was the type of man who could probably crush her with one arm.

She suddenly felt very small and very vulnerable. Weak and at a disadvantage.

Which was just the kind of thing she wouldn't show them. Powerful men got off on causing fear and vulnerability. She'd seen her nephew's father do that enough to have built a mask against it, and she'd worked with and for plenty of men who'd wanted to intimidate her for a variety of reasons.

She could handle whatever this was. Chin up. Spine straight. A practiced down-the-nose look. "Do legends need a cause? A scientific explanation? Or are they simply . . . magic? Do I need to analyze *why* I believe in it, or can I simply believe it happened and continues to? And, more, what on earth does it have to do with my work here?"

"If you're going to work here," he said, his voice low and . . . fierce to match his face, "you will need to understand what we believe about the legend. Because it has everything to do with why we built Mile High Adventures."

"That's not what I heard," she muttered before she could stop herself. Okay, maybe remote consulting *had* dulled some of her instincts if she let things like that slip.

"Oh, and what did you hear, Ms. Preston? That we're the evil spawn of Satan setting out to crush Gracely even deeper into the earth? That we're bringing in an influx of out-of-towners, not to *help* the businesses of Gracely, but to piss off the natives? Because if you think we don't know what this town thinks of us, you don't understand why you're here."

"I know what the town thinks of you *and* I know why I'm here." She took a deep breath, masked with a smile, of course. "I'm here because I think this is an excellent opportunity." *To sell my soul briefly so I can stay where I want.* "I do believe in the legend, and I think it would be imperative you do too if you expect to sell the town on you being part of its salvation."

His eyes narrowed and she knew she was skating on thin ice. He was one of those control freaks who didn't like to be told what to do, only unlike most of the men she'd worked with like that, he wasn't placated by sweet smiles or politeness.

She'd have to find a new tactic.

"I believe, Ms. Preston"—that damn conceited drawl again—"in these mountains. In this *air*. I believe that, if

people choose to look, they can find themselves here. I believe in this town, and that it can be more than what it's become. You'll need to believe that too if you want to work here."

"We've already hired her, Brandon," Will said, *finally* inserting something into the conversation. *After* letting this man act as though she were . . . well, unwelcome, unwanted.

Typical.

"*You* hired her."

"Did I walk into the middle of something, gentlemen? I can just as soon come back at another time when you're ready and willing to be in agreement." She even stood, picking up her bag to slide over her shoulder. Because she might be desperate, but she wasn't going to sell half her soul *and* be treated poorly.

That was not what she'd signed up for. She'd as soon move back to Denver. It would kill her to leave Cora and Micah, but she had some pride she couldn't swallow.

"Have a seat, Ms. Preston."

When she raised an eyebrow at Brandon the Bastard, he pressed his lips together, then released a sigh. "If you would, please." All said through gritted teeth.

Ugh. Men.

She took a seat. One more chance. He had *one* more chance.

"I apologize if I've come off . . ."

"Harsh. Douchey. Asshole spectacular."

Brandon glared at his brother, who was grinning. She didn't want to find it humorous. They were both being asshole spectaculars as far as she was concerned, just in different ways.

"This business and what it stands for is everything to me, so I don't take it lightly."

She met his gaze. Just as she didn't want to find them amusing, she didn't want to soften, but she realized in that

simple, gravely uttered sentence, that he wasn't fierce so much as . . .

Passionate.

She met his gaze with that realization and her stomach did something other than the alternating jittery cramps. Her chest seemed to expand—something flipped, like when Cora drove them too fast down a mountain road.

She couldn't put her finger on that. The cause, what it was, and more, she didn't think she wanted to. If she was going to survive working for the Evans brothers, it was probably best to keep her polite smile in place and ignore any and all *feelings*.